"Quite simply a great read. Once again. Buchman takes the military romance to a new standard of excellence."

—*Booklist* Starred Review

"Readers will be amazed at the attention to technical detail that is expertly woven into the fabric of the story… Multifaceted characters, a good plot, and riveting action."

—*RT Book Reviews*, 4 Stars

"M.L. Buchman's writing is so realistic that one almost forgets it's fiction. The imagery…the events so like the latest news, and the magnificence of people when they rise to be their best for a cause they are willing to die for make *Take Over at Midnight* riveting."

—*Long and Short Reviews*

"A thrilling, passionate story in which love sparks in the midst of helicopter warfare."

—*Barnes and Noble Review*, A Barnes and Noble Best Romance of 2013

"Dangerous top secret missions and sizzling love scenes lead to a satisfying conclusion."

—*Publishers Weekly*

"A fabulous, soaring thriller."

—*Midwest Book Review*

Wait Until Dark

"A must-read for fans of military romantic suspense."
—Fresh Fiction

"Exquisitely written, sensory loaded, and soul satisfying."
—Long and Short Reviews

"With a mix of military suspense, broken lives and emotions, and romantic heat, *Wait Until Dark* packs a leisurely but intense punch for lovers of this genre!"
—Romancing the Book

"A wonderful romance and awesome read!"
—RomFan Reviews

"It was delightful to become immersed in this exciting and dangerous world... An exceptional addition to the series."
—Night Owl Reviews Reviewer Top Pick, 5 Stars

"A slow-building, captivating story...a 5-Star Military Romance!"
—Tome Tender

"High-energy military suspense at its best...this book has it all."
—RT Book Reviews

I Own the Dawn

The Night Is Mine

"An action-packed adventure. With a super-stud hero, a strong heroine, and a backdrop of the world of the Washington elite, it will grab readers from the first page."
—*RT Book Reviews*, 4 Stars

"A gripping, multilayered military romantic suspense."
—*USA Today Happy Ever After*

"Absolutely amazing… The romance and relationship blends seamlessly into the story line… A great first book for a new series, and I cannot wait for the next one."
—*Night Owl Reviews* Reviewer Top Pick, 5 Stars

"Buchman's hard-to-put-down novel, with its nonstop action, surprise villain, and story of forbidden love, will be a real treat for fans of military romantic suspense."
—*Booklist* Starred Review

"Takes kick-ass to a whole new level… I was on the edge of my seat during every action scene. This is a must-read."
—*Fresh Fiction*

"Awesome, intriguing, powerful, and seductive."
—*BookLoons*

"The secrets, the suspense, and the romance just all rocked in every sense of the word."
—*Romancing the Book*

LIGHT UP *THE Night*

THE NIGHT STALKERS

M.L. BUCHMAN

sourcebooks
casablanca

Published by Sourcebooks Casablanca, an imprint of Sourcebooks, Inc.
P.O. Box 4410, Naperville, Illinois 60567-4410
(630) 961-3900
Fax: (630) 961-2168
www.sourcebooks.com

Printed and bound in Canada.
MBP 10 9 8 7 6 5 4 3 2 1

To Mike, for teaching me the joys of flight.

Chapter 1

SECOND LIEUTENANT TRISHA O'MALLEY WAITED TEN kilometers off the north coast of Somalia for the mission "Go!" moment. She held her AH-6M Little Bird attack helicopter at wave height, exactly at wave height. The long metal skids were practically being licked clean by the rolling crests heading ashore from the Gulf of Aden.

Through the large openings to either side of the tiny cockpit where the doors would be hung, the smell of the hot night ocean wafted thick with salt and bitter from the dust blown off the achingly dry land. Nobody flew a Little Bird with the doors on. She didn't know why they even ordered them. The only time they were used was to protect the birds when they were parked in harsh environments; a piece of plastic could do that. When they flew, the doors were off. Having them off also added freedom of movement to the tiny cockpit, and far more importantly, the visibility was much better.

Not that visibility was such a big deal at the moment. Outside the forward glass-and-polycarbonate windscreen, which reached from below her foot pedals to almost above her head, was nothing but impenetrable darkness. That was one of many things Trisha liked about the Little Birds. The console swept up between the pilots' seats but was confined to a narrow column on the front windscreen that stopped below eye level.

Flying an AH-6M was as close to flying with nothing

between you and the sky as existed. No door beside you and bullet-resistant protection from below your feet to farther back than you could tilt your head while wearing a helmet. Everything a girl needed for a good time.

The console itself was dominated by a pair of LCD multifunction screens that could be switched at the tap of a button from engine performance to weather radar to digital terrain map. It made her feel like those science fiction movie heroes in superpowered suits, as if rather than flying a chopper, she herself was wearing a weaponized suit that happened to be in the shape of a helicopter.

Though there really was nothing to see at the moment. Even through her night-vision gear that projected infrared images from the cameras mounted on the outside of the chopper onto the inside of her helmet's visor, there was nothing to see ahead. Except more waves.

To her right hovered the DAP Hawk *Vengeance* with Chief Warrant 3 Lola Maloney commanding, and beyond that Dusty James's transport Black Hawk, the *Vicious*. To Trisha's left, if Chief Warrant 2 Roland Emerson weren't sitting shoulder to shoulder with her in his copilot seat, she'd be able to see the two other Little Birds of her flight formation, *Mad Max* and *Merchant of Death*—*Max* and *Merchant* for short.

When she'd named her bird *May*, everyone thought it was some stupid woman joke. But any fool who teased her about it being the *Merry Month of...*or *Mayfly* soon learned that it was short for *Mayhem*. She never had to explain it twice.

There was no "Go!" command and no need for risking that extra bit of encrypted communication. The mission "Go" had been given fifteen minutes earlier when they'd spun up their rotors and departed the USS *Peleliu* amphibious assault ship floating forty miles out in the Arabian Sea.

Now fifteen seconds to start of mission, she wound up on the throttle in her left hand. At five seconds to "Go!" both the bird and Trisha's body were humming with the need to get moving.

The clock on her dash hit 03:00—and she was gone. The *May* didn't fly, she leaped. Not like a racehorse, like a greyhound. With the collective full up and the cyclic forward, Trisha was tilted nose down five feet above the waves and a hundred meters in the lead of any other bird in the flight, right where she liked to be. They closed formation quickly, but she liked setting a higher standard even on this, her first operational flight. It had been two long years of training, and she was way past ready.

Even with the low-noise blades and engine baffles, the roar inside the craft was loud enough that you wouldn't want to try a conversation without your headset. You could do it, but your voice would get tired really fast. Despite the full-enclosure helmet, she could feel the familiar beat of the machine and whine of the high-speed turbine engine against her body.

Everything in tune and running true. Sounded like an idea for a song, not that she could write music.

Three a.m. should be the sleepiest moment on the Somali coast. Intelligence said the guard change was at oh-four-hundred. Everyone else should be asleep.

Everyone except the Night Stalkers of the U.S. Army's 160th Special Operations Aviation Regiment (airborne). SOAR(a) ruled the night, the most elite Special Operations Forces helicopter team on the planet.

Tonight they'd be ruling the northern coastal town of Bosaso, Somalia, on the Horn of Africa. Or at least one corner of it. They wouldn't be engaging within the third largest city in the country, because the pirates had made the mistake of using a compound outside of town. The local authorities were clamping down hard on piracy and, even if just for public image's sake alone, they wouldn't have been as tolerant of the pirates if they were right in town.

She'd expected to feel some serious nerves. It was her first mission-qualified flight for the Night Stalkers. She'd spent five years with the 101st Airborne flying Cobra attack and Little Birds. She had planned that the day she hit the five-year minimum-experience requirement, she'd walk across Fort Campbell and knock on the 160th's locked gate for an application. Instead, an invitation to apply had been waiting for her that very morning.

Trisha smiled at the memory of that. Her old friend Major Beale had kept track of her despite roaring up the officer ranks. Trisha hadn't West Pointed in, though she could have. Instead she'd made her parents crazy by taking the NYU education that she'd paid for herself, then enlisting and bucking her way up from private. Though stepping back to the basics of Office Candidate School after she'd been a noncommissioned officer for several years had been tough. She didn't want any advantages; she'd long since understood the value of learning the hard way. She'd no more climb up the broad ladder of her father's political heft than she would clamber up the lace-draped tiers of her mother's social one.

Two more years had passed since she'd been accepted to SOAR. She was used to leading entire flights and planning operations for the Screaming Eagles. Not so with the Night Stalkers. They'd spent two years showing her just how little she knew. She was glad to simply be allowed to fly with them.

"One click," Roland said over the headset. She and Roland were the same rank, though he'd been in a year longer than she had. He was there in case she fucked up.

No! Trisha admonished herself. He was there as her copilot. If he were there to cover for her, she'd be in the left seat and he'd be in the right-hand pilot position. All they both cared about was doing this mission and doing it right.

One kilometer out. Fifteen seconds to shore.

Right on cue, the breakwater came into view. A massive pile of car-sized concrete blocks protected the small harbor from storms coming in off the Arabian Sea. But it wasn't ready for the storm that the Night Stalkers could unleash.

———⁂———

Navy SEAL Lieutenant William Bruce squatted in the dust, wearing the standard clothes of a mercenary soldier looking for a quick buck by joining the Somali pirates. Bill wore camo pants, a dark tank-tee, and a black sweatband. He carried a very battered but immensely serviceable M-16 which marked him even more clearly as a merc for bringing his own weapon with him.

Most pirates wielded out-of-date Russian crap, some

of it from all the way back to WWII, that was as likely to explode in their hands as to actually fire. He had a Russian TT-30 semiauto pistol in the back of his waist-band, a reliable enough weapon though he preferred a Sig Sauer, spare magazines in his thigh pouches, and a rusting but very sharp hunting knife strapped to his thigh. He fit right in.

Bill checked his watch. Oh-three-hundred sharp.

The choppers should be here in three minutes, if they were to be trusted. There was a laugh. A decade in the Navy, the last five years as a SEAL, and he still didn't trust the Night Stalkers. He really should try to get over it, but he didn't see that happening anytime soon. They were dead reliable, anywhere on the planet, any time. But this was Somalia, and though it wasn't their fault, he couldn't help himself. He would never trust them on Somali soil.

Well, the time was now or never, and he'd have to bank on them actually showing up and doing it right. He slid up behind Abshir, the night guard assigned to the hostages taken in their latest successful piracy, and dropped him with a hard chop to the neck. He could have come from the front, Abshir knew him, but Bill didn't want to risk his undercover role being identified. Nor was Bill willing to kill the man in cold blood simply to protect his identity.

The local warlord, Mahan, would probably have the man shot for failing his guard duty, but that would be his choice. It wouldn't be any great loss to the world. Abshir was a nasty piece of work with a deep strain of cruelty that even the most hardened pirates rarely possessed.

Bill slipped into the low building holding most of the

prisoners, dragging Abshir with him. Let Mahan think that the prisoners had overpowered the guard.

All of the male hostages were asleep. No one on watch. No one waiting for the least opportunity to escape. It just showed how easily civilians became dispirited, and this was only the second week of their captivity.

He began waking them quietly. At first they'd thought he was attacking them, and he lost almost thirty seconds convincing them they were about to be rescued. The boat's owner, Wilkin something Junior, was the slowest of the bunch. Senator's son. No one ever said he was a bright bulb, just rich and related to the right man to require an immediate rescue. Who would name their kid Wilkin anyway? And Junior was just salt in the wound, like the father hadn't learned from being stuck with it himself.

Eleven, six passengers and five crew, taken off the hundred-and-fifty-foot pleasure yacht *Gracie* in the Arabian Sea. The same number of SEALs that fit in a twenty-two-foot rubber boat along with all of their gear.

What the idiot yachties were doing out there alone in the constricted throat of the Gulf of Aden, he didn't want to know. Anyone transiting the Suez with even half a clue on board would wait for a military escort convoy before braving the waters between Somalia and Yemen. The Somali coast was one of the four most dangerous stretches of water on the planet, and they'd gone sight-seeing. Probably on their way to explore the Straits of Malacca off Indonesia next. There they wouldn't be hostages, they'd just be robbed or dead if they resisted at all.

He knew the civilians would take another minute or two to get their acts together, so he told them to stay silent and be ready. They hadn't even asked about the women of their crew yet, a crime that made him think the men were the ones he shouldn't bother rescuing.

Bill slid out the door and moved in the darkest shadows of the moonless night, tight against the adobe walls on the right side of the street. At the last doorway before the cross street, he turned in. The three women yachties had been separated from the others and were tied to beds. So no guard. They were battered and bruised, but he was pretty sure that they'd only been mishandled, not raped. It had taken some risk, but he'd convinced Mahan that unless he wanted serious retribution after they were ransomed off, he'd better not let his men make a holiday of the ladies.

They were gagged, so he didn't bother to wake them gently. They wouldn't be making any noise. He just slashed their bonds and had them stumbling ahead of him before they were fully conscious.

Just as he reached the first building to collect the rest of the men, he could hear the choppers. The low thud of helicopters with quieting technology, sliding up to the beach. He'd only heard the stealth-rigged choppers once before. It was a unique sound that he would have ignored if he didn't already know it. Bill did his best not to be impressed that they were releasing those assets to any task less than taking out the next Osama bin Laden.

At least the Night Stalkers were punctual. Now if they could just resist being shot out of the sky.

Trisha checked her clock as they crossed the beach. 03:02:54, six seconds early. She liked being early.

That was one of the things the Night Stalkers had taught her. How to hit a mark within a thirty-second window, whether it was a thousand meters away or a thousand kilometers.

Also, no warm dots of infrared heat on her night vision that might be a flock of pelicans. Mission briefing had warned they traveled in large flocks along the Somali coast and could cause problems if you flew over one and spooked it aloft, especially at night.

Their appointed meeting place was by the large compound at the west edge of town. It stood separate from the hovels that littered the edges of Bosaso.

The center of town had some two- and three-story buildings, clumps of scrub grass, even a few carefully nursed palm trees around hotels and government buildings. Out here at the western edge of town any trees had long since gone to fuel cooking fires and any grass was dead. Not much survived the dry season that lasted, well, all frickin' year. This place was dismal. Thorny acacia bushes, about the only thing that grew in the sandy orange soil, were called desert roses when they "bloomed" with multicolored windblown plastic debris.

April got them two of the five inches of rain that fell all year. In September, they were screwed. Dust was a major issue. So the Night Stalkers formation flew in side by side, rather than in a line, so that no one ate anyone else's dust as they arrived over the land.

Thankfully, out at the edge of town where the hostages were supposedly being held, there were few power lines and almost all of the buildings were single story, a lot of tin roofs and a lot with no roof at all. So there was room to maneuver. Even in a brownout of dust beaten aloft by the chopper's rotor downwash, if you were a dozen meters up, you would be in the clear. At least from hitting any obstacles.

Early in the night, the tin of the roofs would have shown as bright square projections on the inside of her helmet's visor because of the release of the sun's heat. The ADAS camera gear laid an infrared-amplified image across her bullet-resistant plastic, so clear that it was almost like daylight.

All the press, and most of the military, thought that the Advanced Distributed Aperture System was just an idea in testing. SOAR had seen it, worked on the quiet with Raytheon to take it to the next level, and installed it. It was frickin' amazing. It was to night-vision goggles what NVGs had been to squinting really hard. And because the cameras were mounted outside the chopper, there were no blind spots, not even straight down. She could see out in every direction as if she were just sitting in the sky with nothing around her. She could even see most of the way through the dust of rotor-born brownouts.

A quick blink and she could switch her focus to seeing directly through her visor to the world beyond her helmet. But almost everything she needed was projected inside, including the heat signature of the tin roofs.

By 3:00 a.m. the sun's heat had dissipated, and the only heat signatures on the roofs now came from the bodies inside. It wasn't much, but the tin glowed a little bit with heat if the space was inhabited. Otherwise they looked solid black.

One of the hottest roofs was close by the compound, the one they'd been told to target. That meant the information was right; a lot of people radiating a lot of body heat under that one particular roof.

Even as Trisha pulled up to hover in a guard position fifty feet in the air, she could see people running from that building, being herded by a man carrying a rifle. The briefing had warned them there was an embedded friendly doing the inside setup. If there hadn't been, they'd have had to bring more choppers loaded with more Special Operations Forces. But this guy was apparently a one-man rescue machine.

They didn't reveal any of his details, other than he was absolutely trustworthy and be careful not to kill him. A "high-value asset." What kind of a crazy idiot, high-value or otherwise, embedded himself in the Somali pirate community? Probably some testosterone-poisoned jerk, some serious adrenaline junkie with a death wish.

Trisha flew the weaponized attack version of a Little Bird helicopter, so she hovered close but didn't go to ground. She wasn't designed for passengers, just a pilot, a copilot, and enough weapons to rip anyone a new hole if they messed with her. The Killer Egg, as it was often called, could take down tanks that were fifty times the weight of her bird. The body of the chopper might be goofily close to being egg-shaped, but that didn't make it one bit less of a "killer."

Merchant and *Mad Max* were MH-6Ms, tactical transport versions of the Little Bird. They could get close in and dump off four to six operators. The chopper was so small that the Special Ops guys actually sat three on a side on small, fold-down benches running along the outsides of the chopper. They were exposed to the wind, but they were fast for load and unload. They had a rope for fast descent into places that even a Little Bird helicopter couldn't land.

They came in quick and low with one Delta Force operator each, who jumped off the benches before the choppers even touched down. In moments they were shoving rescuees onto the side benches with their backs against the sides of the helicopters and tying them on. As soon as they each had four people on the benches and had slapped helmets onto the hostages' heads to protect them from the wind, the Little Birds lifted and were instantly headed back toward the beach.

The D-boys rushed the rest of them toward the *Vicious*, the transport Black Hawk that had grounded a little farther away. Unable to fit inside the courtyard, it had landed outside the front gate.

"*May!* Three o'clock." Wrench, the call sign of Air Mission Commander Stevenson, still sitting back on the ship they had launched from, called down the warning. He had a spy drone circling a thousand feet up and keeping an eye on them. It had taken her forever to break the desire to lean out and see if she could spot the blacked-out eyes in the sky of the high-circling "drone." Though the military kept trying to kill off that word, everyone still used it. It was supposed to be UAV, unmanned aerial vehicle. Yeah, right. She managed not to look up for the drone because SOAR had drilled into her head to keep her attention on her own problems.

"I see it!" Trisha called back to Stevenson. She'd been hovering the chopper and letting it slowly spin on its axis so that she and Roland, her copilot, swept a complete circle of the area every six seconds. Even with that, the AMC spotted the new problem ahead of her. Man was good. She liked that.

With a slight tip of the cyclic, she got her weaponry lined up on a doorway where a whole lot of hostiles were pouring out into the compound's central courtyard.

"Do it!" she called to Roland over the intercom.

Roland fired a short burst from the M134 minigun, a three-second burst that was two hundred rounds. It chewed a line of lead and bright-green phosphor tracers in front of the bad guys. Almost as importantly, the gun had a roar like an angry dragon. It was scary as shit, even when she was the one firing it. On the ground, it heralded imminent death like a hammer blow.

Most of the "bad guys suddenly in over their heads" stumbled back against the front wall of the building. Two even tumbled back through the door where there was no wall to stop their flailing retreat. A couple guys dropped to the ground, probably shot in the legs by rounds that ricocheted off the hard-packed dirt or kicked up rocks.

That drew their attention, and their fire, upward. At least they weren't firing toward the hostage flights anymore.

Trisha rolled left and then pulled hard right, circling around behind the building. Now the front wall blocked the bad guys from a direct line of fire until they moved farther back from the building, which they'd hesitate over. They'd know that would make them even more exposed. It also served to keep their backs toward the ongoing rescue operations.

She could hear CW Lola Maloney in the *Vengeance* handling similar problems further into town with her big DAP Hawk. The Direct Action Penetrator Black

Hawk was the most powerful and effective heli-aviation gunship platform ever launched by any military on the planet. But it weighed almost ten times as much as her bird and moved like it. She'd take the tap dance of the Little Bird over the waltz of the DAP any day.

Trisha slid to a hover behind the building.

That's when the RPG came at her out of the back window, triggering a painfully loud audible warning system over the headphones embedded in her helmet. Someone had stayed inside, someone smart who had guessed where her first move would be. Nothing she hated more than a rocket-propelled grenade. She'd been downed in Iraq by one of those while still flying for the Screaming Eagles. It hadn't been an experience she'd enjoyed much, though she'd managed to autorotate to an okay landing. Truth be told, it had actually scared her right out of the sky until her commander, Lieutenant Beale, had booted her ass back into the air.

She shoved the collective down and drove the bird toward the ground. Even as the RPG shot by with an angry hiss of its rocket motor mere feet over her rotor and a tapering squeal of the audio warning, she leveled the bird and unleashed a pair of 2.75-inch Hydra 70 rockets into the building. One hit the wall and the other went in through the window before exploding. The tin roof spun up into the air, and the four walls blew outward in a beautiful fireball.

She climbed up through the flames and, through the screening smoke, spotted the collection of baddies in the front yard still looking for a target. About half were down with chunks of wall on them. The other half began pinging lame-ass 5.56 mm rounds off her forward windscreen.

"Take 'em!" she called—and Roland did. A five-second burst from the two miniguns bolted onto the hardpoints that stuck out either side of her bird, aimed with a little jiggle on the cyclic to make a figure-eight pattern concentrating their gunfire. That put the baddies out of action.

The clock said 3:04:03. They'd been in contact for a minute and ten seconds. The hostages should be clear by now.

Once she climbed clear of the smoke and flames, she saw that the transport Black Hawk was indeed lifting and Maloney was riding protection. The other Little Birds were long gone.

Trisha was just about to bug out when she saw the lone guy standing where the Black Hawk had just lifted.

At first she thought it might be one of their team, one of the Delta Force boys still on the ground, but he didn't have the small red shoulder-tabs that would glare in the infrared of her night vision. That would tell her he was a good guy. Nor was he a left-behind hostage, because he had a rifle.

It was the embedded agent. He was staying behind. There was no way his charade would hold up after a successful rescue of the hostages occurred right under his nose.

A glance around the neighborhood from her vantage point a hundred feet up in the air told her he was about to be too stupid for words and way too dumb to survive.

A pair of inbound technicals, pickup trucks with big machine guns mounted in their beds, were racing toward the rescue square at high speed.

Cursing loudly, knowing she should be already headed to the beach, she put her nose down and dove into the small square.

―――∿∿∿―――

"What the hell are you doing?" Bill shouted at the pilot who had grounded his craft with the rotor just inches from him. He'd ducked to keep his head from being chopped off, though the pilot had been pretty damned precise with his positioning. They were just fifteen feet apart.

"Get aboard!" the pilot was shouting at him. "I'm saving your ass." Boston. He could hear it in the pilot's voice even over the beat of the rotors.

Bill shook his head and waved them off. The pilot and his copilot wore the full flight suits of Special Operations aviators, FN-SCAR rifles strapped across their chests, and large black helmets with black visors covering their faces. The pilot had a big green shamrock painted on the side of his helmet.

Irish. Boston Irish. It figured. Only an Irishman would be dumb enough to come in and blow his cover.

"Get out of here! You're screwing me over!"

"There are two technicals coming in from the south and west," the pilot shouted as he kept the blades at near takeoff, the chopper actually bouncing its skids on the soil.

Okay, he had to admit that didn't sound good. The technicals were the scourge of the Somali streets. A Jeep or a Toyota pickup with a heavy machine gun mounted in the truck's bed. It would often have a half-dozen other guys with automatic weapons along for the ride.

Then the pilot jerked his hands from the controls, grabbed the rifle hanging across his chest in one smooth upward sweep, and fired it over Bill's shoulder. The light of the muzzle flash was blinding, but thankfully he was far enough back to avoid any powder burns. It had been a damn smooth move, worthy of a SEAL.

He turned to see who the pilot had shot. The muzzle flash of the second shot lit the dingy square.

Abshir. Now with two holes in his shirt even as he fell backward. Good patterning as well; both were probably heart shots. His AK-47 was still aimed at Bill and the chopper, but there was no one alive to pull the trigger.

Okay, maybe the pilot was right and it was getting too hot to stay here. That was one of the problems of running undercover. You started to believe that you belonged. Even though that psych condition was trained for, it was difficult to avoid.

He ducked his head and sprinted to the side of the chopper. It was the attack version of the MH-6, so there were no side benches and the tiny inside passenger compartment behind the pilots' seats was packed with the large ammo cases for the miniguns.

He found a spot to hang on to outside, barely, just behind the little side wings where the weaponry was hung on hardpoints. He slapped the side of the helicopter hard.

The pilot didn't waste time looking back.

They were aloft before Bill had time to catch his next breath.

Three technicals were roaring into the area, one appearing far back of the other two.

He hoped the pilot remembered he was here and

didn't fire any rockets off his side. He'd get serious burns from the rocket motors if he did.

***

Trisha cursed the man for eight kinds of an idiot. Now she was out of balance with his additional weight on the right side and barely off the ground as three technicals roared into the square.

She'd fired a thousand-odd rounds and a pair of rockets that would make up for a third of his weight. And she'd burned about ten gallons of fuel since the start of the mission at six-plus pounds a piece, which bought her another third. Even with that, he made her overweight and it was a major struggle to compensate. Time to dump some more ammo, which was fine with her.

"Open fire, guns only!" she called to Roland and stamped on the left foot-pedal, which would press Mr. Jerk against the chopper rather than flinging him off. He'd still better hang on.

Two feet off the ground, the chopper spun beneath the rotor like a child's wooden spinning top. Roland unleashed both M134s as they rotated about their central axis. A line of fire three feet above the ground arced outward like a buzz saw. It sliced through everything in its sweeping path.

It chewed up the front walls of houses, hammering a line of holes through each burlap door. She really hoped that if there was anyone home, they were lying down on the ground, as any sensible person would be during a firefight. Anyone standing up was about to be shot.

It also dragged a line of fire across the front of each technical. It shredded radiators, engines, front windshields.

Roland was reading off rotor blade and tail clearances from the buildings—she couldn't take time to look at herself. But it was exactly what she needed to maintain flight safety.

By the second rotation of the Little Bird, people were bailing off the truck beds.

On the third rotation, the two lead technicals exploded in balls of fire, and she decided it was high time to be somewhere else, preferably before her engine scooped up chunks of truck shrapnel.

"Off!" she called to Roland, and she leveraged her spinning energy into a rolling climb and a lot of forward speed.

She leaned out and looked back. Their passenger was still there.

The third technical went up in a ball of fire behind them as she cleared the beach. Not a whole lot of ground fire was following them. She dropped back to wave height, resisting adding a victory roll because of their passenger.

3:05:30. Two and a half minutes in country.

"Feet wet." She called on the radio to let the AMC know she was safely clear of the land and back over the water.

Chapter 2

"I didn't want a goddamn rescue!"

The guy was alive on the deck of the amphibious assault ship USS *Peleliu* and complaining about it bitterly. The ship had been scheduled to retire in 2013, but instead it had been given a new lease on life. The Navy had assigned her to the Gulf to anchor United States participation in the anti-Somalia piracy task force, Operation Heavy Hand. She was an aircraft carrier for helicopters—a couple hundred feet shorter, half as wide, and one-third the displacement of her big sisters.

Trisha let him rant while she shut down the *May*. 03:46:10, right on mission schedule, ten seconds late this time. She made a point of chatting with Roland for a moment before she peeled off her helmet and turned to face the raging idiot.

The red deck lights for night operations were bright enough that he'd be able to see her clearly. That usually stopped guys cold.

"Oh fine. A woman. Now I'm probably going to have my ass reamed for yelling at a woman." Then he continued right along, chewing her out without further pause, which was pretty funny. She let him rant, figuring he'd feel better if he could burn off some of his excess, over-righteous macho.

Embedded agent. She'd expected a skinny black Somali with a rusting AKM rifle looking for a ticket to

America. This guy was white as could be and built like a linebacker. Bugfuck crazy to go undercover in Somalia looking the way he did.

Which, she had to admit, was pretty good despite the ratty clothes and smelling like he'd had a couple dozen too many nights in the desert without a shower. Actually, linebacker looked damn good on this guy. She liked them big and handsome. She also liked his temper. Guys who just rolled over and played puppy dog when confronted with a cute woman were dull and predictable. Mr. Agent Man…

She climbed down and set her helmet on her seat. Even standing up straight in her boots, he towered over her. Six foot, maybe six-two. SEAL or Delta. Hard to imagine a Delta Force operator yelling at her. D-boys rarely even spoke and were rarely over five-eight. So he was a SEAL. It was the blue eyes, eyes that blazed with fury at the moment, that were his outstanding feature. His jet-black hair was a dirty snarl from riding out in the wind without a helmet.

"I was supposed to bring down Mahan—"

"If"—Trisha finally had had enough and pushed back—"he was hanging out of the back of the main building with an RPG, I took care of that." And she managed to suppress the shiver at the memory of that bolt of death coming right at her.

"Well, that's something anyway." He stopped his harangue long enough to take a breath. Then crossed his arms, each as big around as her legs, over his chest and glared down at her. "But I was supposed to get to his boss too."

"Sorry." She shrugged. "Can't help you much there

unless he was over for dinner last night and hanging out in the main house."

A smile almost quirked up one corner of his mouth before he got it under control. She could see the nice things it would do to his face if he ever actually let it loose, which couldn't be very often by the look of him. A heavy scar ran from his left ear and down along his jaw. "I'd know if he was, because the food wouldn't have sucked as bad as usual. And it did."

That got a laugh out of her.

William Bruce liked that laugh, despite his better judgment. It was bright, from the heart, and lit her up even prettier than she already was, which was saying something.

And she'd saved him, no question.

Worse, she knew it.

So why couldn't he stop railing at her?

Without the sound of the rotor washing over them and his ears ringing from the gunfire, her voice and accent were even more distinct. Very upper Boston. Very well-bred. He didn't mind the Irish. It was just something handy to be pissed about, as he was pure-blood Scots, or as pure as anyone got these days.

Her voice was also very female, and it sounded good on her. Not low and throaty, but rather midrange and rich with nuance. She'd simultaneously expressed absolute contempt for him and deep humor at his rant, the latter finally cooling his jets.

She stood, hands on narrow hips right above her Browning M1911. Big gun for such a small woman, but she'd already proven she could handle her weapons when she shot Abshir. She didn't even come up to his shoulder, didn't look to be big enough around to stand up in a strong breeze. Her hair, a feathered chop-cut that reached past her jawline and might have been done with the Ka-Bar knife strapped to her thigh, was a rich red without quite crossing over into carrot orange, and her blue eyes were brilliant on a freckled face.

Her smile just shone, brighter than the deck lights on the flat gray expanse of the assault ship's deck. Bright and way too sure of itself.

Damn, was the only thing he could think. This woman was far too cute to be real. Like the sassy sidekick in a cop shop, the one any guy with a brain would be lusting after rather than the main babe in uniform. But she had saved his ass, so she must be real.

"Liked the spinning trick." He wasn't going to admit that he'd never seen anything like it before and that it had taken every last ounce of his strength and training to stay aboard while she was doing it.

"It just came to me." She cleared the magazine and the chambered round out of the rifle still hanging across her chest.

He knew that in that split second after he'd grabbed on, she'd figured out her whole attack plan including which way to spin to make it easiest for him. The other way and the centrifugal force would have thrown him clear without question. She also didn't use the rockets as she'd probably have preferred against the technicals.

Between Abshir regaining consciousness sooner than expected and the three technicals he hadn't even known were in Bosaso…

The three technicals hadn't been in town as of last night. The Puntland militia had driven most of them away in their battle against piracy and warlords, and even the ones the militia maintained would have no reason to be running them around in the middle of the night. He'd have known.

"Shit!"

"What?" The smile slid off her face.

"The technicals weren't there last night."

"And they aren't there now."

Which was true. She'd killed them dead. "But the only reason they'd come to town, especially the west end, was if the boss man was showing up."

She looked grim. "Any chance he was on one of them?"

He liked how fast she switched over from joking to considering tactics. Not even all that many guys were as fast.

"No. Hassan doesn't trust anyone. Always drives separately in his own Range Rover."

"Crap. Sorry about that. Can't be helped now. Can I buy you some coffee?" Just as mercurially as she'd switched into soldier mode, she flipped back into sassy.

"This is a Navy ship. It's free."

"Fine. Whatever." She turned and walked away.

He opened his mouth, but nothing came out. After three months embedded, coffee sounded awfully good. And he'd just turned down an invitation to coffee from the person who'd saved his hide. He'd tossed the proverbial cuppa right back into her face.

She'd decided she was done with him, teasing or otherwise, and simply left—which was far more effective than any girlie slap would have been. No, she was a soldier, a flier for SOAR. If she'd unleashed a strike and gotten past his guard, no question it would have stung.

He watched her go. He wasn't about to go chasing after some pint-sized Night Stalker. But, damn, she was worth watching. There was no way on the planet any woman could make a flight suit and survival vest look sexy, so how did she? *Way too long in the field, Billy. That's how. Gotta get yourself some shore leave.*

He headed over to the control tower to find the Quartermaster. He'd need a shower, fresh clothes, and to check in with command, preferably in that order. Maybe get a meal in there real soon as well.

He stumbled to a halt and looked in the direction the pilot had gone. Already out of sight belowdecks.

Not only hadn't he thanked her for saving his ass, but he also hadn't gotten her name.

Not that he really cared. *He didn't, did he?* No chance he wanted to hang out with either a Night Stalker or an Irishwoman. Two strikes right off.

Still, he cleared the rounds out of both of his weapons as he turned once more for the Quartermaster's. Wouldn't hurt anything if he knew her name.

Chapter 3

TRISHA CLAMBERED DOWN THE THREE FLIGHTS OF stairs from the flight deck, past the massive, mostly unused hangar deck to the main deck where her quarters were. Without the standard U.S. Marines aboard and only a quarter of the full Navy crew, there was plenty of space.

Even though she was enlisted, she'd been assigned her own cabin in the officer's section at the forward end of the main deck, as had been all the women of SOAR. This wasn't a great hardship on space allocation, as there were only the four of them in all of the Night Stalkers, now that Major Beale was retired to civilian life. The other three were married and had their husbands with them in ship's quarters that had never been designed for couples.

So, Trisha enjoyed that great state of luxury held only by the top Navy officers—her own damn space. Even better, her own damn shower. Well, she shared it with the Maloneys, Tim and Lola, but since they were busy delivering rescued hostages to the aircraft carrier, it was all hers at the moment. The shower flow had a three-minute timer for fresh-water conservation, but she wasn't complaining. The men from the flight crews on the choppers were in double-up rooms and the service crews were in the open-berth accommodations.

She showered and changed into a comfortably worn

set of fatigues, running shoes, and a T-shirt that declared "Army" across her chest. She decided that she wasn't going to waste another thought on the ungrateful, ego-ridden, too-damn-handsome-to-let-live jerk she'd rescued.

Though she was sorry she hadn't known about the leader Hassan in the Range Rover. It didn't really matter. At the first sign of trouble, Mr. Pirate-Boss-Bad-Dude would just pull up to some building and shut down his engine and lights. There wouldn't be any real way to pick him out then, especially in Somalia. There were hundreds, maybe thousands of white Range Rovers there. It was the badge of honor, first purchase of any pirate who earned a cut of some ransom. Whoever owned that dealership sure wasn't hurting.

Trisha headed down the narrow, gray-steel passage for dinner. The boat was so lightly manned that only the officers' mess was running, which worked out great. It meant she was a dozen steps from food, not a dozen passages winding through the heart of an eight-hundred-foot-long ship.

The *Peleliu* had been stripped down for this mission, as much as you could strip down an eight-hundred-foot amphibious assault ship. Her total ship's complement had gone from twenty-five hundred to under four hundred.

Seventeen hundred U.S. Marines had been replaced by a platoon of forty-two Special Operations Army guys from the 75th Ranger Regiment and a six-man team of Delta Force. It was the sworn responsibility of the Rangers and the Marines to denigrate each other, so the Rangers made lots of jokes about them replacing forty times as many Marines being a roughly equal exchange of abilities. The Navy personnel still aboard didn't particularly appreciate that.

As usual, the D-boys didn't say much at all.

With the usual twenty-nine choppers being replaced by six of SOAR's birds, who provided their own service and support team, the ship's standard complement of nine hundred Navy personnel was also cut by three-quarters. They had only one big and two small landing craft in the hold of a ship that could usually launch twenty craft or more.

They all practically echoed about the ship. But it didn't feel like a ghost ship, just an efficient use of a monster vessel that had served for forty years and been given this new lease on life at the end of her days.

Now, lean and mean was *Peleliu*'s mission profile, and Trisha was totally down with that. No Somalis would mess with a ship of her size, and she wasn't attached to any war patrol, so her defenses needed only to be lightly manned. She wouldn't be an attractive target for an Iraqi or Iranian with a death wish, as she could still defend herself plenty well even with the short staff.

The mission debrief would happen later, after Maloney returned from delivering the rescued hostages to the aircraft carrier. From there, they'd be shipped out to Ramstein Air Force Base on a C-2A Greyhound transport plane and then back stateside. The captain would be welcome to negotiate the ransom for the recovery of his yacht. At least it wouldn't be for his life and that of his passengers. Trisha bet not a one of them would ever sail with him again, not even around the Washington, DC Tidal Basin in a canoe.

There was also a whole pirate cell that they'd chewed

up pretty good and an obnoxious SEAL who'd had his ass saved when he was too stupid to do it himself. A good night's work.

Trisha followed the amazing scents of burgers and fries and bacon and eggs. Since they flew at night and slept during daylight, it was often the toughest decision of her day. Should she have breakfast because it was now morning, according to most of the planet's population? Or dinner because it smelled so good and she'd just successfully completed her first fully mission-qualified flight with the Night Stalkers? She went with her nose and had a burger with bacon and a fried egg on it, with a side of hash browns.

The service guy behind the stainless-steel chow line had handed it over with a smile and a friendly wink. She knew a lot of women who got all stubborn or pissed about being treated differently. She winked back. Hell, Trisha was different. She squared her shoulders while carrying the tray over to the ketchup and mustard pumps. Only the fifth woman to ever qualify for SOAR, she was a woman in a man's job because she was just that damned good.

"Don't you ever eat anything green?"

Trisha looked up at Colonel Gibson, the commander of the six Delta Force operators aboard. He was a fair bit taller than she was: five-ten, making him tall for a D-boy, and greyhound lean. They'd slept together a couple of times when she was still in SOAR training and their assignments had briefly overlapped at Fort Rucker. She could attest that every ounce he carried was pure muscle and that his stamina was astonishing. It had been fun, but it hadn't taken on anything deeper for either of them, so they'd become friends instead.

"Not if I can help it." His steel tray included a token banana. "And that yellow thing there doesn't count."

"It's closer to green than all that red meat you got on yours."

"Not by much, Michael."

She went for milk because a soda would jazz her up too much. Michael went for coffee, in this heat.

"You're crazy."

He didn't even ask why she was accusing him of that this time. He just shrugged noncommittally toward a vacant table in the corner of the gray-painted mess hall, and she followed him over. If he were any other man, he'd be working a desk job. After all, the whole of Delta Force was commanded by a colonel, most definitely not a field grunt's rank.

Each year he'd receive a set of orders retiring him to Washington. Each year he'd write a simple "No" across the orders and send them back. It felt good to be friends with the most experienced field operative on the planet. She didn't mind the extra bit of self-validation at the moment, though she'd never admit to it aloud, and only a little bit to herself.

Instead of screwing up, she'd kicked ass on her first forward mission as pilot-in-command for SOAR. Damn, but that felt good.

They sat down at the red Formica four-top along the edge of the room. Some of the other crew drifted into the mess and hit the chow line—Roland, Max, and Dennis, *Merchant*'s pilot, along with the other two Little Bird copilots.

She sat down with her back to the room, because she knew that Michael wouldn't be comfortable without his own back to a wall.

"Why do they make these rooms so short?"

Michael took her question seriously and inspected the low-hanging gray ceiling and its impossible nest of strangely labeled pipes zigzagging everywhere, worse than the control wiring inside her chopper. Then he took a bite of his burger, that he'd set up just the same as hers, and chewed as if seriously considering the problem.

Before she could mount her next attack, for she knew that while he was insanely bright, it always took him a moment to formulate his comebacks, he waved a hand beckoning someone over. Apparently there was some initial resistance, as he had to signal a second time.

Trisha turned in time to see the guy she'd rescued coming over. A wake of sailors moved aside for him almost without noticing. You just didn't get in the way of a guy who moved like that. Incoming battleship. No, a destroyer. She liked the analogy—big enough to be unstoppable, lean and long like he was, and enough speed and muscle to be absolutely lethal.

She turned back to scowl at Michael, but it was too late. The damn fool was already on his way. He hadn't looked any happier about it than she had.

"Michael." The SEAL stopped beside the table but didn't set down the tray he held in his big, meaty hands. "Long time."

"Azerbaijan."

Trisha tried to think of any mission she'd ever heard of in Azerbaijan. Man, she'd barely heard of the country itself. Might never have, if it weren't shoved up against Iran's northern border. So, he did nasty secret stuff with a Delta commander, not a big surprise. She offered the guy a welcoming scowl.

"I see there's no need to introduce. Have a seat." Michael nodded beside him.

Untrue, but Trisha didn't need Mr. SEAL's name anyway. Didn't want it. It would just be another thing for her to forget as quickly as possible.

"Don't want to interrupt."

"Oh, sit down, for crying out loud." Trisha hated when guys got all weird around her. She'd been sick of it from the first carefully planned prekindergarten date, arranged by her mother and attended by her nanny. And she was sick of it now. It was much more prevalent for a woman serving in uniform.

The guy waited another beat before settling down beside Michael.

He'd at least gotten some broccoli with his burger and eggs and fries and hash browns.

"There's green shit on your plate."

"Don't worry. I made sure it was dead first."

Okay, he was quick; she liked that even if she didn't want to. She settled into silence, figuring that since he and Michael had sought each other out, they'd have something to say to each other.

Nope.

Like most of the military, especially in the Special Ops Forces, they were such guys. Kinda cute in a way, when it didn't make her want to knock their heads together. So, any conversation was going to be up to her.

"I think something's wrong with the ceiling. It's far too low for the width of the room. They should have gone up at least two more feet and gotten rid of all those pipes." It really was a little oppressive. She'd seen the tallest Rangers duck to clear the gray pipes even though they weren't actually that low; they just felt as if they were. The nameless guy hadn't ducked, though he was taller than many of the guys who did. As if he knew exactly what was and wasn't a threat.

Michael inspected the ceiling again as if it were a target. "Add two feet per story. Nineteen or twenty stories from the bilge keel to the sky control room. That would be an additional thirty-eight to forty feet added to the ship's height."

Sometimes she would just let him ramble. Michael would often go on for some time being all analytical before he realized that she was just messing with him. Soon he'd be talking about extra weight above the waterline and the necessary extensions to the keel to compensate. It was one of the several reasons it hadn't worked out between them. He just didn't keep up with her humor, and as a result, he never knew when to take her seriously. He'd dust her in tactics or situational awareness, but humor not so much.

"Don't go down any more decks," the big guy said.

"Why?" He forked up some of his eggs as if this was a perfectly normal conversation. He cleaned up nice, real nice. The T-shirt they'd found for him, in Navy dark blue, stretched tight across his chest and outlined every muscle. The antithesis of the lean Colonel Gibson. His black hair reached his jawline, slicked down with the shower he'd taken since they'd parted. It emphasized both the nasty scar and the strength of the jaw that bore it. She could see that the scar continued on his chest, ducking below the line of his collar. She wondered how far down it went and how he'd earned it.

And his eyes really were amazing. It felt not as if he

was watching her, but rather as if he saw her. A gestalt view, watching her whole person, not just her face or, more typically, her chest. His intentness started to bring a heat to her face that she suppressed ruthlessly; she was so fair-skinned that even the slightest blush radiated.

"The decks get shorter as you go down. Two more decks and even someone your size would be stooping."

"How short do they get?" Her size, huh? She'd taken men down for less than that when she was in a bad mood. But she wasn't at the moment, so she'd play along. "They have children down there in the engine spaces? Or Oompa-Loompas?"

"Smurfs." He said it like bald truth, not the least hint of foolish in his eyes.

"Color of your eyes."

"What was that?"

"Nothing." Why had she even whispered that to herself? She ordered herself to stop going all mushy in the brain about his blue eyes. Immediately!

His glance said that he wasn't letting her off the hook, so she covered quickly.

"Your eyes. Clearly you have Smurf blood. I'll remember to run if they ever turn purple."

"Do that." He continued eating his eggs as if this were a perfectly normal conversation.

Michael was wincing slightly as he did each time he finally caught up and realized he'd once again fallen for one of her jokes.

～ᴗ～

Lieutenant Commander Boyd Ramis came over to shake Bill's hand and join them. Trisha wondered, who didn't this guy know? At least the Lieutenant Commander's greeting had given Trisha the guy's first name since he was too lame to introduce himself.

Now the four of them sat around the red table in the corner of the officers' mess of the *Peleliu*.

Trisha considered feeling uncomfortable—Lieutenant Commander, Colonel, and Bill Whatever-His-Rank-Was the SEAL were all clearly way above her mere lieutenant—but she decided against it. She'd just think of it as one of her parents' dinner parties, with enough political and social power in the room to light up half of Boston. Unlike those Boston power dinners, these guys still didn't have a clue among them.

At long last, they started discussing some past missions. Everyone aboard this ship had serious security clearance, not even an embedded reporter aboard, so they knew that they could speak freely. But still they didn't, hedging references, casting sidelong glances for her perceived delicacy.

Men seemed to come in mostly one breed, jerk. Actually, she could see Michael glancing her way, but with a different expression. The glance wasn't about her presence bothering him. She'd once explained to him what always happened around women in the military, how men's brains switched over into "stupid mode" almost every time. He'd argued at first but finally had seen it happen to Trisha enough times to believe her.

His slight nod acknowledged that he was making the same observations she was and that she wasn't being overly sensitive. And, typically for a D-boy, he wasn't saying a word.

Fine! Let them have their way.

Trisha grabbed her tray with her half-finished meal, gave Michael a pleasant smile, and rolled her eyes at the two oblivious men, then went to join the Little Bird crews.

She could feel Bill the SEAL watching her back as she walked away. He better not be watching her butt or she'd hurt him big time.

Billy the SEAL. Even better. Maybe she should buy him a one-way ticket to SeaWorld. He could perform scowls, sulks, and grimaces four shows a day. The fact that she'd be willing to pay the price of admission was something she simply ignored.

Bill caught the woman's eye roll as she turned away. He also noticed that she was even slighter than he'd first thought when she'd been in the flight suit. If she weighed a hundred and ten soaking wet, it would be a surprise. Yet she'd survived SOAR training. He knew what the Night Stalkers put their people through. Ranger School, Green Platoon, and worse. It wasn't a BUD/S course, like all SEALs survived, but it was about the closest thing there was in the U.S. Special Operations Forces. That meant she was tough as hell and driven beyond belief, in addition to the cuteness factor.

He dragged his eyes away from her trim form and perky walk—the woman actually bounced on her toes. Light on her feet like some dancer or the very best field operators. As if. But what if she was? Again he had to actively shove her out of his thoughts. Shouldn't be too hard, as he still didn't know her name.

Bill put his attention back on Boyd's story of a messy operation they had been running against a pirate operation off Indonesia back when he was a second lieutenant, but his mind wandered back to the woman.

It didn't take much to figure out what caused her disgust. He'd served with the Lieutenant Commander before, back when Boyd was on his first tour. The man had gone through the Naval Academy at Annapolis and started out as the greenest ensign the planet had ever seen. By that time Bill, who had enlisted straight from high school, was a petty officer third class, not long before he went over to the SEALs.

The nice thing about Boyd was he'd listened and learned. Now, at thirty-two, he was a lieutenant commander and had been given charge of this overage vessel on a solo special operation, a low-stress posting for the Navy. It boded well for his future career. He was a good guy, as far as it went. Bill made a bet with himself that Boyd would never break the rank of captain and would probably never command a warship. He was cut out for supply and service vessels; he'd never make it to a destroyer or carrier except as a second- or third-ranker.

Boyd's problem was that he thought lower ranks were useful, to be treated well, but that they were indeed lower ranks. And the woman—damn, he wished he knew her name—was Army rather than Navy, which was its own crime in Boyd's eyes.

Bill would have to corner Michael later and see what he knew about her. That they'd been sitting together had said a lot in her favor, though Bill still didn't know how to interpret it.

Of course, getting information out of a D-boy like Colonel Michael Gibson would take some doing.

Maybe Bill needed a different tack, like maybe just asking her.

He turned his attention back to Boyd's story, for now.

<center>~~~</center>

"So what were you doing back there?" Max Benjamin waved a piece of bacon over his shoulder. Sitting in the windowless bowels of the ship, there was no way to know in what direction Bosaso now lay, so over the shoulder was as good a direction as any. It wasn't toward the table she'd just left, which was fine with her.

"Covering your behind, Max. Covering your behind." Trisha had only been flying with this particular group for a couple weeks and tonight had been the first action she'd seen with them, but already they were comfortable. It helped that there had been four women before her, but even during training, the Night Stalkers had been a significant improvement over her former Army unit. In SOAR only one thing really mattered—how good you were. And she was damn good.

She wanted to laugh at her own arrogance, sitting around a table with far more experienced fliers, but she knew how to assess her own skills objectively. Okay, fairly objectively. Any decent pilot had at least some dose of arrogance. But she belonged at this table. She belonged or they wouldn't let her sit here.

"That blockhead SEAL." She tilted her head over her shoulder toward her former table. "He was standing there in the brownout dust of Bosaso yelling at me for wanting to rescue his sorry ass. So, I had to kill a couple technicals before they erased him."

"Next time you want to be a little more careful."

The voice behind her was some kinda pissed. Army-superior-officer pissed.

Trisha spun to look at who had come up behind her, then bolted to her feet and snapped to attention.

Chief Warrant 3 Lola Maloney stood close behind her, still imposing in her flight gear. She was flanked by Sergeant Kee Stevenson and the massive Master Sergeant John Wallace. The Black Hawks were clearly back from delivering the hostages to the aircraft carrier. Kee Stevenson was Trisha's own height, but built like God had meant a woman to be, seriously curved. Trisha had to look a long way up to see the dark eyes of Chief Maloney, and Big John Wallace towered another couple inches past her.

"I killed them, sir. All three technicals."

"No." Lola Maloney shook her head. "You killed two. The third had you in the sights of both their .50 cal machine gun and an RPG launcher when I put a pair of rockets in them. John gave them several hundred rounds for good measure."

Trisha could feel her knees go soft. If Chief Maloney hadn't been there, she, her copilot, and Billy the SEAL would all be very dead right now. No way to dodge an RPG from straight behind. But she'd been so sure she had done it right and gotten away clean herself.

And she hadn't even seen it happen.

Damn! Another goddamn RPG! They had it in for her.

Maloney nodded once, seeing that the message had been received. "Nice job pulling him out, by the way."

Trisha swallowed hard past the tightness in her throat.

"Thank you, sir. He didn't appreciate it much."

Lola smiled brightly as if she hadn't just finished

whittling Trisha down to boot-tall. "Men never do. And no, you won't get used to it. It will keep pissing you off. Next time, call for help before you head into trouble. We were right there, but we might not have been."

Then the three of them were gone, moving as a unit toward the chow line.

Trisha sat back down slowly and took a bite of her burger without really tasting it, just for something to do. She kept an eye on the DAP Hawk and transport Black Hawk crews. The three women and five men moved as a unit down the line and gathered all together at a table beyond some Navy officers. The Air Mission Commander, "Wrench" Stevenson, and a young girl joined them. They made a tight group, impenetrable. Other.

Usually, Trisha was amused by the dynamic. When there were only a few of them, Night Stalkers would gather together as a group. But as soon as the density of helicopter crews was high enough, they divided by type of craft. The Night Stalkers only flew three different craft. And the other three women of SOAR were all flying on the Sikorsky MH-60M Black Hawks, as were two of their husbands. So here she was the outsider.

But she wasn't. She was the first woman to fly in the Little Birds. The Hawks might be the hammers of the outfit, but the Little Birds weren't called the Killer Eggs for nothing. They went in close. She'd rescued Billy the SEAL from a place a Black Hawk would barely fit. And they'd never have room for her spinning-top maneuver.

"You actually killed two technicals?" Mad Max leaned in, keeping his voice down so that it wouldn't carry past the Little Birds' table.

Roland, her copilot, answered for her while she continued to chew slowly because her throat was still too tight to swallow.

"Sweet as could be. Never seen anything like it." Then he started explaining what she'd done to the controls to pull it off while compensating for the weight of the SEAL.

She was content to focus on her hamburger and let the feeling of belonging spread over her again as she ate and the Little Bird crews laughed around her. Together they reviewed every control detail of what she'd done. She had something to teach here, something to give.

One thing every Night Stalker cared about—how to fly it better the next time.

What did SEALs care about?

Chapter 4

TRISHA WAS HALFWAY THROUGH HER LATE-AFTERNOON run in the helo hangar of the *Peleliu*. The aft half of the ship and a stretch up the side of the main deck were an open area for parking and maintaining helicopters. The space was empty, since all of SOAR's craft fit on the ship's flight deck thirty feet above that covered the helo hangar. This saved time because rotors didn't have to be folded back for storage.

That left the hangar open for running. Briefing for tonight's mission wasn't for an hour yet, which would leave her plenty of time for a shower and breakfast. For now, she worked the roughly half-kilometer running loop down the length of the helo hangar and back.

Up top, heat waves still shimmered off the flight deck in the late-afternoon light. A person could get heatstroke just standing on the steel surface, assuming their shoes didn't melt first. Here inside the body of the ship, the covered but wide-open helo hangar wasn't that much cooler, but at least it didn't have the sun hammering on it.

The Navy guys had shown them a running track that had been worked out on a couple of the lower decks, but you kept having to hop over hatch frames. They'd also included up and down ladders to the workout, but she preferred simple distance running. Here, the path was wide open except for the equipment racks in a couple of the service bays.

Only a half-dozen others were running at the moment, scattered over the length of the ship, so she was practically alone. For company, she had the echoes that rattled around the massive deck. Three stories high, two football fields long, half of one wide, and all steel, the hangar had serious echoes. Even with just the slap of rubber-soled shoes, it was quite loud.

That's when she spotted Michael doing warm-up stretches by the big elevator that raised and lowered aircraft between the helo hangar and the flight deck. She eased up to him and continued jogging in place.

"Morning."

"Hey, Trisha." In moments, he fell in beside her.

She kept her pace down for the first lap or two as he warmed up, but soon they were both back at their normal pace. It was one of the ways they'd been compatible. They ran well together, neither holding the other back.

She kept running longer than she'd planned, just enjoying Michael's quiet company as they looped along the track for a quarter of a mile per lap.

"So, did Billy the SEAL get even more charming?" She put enough sarcasm in her question for Michael to get it clearly. Trisha wasn't quite sure why she was asking about the SEAL, but it was a morning conversation starter.

They ran past the flight-ready room and along the forward service bays delineated by broad stripes of worn yellow paint just barely an aircraft-width apart. Turning at the forward gunnery station and gunnery crew berths, they were heading back down the length of the ship before he answered.

"Bill's a good guy."

Trisha almost dismissed the comment, but this was

Michael. He didn't praise anyone who didn't really deserve it. And the only way to earn Michael's respect was the hard way.

"What else did he have to say?"

They passed the chopper-sized opening in the side of the hangar deck where the elevator would come down. It offered a blinding view from the otherwise dim deck. The Gulf of Aden shimmered in the brilliant light. They were steaming slowly east, so the opening was to the north. That meant no direct sunlight, but still the ocean glared and she had to squint to see that the waters far below were pretty calm. All quiet for now.

"He wanted to know your name."

"That's it?" It was a start anyway. A start of what? She wasn't really interested in Billy the SEAL…so why was she asking about him?

"No."

Trisha laughed. Michael was always such a font of information.

"And…" she prompted him.

"When he asked about more, I told him that he'd better watch himself around you. Because anything you left after taking him apart, I would see to personally."

That shut her up. They turned at the afterdeck, the second major opening in the helo hangar for the aft aircraft elevator, now filling with the orange light of the setting sun.

Michael only spoke truth; it was just a part of who he was. That meant he thought she could probably take on Billy and win. He was one of the few people who knew about her past, or at least that part of it. But there was more than that. One of the most decorated and able soldiers on the planet had just threatened a Navy SEAL on her behalf.

She wasn't going to tear up because of that, despite the tightness in her throat. She wasn't going to hug Michael, as she'd like to. Not even punch his arm as they ran side by side down the long side of the deck marked for a dozen empty maintenance bays, stripped now of aircraft, tools, and even equipment racks.

Trisha said the only thing she could think of that wouldn't leave them both totally uncomfortable.

"Thanks."

He nodded once and they kept running in silence.

William Bruce climbed up the decks toward Boyd's office. He'd gotten a call that new orders were in, and could he report to the Lieutenant Commander? A bit unusual. Typically someone would just tell him when his flight to rejoin his team would be, but Boyd was an old acquaintance and must want to handle things personally.

Bill climbed past the main and 01 level decks. At the 02 level deck, the highest level below the flight deck, an opening in the stairwell let him look down over the vast helo hangar. The sunset was streaming into the stern of the ship, lighting the length of it. A half-dozen guys were running the loop. The sun also lit the color of fire off the hair of one particular redhead.

Lieutenant Patricia O'Malley absolutely glowed in the belowdecks light. He automatically assessed her gait. Smooth, long, not practiced. There was something about how a practiced runner ran, and she didn't have it. Patricia ran as if it was the most natural thing on the planet, as if she'd been born to it. That meant she'd run a lot as a kid. Not around the playground, but really run. Like it was important.

That didn't fit the mental picture he'd been building. She sat with Colonel Gibson, which few did. She was just a second lieutenant, but had at least seven years in the service to be flying for SOAR, which meant she'd started out enlisted and had only recently flipped over to being an officer. The only way to do that was to enlist and then earn it through hard work and exceptional service. Couldn't be more than mid-twenties, so she'd earned it fast. She sounded like a college girl. Add five more years of service before you could even interview for SOAR, plus a minimum of two years before you commanded a bird in the field, so late twenties.

Only at this moment did he register quite where she'd been sitting when he first saw her. She'd been sitting right-hand seat in a Little Bird for the 160th SOAR. That meant she was pilot-in-command, not ride-along copilot in training. Beyond good, she had to be exceptional to fly right seat for the Night Stalkers.

Still, he'd figured her for some comfortable middle-class girl who'd decided to go military for reasons as yet unknown. She had some of that entitled attitude and poise that he pegged as having been brought up in a far nicer world than he had been.

But then there'd been Michael's twofold warning. That Patricia was actually a skilled fighter and would stand a chance against him, though she couldn't weigh half as much. Which Bill would have dismissed as impossible coming from any other source. And the second that Michael would defend her if she couldn't.

That's when the Colonel's shield had come down. They weren't lovers, that much was obvious, but Bill took the Delta operator seriously when he threatened to take Bill apart on Patricia O'Malley's behalf, if necessary. And though he knew that only a few men on the planet could take him down in a fair fight or even an unfair one, he'd bet that Gibson was one of them.

Bill continued to look down, watching Patricia run the length of the helo hangar and back. He sure as hell couldn't look away. How in the world had she crawled under his skin? He'd watched her laughing with her teammates for the second part of dinner. Seen her and her commander discussing something, with her showing the sharp military she could present but then slide back into being her casual self. He sure hadn't minded watching what her gait did to her body as she'd walked away from them, either.

And the way she ran was something impressive to see, as well. Her gait had an odd break when she hit corners. Not the plod, twist, plod, twist, plod, finish turn of most runners on a narrow course. Instead it was a sharp lean and quick offbeat shuffle. She practically turned a right-angle rather than a curved one. A necessary skill to disappear down an alley or into an opportune doorway.

That was street. He knew how a street fighter moved, had grown up surviving on the bad side of Detroit and later Chicago. And she had it. How could a pretty little thing like Patricia O'Malley and her upper-crust accent have survived that hell?

Then he refocused.

She wasn't running alone. She ran beside Colonel Gibson. They were coming down the deck toward his lofty position at the head of the stairs, which was nearly lost in the girders that supported the flight deck.

As they drew close, Patricia said something to Gibson.

Michael Gibson looked right up at him. One quick, assessing gaze, despite Bill being back in the shadows and three stories above them.

As Gibson looked down, Patricia nodded without even looking up herself. She'd already spotted him, and he hadn't even noticed.

Just before she ran out of sight below his position, she looked ready to laugh. He rubbed a hand over his face. He really needed to get off this ship and far away from this woman, or she'd really lodge herself in his brain. He climbed the last story into the command tower.

Bill knocked on the squad room door and was admitted immediately. The Lieutenant Commander had taken over one of the flight-level ready rooms as an office. It placed him closer to the communication and navigation platforms that made up the ship's tower and was a good choice. The Lieutenant Commander's formal cabin was at the forward end of 02 deck, awkwardly out of the way with so few people aboard.

Boyd shook his hand and offered coffee, which Bill accepted. A table with a long bench down either side only took a small part of the room. He could see painted-over bolt holes that indicated a much larger table had been here before. Now some comfortable chairs and a couch had been placed in the extra space and then bolted down in preparation for bad weather.

On a short couch sat Captain Archie Stevenson, the SOAR Air Mission Commander, and Chief Warrant 3

Lola Maloney, the commander of the *Vengeance* DAP Hawk. This wasn't some casual handoff of orders.

Bill felt a sudden itch between his shoulder blades and did his best not to show it.

Introductions were barely completed when Colonel Gibson came in after knocking once. He had a towel around his neck and sweat dripping down his face.

"Sorry, wanted to finish my run before the meeting." He took a large bottle of water and perched on a chair facing the door. His look at Bill revealed nothing beyond a pleasant good morning.

The itch between Bill's shoulder blades started feeling more like a target.

"Your commander has left the option up to you." Lieutenant Commander Boyd Ramis was not being the least bit helpful.

Bill translated that one easily. Lieutenant Commander Luke Altman, Bill's commander back at SEAL Team Nine, would kick his ass if he didn't make the right choice, but, per usual, Altman wasn't giving any hint about what the right choice was. That at least felt normal. About the only thing that did at the moment.

The others were here in the Lieutenant Commander's conference room to make a full-court press for Lieutenant William Bruce to remain aboard the *Peleliu* and assist in the ongoing antipiracy operations. To make the pitch, they'd gathered Boyd Ramis, the top-ranking Navy asset, the two ranking SOAR assets, and the top Delta operator.

"Experience in-country."

"Unique intelligence asset."

"Provides us with significant advantage."

Bottom line, he knew too much about Somalia, the Somali pirates, and their tactics. After six months studying them and three months embedded with them, there was probably no one in the U.S. military who knew their ways so well. Now this team wanted to leverage his knowledge and skill set, and Luke had left it up to him.

Bill tried to weigh the advantages and disadvantages as he sipped his now-cool coffee. The others were all trying to look casual, sitting back in their chairs, pretending to have some side conversation about the ship's food, while he digested the load they'd just asked him to swallow.

He didn't want to be their adviser or anyone's. He was a SEAL. If he wasn't on an op or training for one, the edge would come off. Not only physically, but also mentally, and that's where the game was really played. He knew he'd perform to his own personal best when challenged as only a fellow SEAL could challenge him. The need to never let down your teammates, no matter what, elicited a level of exceptional performance unattainable elsewhere.

But neither were these people slouches.

Archie Stevenson's reasons had been all about strategic advantage, as you'd expect from an AMC. Maloney had combined being a fine-looking woman with having a fine-functioning brain. Tactics, methods of protection and attack, patrols and guards. She'd been hard pressed not to ask him a thousand questions so that she could enhance her own flight crew's safety and nuance their attacks and defenses. If he stayed, she certainly would be hounding him.

Commander Boyd Ramis liked the idea of having an old buddy on board, even if they'd never been all that close. He also liked having a new liaison—make that a buffer—of someone besides himself to deal with the Night Stalkers. That was probably a more important reason to him.

Their conversation was running down. Bill would have to make a decision soon or they'd start battering at him again. A verbal battle was not one he was well equipped to tackle. He had about as long as it would take them to refill and complain about their Navy coffee.

Working more closely with the Night Stalkers was a big downside for him. They were among Bill's least favorite people. Okay, that wasn't quite right. After seven years as a SEAL, he'd been on dozens of missions and hundreds of training flights on the helicopters of the 160th SOAR. They were exceptional pilots to the very last man, or woman. He'd never flown with any of the other women of SOAR, but after last night he didn't question their standards.

CW2 Patricia O'Malley was clearly exceptional, and no question that she'd be pushing on him if he stayed aboard.

But he would never wholly trust them, which was a near-disastrous problem on missions. It was like not trusting your gun to fire, your knife to cut, or your buddy to stand right beside you ready to die, if necessary, when things went sideways.

Because of one deed, an event more than twenty years ago, he would never trust them completely. The Battle of Mogadishu should never have been a battle. It was a smash-and-grab operation. Capture a couple key advisers of Mohamed Farrah Aidid, the most powerful warlord in Mogadishu, and gut his powerful rule over the Mog. Instead, two of their choppers had been shot down, turning the smash-and-grab into a total cluster-fuck. It had been an awful day for them and, as a result, an awful day for his own father. It nearly broke the family he left behind.

The Army stipend for a young private first class had done almost nothing to stave off the brutal poverty that had ruined his mother's life and made his a living hell.

As an eight-year-old kid who'd lost his father, he'd sworn to pay back the Somalis and the Night Stalkers both. He wasn't sure which one he was angrier at. As an adult, he understood the Night Stalkers' devastating loss as well and he was a little more mature about it. A little. But something had made him stupid enough to volunteer when the assignment to penetrate the pirate crews of Somalia had come up. And now they were asking him to trust SOAR in the one place he was least likely to do so.

Even two decades after his father's death, Somalia was a total train wreck. Except they weren't even that fortunate. Those in power weren't there long enough for strategizing, something totally out of their mind-set. They were simply reacting to warlords, Islamic extremists battling for control, and a massive depletion of fishing stock by foreign fleets taking advantage of Somalia's anarchy, which made the country unable to guard its own seas.

The question was: Could he help fix something if he stayed on with Operation Heavy Hand to quash the pirates? Answer to that much, at least, was "yes."

Could he resist the urge to blow the damn country even further back into the Stone Age than it already was? Well, implementing a major invasion was beyond his circle of control, so it was a moot point.

Was he willing to fly with people like Patricia O'Malley to do what he could? He didn't like his own answer to that one, or that it was even a question he'd asked himself in that way.

What the hell was a female Boston-Irish Night Stalker doing in his head? Crap, but that woman was there every time he turned around, even when she wasn't. And he was sitting still…trying not to remember how she'd grinned at him when he warned her about his eyes going purple. And—time to focus.

He looked over at Michael, the only one who hadn't spoken in the half hour the others had used to try talking him into this. Speaking of exceptional people, he would have the chance to serve alongside the best warrior on the planet. That opportunity was damn hard to argue with too.

"Well, Colonel. What are you thinking?"

Michael did his slow assessment of each person's face around the suddenly silent room.

Then he turned and studied Bill long enough for Bill to begin counting his heartbeats.

"You already made your choice. Why are you asking me?"

Bill shrugged, but it did nothing to ease that target itch between his shoulder blades.

Chapter 5

"Tonight's flight is a wide-area sweep." AMC Stevenson stood at the small podium at the front of the 02 deck briefing room. It was a twenty-by-thirty-foot room on the closest deck beneath the flight deck.

Trisha slouched in the last of a half-dozen rows of comfortable chairs. It was cushy enough to let a pilot forget she was about to launch on some mission that would pound her butt sore before the night was through. The only other feature of the room was a whole lotta gray-painted steel.

What was it with these guys? The Coast Guard boats were all pristine white with orange accents, and their choppers were orange with white accents. Their mission was to be seen. The Night Stalkers' machines were nonreflective black-on-black, but inside Fort Campbell, Kentucky, the rooms had a bit of color and some nice pictures taken by various Night Stalkers, mostly of helos in exotic locales, but some of them were really good shots.

The Navy could just as easily have gone with blue or pastels. It wasn't as if there were any outside windows to the briefing room where a bad guy could peek in and critique the color scheme. Sure, gray was the best low-visibility coloring for the sea and the sky, but using the same color inside simply showed a lack of imagination. They definitely needed to start recruiting more interior designers.

The briefing room was weary with the scuffs and aging of ten thousand missions over the thirty-five years since the ship's original commissioning. No amount of blah gray paint hid the dings from years of service. What in the world had dented the wall just above the Air Mission Controller's head? Something had run into it hard, from the other side. Trisha pictured the ship's layout.

The only thing out there was the elevator shaft for shifting the jets and choppers from the hangar up to the flight deck. Some kinda monster sea roll must have sent a plane slamming into the other side of the wall. Guess it was better than going overboard.

Only about half of the chairs were occupied, with everyone still in their off-duty clothes until they heard the night's task assignments. It was a veritable sea of green T-shirts, camo pants, and sneakers. Dennis, Max, and Roland were there, so that accounted for all of the Little Birds. Lola Maloney and her DAP team were there. Dusty James, who had only recently made the jump to a front-seater of the *Vicious* after four years as a gunner and mechanic for Major Henderson on the *Viper*, wasn't. Apparently no need for the transport Black Hawk tonight. The AMC would be working from the ship's communications platform in the upper stories of the *Peleliu*'s tower.

All pretty standard. Even having Michael Gibson in the room appeared to be standard. No one else commented on it anyway, so Trisha assumed it was normal. His rock-steady nerves and the presence of the top D-boy served as a constant reminder that this was a serious operation with the highest levels of support.

There was only one break in the familiar sea of green,

one spot of Navy blue. Only one blemish of a person here who didn't belong.

Trisha glared over at Billy the SEAL sitting in the front row beside Michael. Couldn't they find off-ship transport for the man? Instead of being gone, he was in a preflight mission briefing. Something was wrong with this picture, but no one was telling her a damn thing.

A glance at her copilot revealed that Roland had no more idea what was going on than she did.

"O'Malley!"

"Sir!" She jumped to her feet when the AMC called out to her. She did a trick that every soldier learned by second year if they were going to survive the Army—she rewound the last few moments of conversation that she'd been hearing but not really paying attention to.

She was supposed to take Lieutenant Bruce under her wing.

Who the heck was Lieutenant Bruce?

That's when she caught Billy the SEAL glaring at her with those wondrous blue eyes that had cost her half a day's sleep and looking very unhappy. Lieutenant William "Billy the SEAL" Bruce? Crap. Bloody Scotsman.

"Yes, sir! Glad to, sir!" she repeated and dropped back into her seat after carefully ignoring the Navy SEAL.

Maybe this was some kind of newbie hazing. But she didn't think SOAR did much of that. Or maybe they did, but still, they wouldn't do that when a mission was involved.

She'd flown for two years with the toughest instructors ever fielded in heli-aviation, and that was after five years with the Screaming Eagles. Her final months had been the best. Her friend from their days in the 101st,

Major Emily Beale, had taken a final rotation as a training instructor as she was leaving SOAR. For three glorious months Emily had shown Trisha what you could make a helicopter really do.

Trisha came into the field and flew copilot with Lola Maloney and learned even more during her initial skirmishes. By the time they seated her in a Mission-Enhanced Little Bird beside Roland, she was all set to prove just what a MELB could really do. The Little Bird was the best toy a girl had ever been given to play with.

So, why were they saddling her behind with Billy the Lieutenant SEAL if it wasn't hazing?

"You two seem to have a rapport." Chief Warrant Lola Maloney was standing right in front of her.

"A rapport, ma'am?" Trisha had missed the rest of the briefing. Even the rewind trick wasn't working. Everyone else was streaming out of the room. She'd have to catch up with Roland to find out what was going down tonight. They hadn't called her name again, so she'd be background, standard operations.

"Yes."

"Chief Warrant?" Trisha tried to make sense of what Maloney had just said. She and the SEAL had a pretty fair feeling of mutual disgust going on—if you ignored the bit of heat she couldn't seem to stop from running up and down her system—but that was about all.

"What is it, O'Malley?" Maloney stood with the casual ease of a magazine model on break. Her long, mahogany-colored hair draped down to her shoulders and framed a face and dark eyes that made a lot of men stop and stare. But Trisha had flown with her, and the woman was an amazing pilot, as well. If it weren't sacrilege in the Trisha Personal Handbook, she'd say that Lola might even be as skilled as Emily Beale. The woman definitely wasn't here because of her looks.

"Why me?" Trisha blurted it out and hoped she wasn't stepping over the line.

The Chief Warrant merely smiled. "You are the one most recently through training. And we always need to consider our customers whether they be Ranger, Delta, or SEAL. A chance to work one on one with a highly decorated SEAL is good practice. Second, he'll be mostly flying in the *Vengeance* with me, and if he is to recommend 'best use' tactics, he needs exposure to what each bird can do. Your skill with the Little Bird makes you well suited to the task."

Okay, if the number-two-ranked Night Stalker on board the *Peleliu* wanted to pay her a compliment like that, she'd do her best to not let her ego run rampant.

Reading her expression as acceptance, Lola Maloney nodded and was gone.

Now the only people left in the briefing room were Trisha herself and, standing by his seat in the front row, Billy the SEAL, facing her with his arms crossed over his ever-so-pretty chest. He wore that near-permanent scowl he seemed so glad to hand out at every opportunity.

"Okay, sailor. We have over an hour to flight." So, some part of her had been listening and caught the mission start time at least. "We might as well make use of it. C'mon."

She turned for the hatchway nearest the stairs leading up to the flight deck without waiting to see if he followed.

Trisha was halfway up the ladder before she felt vibrations through the steel indicating that he was following behind her. The footsteps were no heavier than a child might make. The man could certainly move quietly.

At the head of the ladder, she grabbed a sound-muffling headset and draped it around her neck in case someone was running up their engines.

She resisted the urge to look back and gauge if his mood was as foul as hers.

—⁂—

Bill grabbed a headset and followed Patricia out onto the flight deck. He was still trying to figure out why in the hell he wasn't flying back to his team right now. He missed the guys. They would be running some new scenario on something that would kick all their asses and set the bar just that one inch higher. And here he was with Night Stalkers, Somali, and one more time following this stunner of a woman from behind. That part at least he could really learn to enjoy.

The heat of the flight deck slapped at him. The gray-steel surface had been baking all day in the East African sun, which had only just ducked below the horizon. The heat shimmers were so thick in the early evening light that the horizon danced as if it were a live beast and not merely a quiet ocean of rolling waves. Even the bow lights a mere four hundred feet away flickered as if they were erratic strobes rather than steady white lights.

Patricia O'Malley did the same thing. She shimmered with the anger that coursed off her in waves.

"Why me?" Her voice and her displeasure had been clear enough, despite the shuffling of the fliers as they emptied from the briefing room. Perhaps for a normal person, the distance would have masked her words.

But like most Special Ops, he spoke three languages and had learned to mostly read lips during quiet operations where a whisper could give away your position and possibly get you killed. Even the slightest bit of a word through crowd noise, and he could tell the general purpose of the conversation.

And he didn't need any of that to read Patricia O'Malley's displeasure three rows away in the briefing room. So she had no use for him? Fine. He'd just have no use for her, no matter what the hell the pint-sized twerp was doing to his libido.

She led him aft past the line of tied-down helicopters. Parked, silent death, waiting for their next chance to strike out. He was used to the transport Black Hawks. He'd ridden in them hundreds of times, both SOAR's and others when SOAR wasn't available. And he'd give them credit—the Night Stalkers' birds were immaculate. They had the highest percentage of equipment availability of any unit that flew, Army, Navy, or Air Force.

Most units were glad to have their birds mission-capable eighty-five percent of the time. SOAR's helicopters pushed that percentage into the high nineties. He'd heard that the Night Stalkers considered a bird not ready for even a training flight a "mission failure" and treated it that way, including a full investigation. It didn't happen very often.

They walked past the nose of the *Vengeance*, the Direct Action Penetrator Black Hawk flown by Lola Maloney. He knew the DAPs well, or so he'd thought. But now that he considered it, he'd rarely been so close to one. They lurked carefully in the high-guard position, only rarely coming to ground. Up close, especially in the falling light of evening after the sun was down but before the deck lights came up, the machine looked terrifying.

There were only about a dozen DAPs on the planet, designed by and built solely for the Night Stalkers. No one else had them. No one else even came close. It was the most lethal heli-platform ever assembled. And that was if you discounted the people, who were actually the bird's true strength.

And this wasn't a normal DAP. Rumor, again only rumors available about most of what SOAR did despite his being a SEAL, whispered that only two DAPs had ever been converted to the stealth standards used on the raid of Osama bin Laden's compound.

The *Vengeance* was one of them, the other apparently destroyed on a mission. The whisper said it was in a fire on an oil platform in the Gulf of Mexico, which made no sense. That meant this bird was truly unique. Five blades instead of four. A large sound cap covering the lifters at the center of the rotor. Angular shapes and odd forms rather than a Black Hawk's normal rounded lines. The thing looked vicious.

More of the Mission Enhanced Little Birds had been built than the DAPs, but that didn't make them exactly common, either. This particular operation only had one, and they'd given it to Patricia O'Malley. He knew that SOAR had done some work on the design, but how much could you do to a bird that only weighed fifteen hundred pounds before you added crew, fuel, and weapons?

This was going to be really sad. He was a licensed pilot. Granted, he wasn't combat-rated, but he knew his way around a chopper plenty well, especially the

OH-6 Cayuse frame that SOAR's Little Birds were built on.

Then Patricia stopped in front of her helicopter. He hadn't been paying close enough attention last night. This chopper also sported stealth modifications. Six-bladed rotor, instead of the normal five. Angular body shapes that would be carbon-fiber rather than metal. The outboard weapons were encapsulated in radar-nonreflective pods. Damn. Another stealth conversion.

"Okay." Patricia's voice was completely different than at the meal or in the briefing. Suddenly the woman who'd hauled his ass out of Bosaso stood once more before him. She hadn't grown any taller than her normal shrimp-sized self, but it felt as if she had.

"You've flown?"

He nodded.

"Little Birds?"

Cayuse, close enough. Almost five hundred hours in this class of aircraft. He nodded again.

"That's a problem."

"Why?"

"Because it means that you've flown OH-6 Cayuse, the OH-58 Kiowas, or something similar."

Shrewd. He'd give her credit for that. He was aware of crossing his arms over his chest, not a "friendly" gesture per his training on blending into a crowd. So he shoved his hands in his jeans pockets, which at least upgraded unfriendly behavior to merely petulant, and leaned against the side of the Little Bird.

He jerked away and rubbed a hand up his arm. The flat, black skin of the chopper was still blazing hot with the sun's setting heat, though the equatorial night was fast darkening the sky.

She didn't laugh, but just watched him and waited.

So he offered a shrug. "And why is that a problem?"

"A Kiowa is a spotter bird. Designed to peek over obstacles, attack, and run. The Cayuse is mission-profiled to deliver teams and fetch them back."

He nodded. That's exactly how he'd used each of them.

"The Mission Enhanced Little Bird AH-6M—'A' for 'Attack'—has only one purpose: to deliver serious firepower where no one else can get in. It is a wholly different mission, and this bird has been crafted specifically for that. It's as related to the Cayuse as an armored Humvee with a turret gun and infrared night-vision gear is to a Jeep Cherokee with a Blaupunkt stereo and Bluetooth for your garage door opener."

"Is that why you like it?" What made him ask that? No reason to get personal with this woman. Yet the chopper fit her somehow. She belonged here, right here beside her bird. He'd watched her for the rest of that first meal and through the parts of the briefing that he could. She was rarely at rest. Like her helicopter, she was about the attack. Fast, always in motion.

Another question about what she did with that energy in other situations came to mind, which he quickly suppressed, and suppressed hard. She was a fellow serviceman—serviceperson—standing on the deck of an amphibious assault ship, not some potential stateside recreation in a bar, no matter how good his body seemed to think she'd be.

Patricia O'Malley stood, hands on hips, and stared at him for a long moment. Then a slight smile pulled up the corner of her mouth and sparkled in those blue eyes of hers.

Slowly, she held her hands out toward him, side by side with the palms up.

Bill recognized the game. It was a speed test. Who was faster. Something you did when you were bored and wanted to prove you were still in top form. Well, screw her. He was the fastest in the unit. Let her just try.

He stepped up and immediately realized this was the closest he'd yet been to her. Even in warrior mode, you could see her smile threatening to dimple, her ever-so-fine hair fluttering in even the mere rising of the deck's heat. He shut it off and compartmentalized it as only a SEAL could do. Focus on the task, or rather the game at hand.

He placed his hands palm down over hers, not quite touching, but so close he could feel the heat off her palms radiating against his own. The trick was to pull your hands back before the person jerked their hands from below and slapped the tops of your hands.

Bill tried not to gloat. It was a game he rarely lost. He hadn't had his hands slapped in years. Why she wanted to lose at a power game was beyond him. He softened his vision so that it encompassed her whole upper body and face. There was always a tell, a sign, some shift in weight or narrowing of the eyes to telegraph the motion of the opponent's hands to twist aside, over, and slap down. Plenty of warning to withdraw his own hands.

Practiced reflex had him jerking his hands back before he was consciously aware of any motion. But he'd barely moved them before his conscious brain informed him there was a sharp pain. It wasn't coming from his barely moved hands, but rather a very sharp pain in his solar plexus as the air whooshed out of his body making him instantly light-headed.

It was only as he was trying to fight his body's natural reaction to keep exhaling, struggling against instinct with his training to pull in that first breath past the pain, that he reconstructed what she'd done.

She'd already preset for her attack when she'd taken the stance. Her weight forward, her feet braced a half step apart. That way, there had been no telegraphed warning signal. Then, rather than attempting to jerk her hands from beneath his fast enough to slap, which he had to admit might well have succeeded, she'd locked her fingers together and driven them straight into his chest with no warning of a change in posture.

And it had been so damn fast, he hadn't seen it. He couldn't even blame it on the failing light. She was just that quick.

"That's what my bird does that you don't understand. Your training hasn't prepared you for it. The Little Bird's job is to be the unexpected point of the spear. It's a different machine, different thinking, different flying."

He managed to stand up straight again, though his body complained bitterly, and he resisted the urge to rub where she'd nailed him. It was an effective way to make an opponent fight one-handed—give them a pain that they would instinctively clutch. That had been trained out of him, but shit, it hurt.

Patricia O'Malley simply stood there waiting, palms up, perfectly balanced. Ready for another go at it. He considered surprising her just as she had him, but decided that it was a set of bruises neither of them needed.

What the hell! Common sense had never been his strong suit.

So, instead of placing his hands just over hers, he grabbed down and captured her wrists. Soft skin registered, and impossibly slender wrists for how hard she'd caught him.

He barely turned his hip in time to take the brunt of her kick. Though holding her wrists tightly kept his own hands occupied so he couldn't use them. He went to trap both her slender wrists in one of his big hands, but didn't have a chance.

He felt her pull against his grasp, not for freedom, but rather for leverage.

He barely tightened his gut in time to block the head butt to his solar plexus. It hurt, especially on top of her first strike, but at least he kept his air this time.

While trying to butt him, she must have gotten a foot up on the deck edge of the helicopter behind her. She drove at him, using her body as a battering ram. If she'd weighed even five pounds more, he'd have crashed to the hard deck with her atop him, but he managed to stand fast.

She was so close, so wound up, that she made his head spin. She smelled of fire and summer. Of grass fields at the height of their growth, filled with so much life that it practically burst forth.

In the near-darkness, he could see the flash of her bright smile, almost feral.

Because he still held her wrists, it only took a small step to push her back against the side of her now-just-warm chopper and lean down to kiss her.

Her mouth opened without hesitation, consuming

him, filling him with her scent and her taste. He could feel her smile against his lips.

He wasn't smiling. He was filled with a need so strong that he barely recognized it as his own.

She slid one cool hand, that he didn't remember letting go, along his cheek and held him tight to the kiss, offering no escape. As if he'd want to. Her taste was even more captivating than her smell, like comfort food if it was made into a hot, sensual woman.

Then he felt cold steel against the scar that ran down the other side of his face and froze. He didn't have to see it to know that a large, sharp knife now lay against his cheek.

Patricia eased back just the slightest inch, making it clear she could cut his throat if she wanted to, or leave him with a fresh scar.

"Uh." He managed to clear his throat, though it sounded rougher than he liked. "I shouldn't have done that." He could feel the knife biting his skin so he made an effort to move his jaw as little as possible as he spoke.

She nipped her teeth lightly on his chin, without removing the blade.

"Maybe some other time, sailor. For now, I think the lesson is done." She shifted out from between his body and the side of her helicopter.

The cold steel edge moved away with just the slightest rasp, as if she were shaving him with it.

A shimmering twist of steel spun between them, highlighted by the few work lights on the deck. She caught the knife by the blade and held it out to him.

He wrapped his fingers around the hilt and she was gone.

Just before she disappeared around the next chopper,

she called back, "Time to gear up, sailor, if you want to go flying tonight."

The deck lights, red for night flight operations, began flashing on.

By their light he could see what he'd known the instant he'd wrapped his hand around the hilt.

It was his own knife and he never felt her take it.

He slipped it back in the leg sheath and did his best not to smile.

Trisha entered the gear locker room to get her flight suit and survival vest but collapsed back against one of the locker doors. Turning her face to the side she was able to lay her cheek against the cool metal. It burned with the heat of Billy's kiss and the heat of his body pressing hard against hers.

She'd had her share of good times, but no one had ever fired her up like that. Not so fast, not so far.

The kiss should have been a joke, a distraction. It was supposed to be, or she wouldn't have let him push her back to begin with. After all, everything's unfair in love and in war. She'd learned that long ago. But if she'd learned it so well, why had she used a kiss rather than one of several dozen other tactics that now came belatedly to mind? And why had she suggested, practically promised a rematch? And why was her heart still beating so damn hard?

"Hey, O'Malley." Kee Stevenson came in and popped her locker open with a sharp rap from the side of her fist. Her daughter, Dilya, almost shoulder tall, drifted in carrying an e-reader in a bright pink cover.

They were a funny-looking pair. It had been obvious the kid was adopted and of a whole different race, but still they looked somehow alike.

Kee was Trisha's height, but with all of the curves Trisha had never grown. As a matter of fact, she was so generously built that Trisha wondered if that's where the rest of her own figure had gone. With sun-kissed skin and almond-shaped dark eyes, she was clearly an exotic mash-up of the American melting-pot gene pool.

The kid was starting to come into some shape, though it was too early to tell how she'd finish. Her skin was significantly darker. Uzbekistani, someone had told her. Refugee.

They both wore dark T-shirts. Kee's showed a large handgun. The words "Protected by Smith & Wesson" stretched over her breasts. Dilya's sported a large feather, a sparkling magic wand, and Hermione's words, "Wingardium Leviosa." Protected by magic. Both wore dark jeans and sparkly red sneakers. Their hair was even the same length, though Kee's was straight and pure black, and her adopted daughter's ruffled its dark brunette waves down to narrow shoulders.

The two of them gazed at her, dark eyes and soft green ones.

"You okay?"

Fine. But her throat wasn't working and the word didn't come out aloud.

She nodded. She was fine. It was just her blood that wasn't. It still roared about her veins in ways that it really wasn't supposed to. She turned to change as Kee did the same.

But Dilya drifted over to stand beside her.

"Why is your hair that color?" Her voice was a strange mix of modern English and the hint of a roll on the *r* that must come from her native language. It also had a lilt to the end of the sentences that went up, but not like a question, even when it was a question.

Dilya reached out a tentative hand and Trisha tipped her head down. The girl stroked a hand over it.

"It feels thinner than mine."

"Red hair is thinner." Trisha tucked it back behind her ear. Maybe she'd let it grow again. Regular Army kept it short; jawline was the lower limit. But this company of Night Stalkers wore their hair more like their customers. SEALs and Delta often went undercover, so many of them had longer hair or beards. Billy's dark hair was almost long enough to catch in a short ponytail, though his cheeks were clean-shaven. Even standing here, she was aware of how soft his hair had been against her palm.

"Is it color or were you born with it?" Dilya was still inspecting her carefully. "Like Ron in Harry Potter? Does your whole family have red hair?"

"Only my mother and me." The problem was that she was the spitting image of her mother. Everyone had always commented on it since her first memory, until she became only a shadow of her mother and was expected to grow up that way. Wow, that sure hadn't worked out the way her mother had planned.

Dilya looked at Kee and then back to Trisha. With an idle hand she tugged on her own hair, as if testing its length.

Kee was watching them closely. Assessing Trisha. Was she an overprotective parent? Or was there something else going on here?

Trisha peeled down to her underwear and stepped into the fire-retardant flight suit. It weighed about thirty pounds with all of the armor plates. One of the drawbacks to flying a Little Bird with no doors was not having a lot of protective armor around you unless you were wearing it. But since she'd worn it almost every day of the last half-dozen years, it felt more unnatural to be in civilian clothes, so light it was as if she was prancing around naked.

Before she zipped up the flight suit, Dilya was holding her arm near Trisha's stomach, comparing the color.

"You are so white."

Indeed, while the girl wasn't African dark, there was a startling contrast.

"It comes with the red hair."

"If I make my hair red, will my skin turn white?"

Trisha had to blink at that one.

Kee had stopped dressing and was waiting for her answer. Clearly used to Dilya's strange inquiries, she didn't step in, but Trisha could feel pending judgment. Kee was the woman with the longest term of service in SOAR, so Trisha valued her good opinion. She usually didn't care what other people thought, but this time she did.

"No," she informed the child. "Our skin color stays the same no matter what we do to our hair."

"Good." Dilya nodded seriously, clearly filing away that tidbit. "I like red, but I wouldn't be me if I was your color." And then she turned to leave.

Trisha glanced over at Kee.

"If my kid dyes her hair electric red, I'm going to blame you." It was said dead seriously, but there was a light in the woman's eyes.

"Guilty and proud to be."

Sergeant Kee Stevenson barked out a simple laugh, then continued dressing.

It was Trisha's first break into the camaraderie of the women of SOAR. She'd flown with them, been accepted by them, but was clearly an outsider.

She zipped up the flight suit and tapped the various pouches to ensure that all of the armored plates were in the right place. Then she laced on her boots over the cuffs.

Trisha hadn't wanted to be identified as a "woman of SOAR." She didn't like the image or the stamp of it. She wasn't a WOS. She was Lieutenant Trisha O'Malley of the Night Stalkers. Flying her own bird gave her some of that distinction. The DAP Hawk had Lola Maloney for pilot, Kee Stevenson for gunner, and Connie Davis for mechanic. She'd been half afraid that some stupid Army public relations guru would insist she fly copilot in the DAP so there could be an all-female crew.

But they hadn't gone there. This was the first time since she'd climbed aboard her own bird that one of the women had done more than say hello. The line between Black Hawk and Little Bird ran deep. As did the line of those who'd flown combat with Emily Beale and those who hadn't.

In addition to final training, Trisha had flown plenty with Beale back in the 101st, but she wasn't going to trade on that card any more than she had on her parents'. She was going to make this a go on her own standing, by her own skills.

So she chose a neutral topic as they slung on their heavy SARVSO survival vests covered in pouches containing first aid, additional ammo, and survival gear if they were downed, including an emergency radio and beacon, and a dozen other essentials.

"So what's the kid reading?"

Kee laughed as they left the locker room forty pounds heavier than they'd entered it and climbed back to the flight deck.

"Damned if I know. She blew through Harry Potter last year. Didn't like *The Wizard of Oz* because it was too unrealistic. Go figure. I think she just started on McCaffrey's Dragonrider books, as if that makes more sense than Oz. I can't keep up anymore, now that she reads on her own. Kinda miss reading to her."

Dragons made perfect sense to Trisha.

Kee turned aside at the DAP Hawk. Trisha noticed Billy the SEAL standing in the shadows getting briefed by Connie, the other DAP Hawk crew chief, and did her best to ignore him. Which wasn't as easy as it should have been. Her body definitely leaned that way, even if she didn't.

Of course, Dilya would read those books. It made perfect sense. Her mother flew every night in a beast that spit fire on command.

Trisha headed to her own chopper, ready to do the same.

Chapter 6

TRISHA BUCKLED HERSELF IN AND CHECKED THE LIE OF her rifle across her chest. When she reached for the engine starter, her copilot blocked her hand.

"Where's your head, O'Malley?" So Roland was still giving her shit for spacing half of the briefing. Just because she deserved it, she wasn't going to eat it.

"In the sky, Chief Emerson. In the sky. What else did I miss?"

He released a long-suffering sigh, though they'd only been together for a week. They shared a laugh. They'd hit it off right out of the chute when she found out he was from Philadelphia and was a huge baseball fan. Being Phillies and Boston Red Sox fans had made for an instant bond, all Phillies and BoSox fans instinctively hated the same team.

"It's a good thing you're not a Yankees man," she informed him.

"Because you'd have to hate me on principle?"

"Bingo."

"We also have cheese steak at our home games."

"Another point in your favor. Though you were also named the number one ballpark for vegetarian options. What's up with that crap?"

"Damned if I know, O'Malley. Damned if I know."

"So give. Why am I sitting in my chopper and we're not in the sky? Mama is itchy. She wants to kick some more bad ass."

Roland grinned at her. They'd also hit it off even before their first flight because their flying attitudes fit together like oil and oil. The fact that she liked him in addition to respecting him was a great bonus.

"Drones, run from the *Peleliu*'s communications platform." Roland cocked a thumb toward the tower superstructure behind them. "They'll be doing a sea sweep. Lieutenant Bruce has identified the pirates' primary points of land departure, and they'll be focusing there. Then we sweep in on anything the drones identify for cleanup. We stay hot-ready here for the first thirty minutes, then we'll shift down coast to the carrier and be hot-ready from there as the drones move farther south."

"Lieutenant Bruce." The name was a foul taste on her tongue even if his kiss wasn't. She fussed with the seating of the electrical system connectors to the helmet that still rested in her lap.

"He said that because of the damage we did, it will take Bosaso and the surrounding ports a bit to recover. So we're going to circle the Horn and head south along the coast where the action is heavier. Ramis already has the *Peleliu* underway."

So, Billy the SEAL speaks and their entire task force jumps and moves to a whole new position? That just wasn't...

Why did the man irritate her so much? He was a SEAL, which meant he was amazingly well trained. A lieutenant, which meant he'd been at it a while. A big white guy who'd embedded himself in Somalia, meaning he clearly had more bravery than common sense, a trait they shared.

It wasn't the kiss. It definitely wasn't the kiss that

pissed her off. She could have stopped that easily if she'd
wanted to, but she hadn't wanted to. Her brain still sizzled
with the memory of it. All of that raw male power and her
control over it made for a pretty heady mix. Even now she
had to admit she was looking forward to trying it again,
maybe without the knife this time.

So why was the man so maddening?

Other than being too damn sure of himself, she still
didn't have an answer twenty-five minutes later when
they got the command to shift to the carrier that was
already operating further down the gulf. The carrier's
primary mission was servicing jets in and out of Iraqi
airspace. Piracy was just a sideline for them, but it was
the *Peleliu*'s mandate.

Bill pulled on his helmet, which blocked most of the
DAP Hawk's noise, thankfully cutting the high whine
of the starter as it began cranking the turbines. Once that
cut out and it was just the two main engines, he worked
his jaw to pop his ears. The thick smell of burned Jet A
fuel filled the cabin, replacing the sea-salt air with the
sharp bite of burned kerosene and the slight tang of hy-
draulic oil that always hung around a chopper. Once the
jet engines were up to temperature, most of that kero-
stench would go away. And then they'd be aloft, which
would clear the air through the two wide-open cargo bay
doors on either side of the Hawk.

They'd rigged a station with two seats against the rear
cargo net, aft of the big ammo cans that fed the outboard guns. In some ways it was immensely spacious,
especially compared to the Little Bird where there was

barely room to wiggle your toes. If empty, the DAP's cargo bay was almost a dozen feet long, eight wide, and over four feet high. But it was anything but empty. It was amazing they had the room for the two seats for himself and Michael Gibson in a space where normally a dozen troops could fit.

The more Sergeant Connie Davis told him about the bird, the more impressed he became with both her and the chopper, though he did his best not to show it in either case. For one thing, her husband was even bigger than he was.

Her passion for the craft was immense, and she seemed to know every bolt, screw, and cable personally and would have been glad to introduce him to each one by name if he'd let her.

The DAP Hawk had overlapping weapons and detection systems, some of which he'd never even heard of. And he got the impression that there was more she wasn't telling him. She, too, had a reputation that reached beyond SOAR. He'd heard the rumors about a mechanic who had personally improved overall aircraft reliability by three percent. He'd just never expected to meet him or, as it turned out, her. Maloney had informed him that the team of Connie Davis and Big John Wallace had done that together.

What in God's name had he landed in the middle of here?

The DAP's primary weapon systems were on the outboard hardpoints. An M134 minigun that fired eighty rounds a second, a 30 mm chain gun that threw rounds bigger than his thumb at ten rounds a second, and a pair of nineteen-rocket pods of the Hydra 70 FFAR,

Folding-Fin Aerial Rockets. The secondary weapons systems were in the control of the two crew chiefs stationed close behind the pilot and copilot positions. Kee Stevenson and Connie Davis each wielded a steerable M134 minigun of their own. He really needed to remember not to mess with these women.

Sergeant Davis was so soft-spoken that he thought he'd heard wrong when she identified her fellow sergeant as the two-time winner of the President's Hundred, the top sharpshooter in the United States, military or civilian. He'd heard that the nation's current top shooter was a woman. That he found it hard to believe didn't make it any less true. But since she was a crew chief on a DAP Hawk, maybe it wasn't so odd. And that would probably explain the locked rifle case mounted beside the starboard gunnery position.

He'd lost track of the protection and detection systems after the first five or six. Maybe O'Malley hadn't been exaggerating when she said these choppers were wholly different creatures from what he was used to. Could her tiny Little Bird also detect the direction of fire of a single bullet and project return-fire coordinates onto her visor? How much information could she process at once?

He was good at multitasking. Could be giving status to a remote commander, calling in supporting-fire coordinates from a ship while lasing a site for a bomber overhead, and still keep an eye out for a combatant sneaking up on their position. Was it possible that Patricia O'Malley was at that level? Or even some whole other level?

And what the hell was he doing thinking about her during an operation?

He looked back to the three screens they'd set up in front of his seat. Two were overlapped video and infrared feeds, one screen for each of the two drones. The third was a satellite positioning map showing the drones' relative routes across the Gulf of Aden and around the Horn into the Arabian Sea.

"Damn things make my eyes hurt." Michael Gibson was in a seat close beside him and leaning over the screens as well. He wondered if Michael was there to assist him, make him feel better, or assess him. Probably all of the above.

"You get used to it." Bill had done several hundred hours of training with the drones over the last few years. Michael would mostly have others do that for him. As a colonel, even one in the field, his job was to think and function at whole-team levels, not basic operations. It was rare enough for a lieutenant like himself, other than a SEAL or a Delta operator, to be doing this. He was often odd man out at the manufacturer training sessions, several ranks above the other students.

Drone control and interpretation was the role of a specialist, focused on that single task, from a deep bunker back in Utah or Nevada. But no SEAL or Delta team was likely to let someone else, no matter their clearance, have a chance of impeding an ongoing operation. They learned for themselves. SEALs did their best to be heavily cross-trained, no room for a specialist with a focus area as narrow as just drone control during a black ops mission.

These drones were flown by teams on the *Peleliu*, but Connie informed him that she'd insisted that the data was a straight feed to Bill's screens on the DAP Hawk.

His kind of woman. Not that he really had a kind that he knew of. He knew what wasn't his kind. A feisty, pint-sized, pain-in-the-ass chief war—

"Welcome to Air Lola," Chief Warrant Maloney chimed in on the intercom. "Tonight is predicted to be hot but with low turbulence, so you get to keep your breakfast. The extended forecast is for stretches of immense boredom, possibly interrupted by intense but hopefully brief squalls of piracy."

"You should have been an airline steward, Chief," Bill teased back.

"My daddy wanted me to be a stripper."

Bill prepared to laugh and make a joke about how he bet she'd be good at it, but something in her tone, though it was light, stopped him. Was this, too, some sort of a test? No one else was laughing. A quick glance at Michael showed that he had accepted the statement as dead serious. He reconsidered his comment and instead said, "All of male-kind's loss is SOAR's gain."

"Thanks, Lieutenant."

She was a looker and definitely his type, if she wasn't married. Another man's woman had never been one of his weaknesses, though it didn't stop him from looking. Lola Maloney was almost tall enough to face him eye to eye. And again the image of a woman who barely came to his shoulder came to mind. Of the shape of her lips and the sharpness of her teeth as they'd scraped over his chin.

He'd always scoffed at the big guys who picked up small, delicate girlfriends as if they were flowers to be kept in a vase. Though that sure as hell wasn't Patricia.

He forced his attention back to the screens as they

flew toward the aircraft carrier. The ships were about a hundred and twenty nautical miles apart. Cruising easily, they'd be there in just under an hour and the Little Birds could refuel at the carrier.

He glanced out the cargo bay door. The running lights of O'Malley's Little Bird blinked in the dark, just fifty yards off the starboard side.

Michael noticed the direction of his distraction.

Bill didn't need the faint illumination of the screens to read the Delta operator's expression. He returned his attention to the displays and watched the endless ocean rolling by beneath the drones just as it rolled by between his chopper and that of Lieutenant Patricia O'Malley.

Chapter 7

"CONTACT AT THIRTY MILES, BEARING TWO-THREE-five." Lola Maloney's call over the radio broke the drudgery of the transit flight over water.

Trisha was always amazed at how long such flights felt. Especially since that was most of what a pilot did. Long patrols, transport through safe areas, flying from a safe base to the mission's target zone, and keeping alert while flying back as the mission's adrenal-high cooled in her blood. Especially tough because the flight home always seemed to last forever.

Battle exercises were almost always more intense than the real thing because they were designed to use every minute possible for training. And prior to Iraq and Afghanistan, there was always more training than missions. She wondered how that would be changing with the troop drawdowns.

Shuttling from the *Peleliu* to the aircraft carrier was all about patience, and looking at nothing but your instruments and the other choppers in your flight as you slid over the featureless black of the nighttime ocean.

Now they had a contact, but would it be a "contact of interest" or just some night fisherman? Whoever they were, they floated just a twelve-minute flight to the southwest. Trisha checked her fuel. Just past halfway to the aircraft carrier, they'd only burned twenty minutes of the two hours in her tank. She was fine for now.

"Close in but don't engage."

Trisha was already rolling to the new heading before the command was complete. *Merchant* and *Max* lagged until the order was complete, but were slightly behind her in the flight so there was no danger of collision. The *Vengeance*, despite being a faster ship, also trailed because she'd been holding formation and was on the outside of the turn.

They all doused their running lights so that, except for the slight glow of their consoles, their choppers were fully blacked out. With the stealth modifications that had been applied to the two attack birds, they'd also be very hard to locate directionally. Stealth made them quieter, though far from silent. Much more significantly, it made their sound very nondirectional. So they could still be heard, but you couldn't tell from which direction if you were on the ground. Likely as not they'd sound like a stealth helicopter that had come out of nowhere and was heading away, when it was actually headed straight in.

In the lead as she liked, Trisha dropped down from the five-hundred-foot transit altitude to ten feet above the waves. The rest of the flight followed her down and then spread wide to allow multiple approach angles. They did it without any communication needed because it was embedded in all of their training—how to take best advantage of many different types of situations. *Merchant* swung a bit west of the mark and *Max* a bit east, leaving her and Lola's DAP Hawk to run up the middle. They'd approach this target from three sides.

"The things to watch for here…" Billy's voice rumbled into her helmet's earphones like a caress. She knew he was talking to all four choppers in tonight's flight, but she could feel herself responding to the voice practically whispering in her ear. She shook it off and focused on his words.

"It appears to be a standard twenty-foot, open fishing boat. If she's a pirate, she'll probably have two engines. A small one that's typical on these fishing dories to save gas and a bigger one for final pursuit of their target. So watch for bursts of speed."

Like that was news. Wasn't Billy the SEAL supposed to be some kind of expert?

"If it is financed out of Garowe, it will be a seventy-horsepower engine."

On a heavy twenty-foot wooden boat, that was fast but not exciting.

"If Galkayo, they favor the Mercury two-fifty."

Okay, that was serious. Trisha decided that maybe Billy the SEAL had his uses. With two hundred and fifty horsepower onboard, the boat would be able to do some pretty amazing things, if the motor didn't shake the boat apart.

"The bosses send them out into the shipping channels with two tanks of gas. They run the smaller engine until it's dry, which gets them into the shipping channel. The big engine only has enough fuel for the pursuit, not enough to return home."

"Cortez," Trisha mumbled.

"Exactly," Billy responded over the radio. "They operate just like Cortez and burn the path home. Put the crews out there, and the only way they're coming back alive is if they capture a boat. Makes them very motivated."

"It's a goddamn suicide mission. Why do they do it?"

"In Somalia, the average annual income is six

hundred dollars American. Average ransom is in the hundreds of thousands, a good one in the millions. Even a one percent share is life changing for both the pirates and their families."

Trisha considered. She could barely support her music habit on fifty dollars a month, never mind an iPod to play it on while she was working out. How did these people live on that little? "In abject poverty" was the answer.

She checked all systems as well as flashing one of the center console's screens momentarily to a weather-radar sweep. No surprise thunderstorms anywhere about, just clear skies. She flipped back to a tactical sweep, peripherally aware of Roland's confirming nod that they were ready.

Hard not to be aware of every motion of someone sitting less than six inches away. If it were Billy instead of Roland in the copilot seat, they'd probably be rubbing shoulders because his were so wide. When two guys were flying Little Birds in full flight gear, their outside elbows always stuck out into the wind. Yet another reason to fly without doors—two bigger guys and their survival gear just wouldn't fit otherwise.

"There will be ten to fifteen pirates." Billy the SEAL must love lecturing. "The leader won't be the one at the tiller. He'll be the one with the RPG launcher or the largest-caliber automatic weapon. They're his badge of honor. Probably only a 7.62 NATO round, not a .50 caliber on a craft this small. Most of the others will have the smaller 5.56 NATO round or something similar."

At least Billy didn't sound all superior about it like a Ranger, whose job it was to be cocksure of himself, or regular Army who often had an inferiority complex on the rare occasions they were aboard a SOAR craft. He was just sharing needed information.

"That's some comfort," she shot back at him just to keep him on his toes. The bigger NATO round could crack her windscreen pretty good, and if it came in the side, even if her armor did stop it, she'd be hurting like hell afterward. A .50 cal could probably punch the windscreen, and definitely her armor. That was all assuming the RPG didn't get her.

"If the heat gets too hot for you, Army, then—"

"Five thousand yards to target," she cut him off sharply. One minute at her present speed. Maloney tolerated a little chatter, but not much. So she'd spare him learning that the hard way.

"Are we sure these guys are pirates?" Max asked.

Trisha hadn't even thought about it. She was about to answer with, "Who else would be headed straight out into the ocean a dozen miles off the coast at near enough to midnight?" But she thought better of it. She knew nothing about fishermen. Did they fish at night? She left that one for Billy.

"About a five percent chance they're fisherman."

"*Vengeance* will overfly," Chief Maloney answered. "Then we'll turn to cover from the south. Let's see what they do." Then she lay down the hammer on her big DAP Hawk and began pulling ahead. That was one thing to say for the big bird—she could sure hustle her butt when she had to.

The DAP flashed over the fishing boat at twenty feet up and going nearly two hundred miles per hour. No way someone could get a bead on the chopper.

But someone tried.

In her helmet's infrared view, Trisha could see the heat of the bullets streaming upward.

"Kill their engine."

Trisha slowed. She was directly to the side of the boat. So she aimed the target circle projected on her visor well off the stern of the boat. She'd sweep up from behind so that she shot the engine first, but not the boat or its occupants.

The moment before she opened fire, the boat leaped away.

"Shit!"

"What was that, O'Malley?" Chief Maloney clearly didn't like the loss of focus.

Trisha checked for *Merchant* to make sure her airspace was clear, then swung to follow.

"He's running the two-fifty. Am in close pursuit."

A low squeal in both earphones of her helmet told her that an RPG was coming straight at her, little more than a red dot on her visor.

She slewed left as Roland released a flare set to starboard that should attract the RPG's attention if it had a heat- or light-guided head.

The Dopplering squeal, shifting from low to lower, told her the threat was past. Before the guy could rearm, she called out to Roland.

"Now!"

He lit off one of the miniguns and she steered it right toward the stern of the boat.

High whistles reported incoming rifle fire. The bullets were occasionally pinging off her windscreen as she slewed to the other side, but not piercing or even cracking it. Again, Billy had been right, 5.56 mm ammunition. In the infrared-enhanced projection inside her visor, she could see one of the pirates firing from the middle of the boat accidentally execute the guy seated high in the stern to steer the engine.

As the man's body toppled backward into her field of fire, she finished him off, if he wasn't dead already.

No time to think about it.

Driving the fire low and behind, she finally found her mark. Under the water of the stern wake, Roland's bullets began sparking off metal. After what felt like forever but couldn't have been more than a second, second and a half at most, the boat lurched forward. They'd shot off the propeller, and the boat buried its bow in the next wave. Everyone still aboard was tumbled forward off their seats.

She twisted aside just in case Roland didn't get the minigun stopped in time, but he did.

Her side of the helicopter was momentarily exposed to the boat, but that couldn't be helped.

A sharp sting on her thigh and hip. Another on her ribs, but missing her unarmored shoulder, and then she was past the boat and clear.

"You okay?" Roland called out.

Trisha didn't have time to check, just swung the bird left to make sure she didn't run head-on into *Merchant*. Sure enough he was coming up from the bow, right where he was supposed to be. He slowed to a hover before he got quite close enough to draw their fire.

Trisha circled out of easy target range and then spun to bring the weapons to bear once more on the small boat now wallowing between the waves.

"Uh, I seem to be fine." She flexed a few muscles in her leg and arm without either screaming pain or spastically affecting the foot pedals or the cyclic control in her right hand. Her ribs stung like hell; she hoped she hadn't cracked one. She'd never been shot before. A wave of panic threatened to overwhelm her, but she slammed it aside. Time to deal with that later.

If she'd trusted Roland's timing and Dennis to know his place, as she should have, she could have climbed out right over the *Merchant* without exposing herself to gunfire from the skiff. The chopper's armor was much better than hers. It even had redundant systems in most areas in case something was hit.

She keyed the radio.

"One down, accidentally shot by his own crew, then fell overboard into my path of fire. Max, there's no way he survived, but if he did, he's a couple hundred yards back in your direction off the stern."

"Roger." Max's problem now.

She focused on the boat, rolling a thumbwheel to zoom in her display. The pirates were all hunkered as low as they could get in the boat. It looked as if they'd shipped on a foot or so of water when the bow had nosed under, but they were still afloat.

Sure enough, a couple of them began wielding bailing buckets with one hand while resting their rifle muzzles on the thick side rails and aiming outward. None of them were aimed quite at her. Two guys in the bow must have lost their rifles overboard as they now held up handguns.

Though they were all facing in her general direction, at two hundred yards out in the pitch darkness, she was invisible. They didn't know where she was. She kept a special eye on the guy with the RPG launcher. Somehow he'd reloaded it and held on to it, despite what they'd just been through.

Billy called something over the loud-hailer that she didn't understand. Then he followed in English, "Lay down your arms. The U.S. Navy has been notified and a patrol boat is coming."

The boat's crew spun in shock to face the DAP Hawk hovering in the darkness to the south. Unlike the deceptiveness of the stealth-masked sounds, the loud-hailer was a point source of sound.

Sure enough, the pirates began firing blind into the darkness.

"Four away," Maloney called out.

So close to simultaneously that it appeared to be in perfect unison, Roland and the DAP Hawk copilot, Guy Nelson, each unleashed a pair of the Hydra 70 rockets toward the boat. With a sharp sizzle of rocket motor as they zipped past the open sides of the Little Bird cockpit, the 2.75-inch rockets hammered down into the water on the sides of the boat.

Tall columns of water fountained upward to either side of the boat, sending another six inches of water aboard to add to what the crew had barely begun bailing.

Most of the guys were laying down their guns. But the leader with the RPG launcher was dumber than should be possible. He was rising again to take aim at the DAP.

Bill couldn't believe the guy's audacity.

Of course, the pirate leader in the boat wouldn't truly

understand the abilities of a DAP Hawk, but even he had to know it was a no-win scenario against a vastly superior force. He must feel such hate or fury at being stopped that he'd risk everything on the off chance of wreaking death on even one of his enemies before he died.

Bill could feel that anger. Every time he thought of his father and the Battle of Mogadishu, he felt it burn deeper. With each mile they had progressed south along the coast, he had become angrier. Serving up north in Puntland, he hadn't felt it so deeply. But with each mile toward the Mog, he could feel the force of it like a strike to… He almost smiled. To his solar plexus.

He stared at the image projected on his visor of the pirate leader bracing to steady his aim. He still had to be guessing, but he wasn't far off. An explosion would be very close to aboard even if it didn't hit them.

If it were up to Bill in this moment, he'd dump the chopper's remaining thirty-six rockets and blow the whole boat to hell.

"Oh, for crying out loud," Lola Maloney cursed over the intercom. "Kee."

"Ready."

Bill glanced through his visor rather than at the projection inside it. Sergeant Kee Stevenson had pulled her weapon out of the steel case bolted to the bulkhead. She'd left her seat and attached a three-meter monkey-line tether from the D-ring on the front of her vest to the ceiling of the chopper so that she could move around the cabin without being thrown out.

He whistled to himself as she dropped into kneeling posture in the cargo bay door. A Heckler and Koch MSG90A1 with a night scope and flash suppressor.

He'd fired one when he did some training with the FBI's Hostage Rescue Team, one of the sweetest guns he'd ever shot. And Kee Stevenson was carrying one around in the helicopter.

Bill glanced at Michael beside him, but he was wholly focused on Kee. One heartbeat. Two.

Then a small blink around the flash suppressor and a sharp crack.

Even with all his training, he'd have a hard time settling for a shot that fast.

He looked back at the projection on the inside of his visor, the feed from the infrared camera system, just in time to see the pirate boss' head snap back. Bill couldn't see the shot actually hit him in the forehead, but there was no question that's exactly what happened.

As the pirate tumbled backward, his reflexes pulled the trigger. The RPG shot up at a steep angle before arcing well over the DAP Hawk and exploding somewhere behind and above them.

What kind of a person went for a head shot from a vibrating platform like a helicopter? He'd have shot center of mass, and if he'd hit the heart, he'd have been thrilled.

Kee remained in her crouch for several long seconds, then the rest of the pirate crew began tossing their weapons over the side of the boat with a show of great reluctance.

That created a problem Bill had never solved. Without the weapons, there was no "proof of intent to commit piracy" that any international court would uphold. But if the pirates were dragged back to shore, the boss man who had financed the operation, including paying for the weapons, might be just pissed enough to execute the whole crew. Yet what choice did they now have?

Kee Stevenson finally stood up into a low hunch, which was all the DAP Hawk cabin allowed, and moseyed back to her position, clearing her weapon. Michael relaxed as if someone had plugged him back in.

"What?"

Michael shook his head.

"What?"

"I've watched her shoot dozens of times. I still don't know how she does it."

Bill blinked at that. He was amazed by the shot. But the man sitting beside him was the senior Delta Force operator on the planet, and even he couldn't unravel the technique.

"It's pure instinct. That's the only possible explanation."

Michael looked over at him. "Is that what you do?"

Now it was Bill's turn to feel uncertain. He had trained thousands of hours to turn learned skills into instinct.

"No, because I don't have a gift." He'd seen it in his SEAL team. There'd be one specialist who could run, jump, shoot, and swim with great practiced skill, but when it came to languages, he picked them up in weeks rather than months or years. Rawlings made explosives do the strangest and most interesting things. Need a guy who could get comm gear to still work, even after it had been shot a couple times? Axel was the dude you wanted. Bill could barely align his mother's antenna for satellite television, but Axel could nail the angle through a hole in the trees that every manual said wouldn't work.

O'Malley ran that way, as if she were just a natural. And flew that way. What else did she do so "naturally"?

"No," he answered Michael. "I'm really good at CQB." Close Quarters Battle, often becoming hand-to-hand combat. It required many skills including a very fast reaction time and no identifiable patterns or timing to your attack and defense techniques. "But I have to train like any other fool."

Michael just watched him closely, not saying anything else.

And Bill wasn't about to explain further. He'd grown up on the streets of Detroit from age eight, fighting for food, somewhere to sleep, for everything so that he and his mother could survive. He knew where he'd learned to fight, learned to stay alive. But he sure wasn't going to be talking about it to anyone real soon. He hadn't even mentioned much of it during the psych evals they put him through when he went into the SEALs.

He turned his attention back to the drone screens, which had turned up nothing else as the *Peleliu* controllers continued winging them down the coast.

The DAP Hawk held station, releasing the Little Birds to head for the carrier. A SOC-R, Special Operations Craft-Riverine, sent out by the aircraft carrier and loaded with heavily armed Marines, pulled up alongside the pirates' boat. The craft was intended for near-shore and river work. But with two miniguns, three machine guns, and a pair of grenade launchers, added to an ability to travel at forty-five miles per hour through almost all weather or wave conditions, the SOC-Rs were pressed into service in many areas.

In minutes, the Marines had tossed a hose into the pirates' craft, emptied the boat of water, frisked all of the prisoners, and confiscated an array of handguns and knives. Then they tied the pirates bowline to their craft and began towing it back toward the shore.

They determined that the big engine was leaking oil and therefore an environmental hazard as an excuse for confiscating it. The Marines left the pirates with the broken smaller engine to fix if they could for their fishing. Tonight it would be a good thing that they'd brought along a pair of oars, because the Navy dumped them off a half mile from the beach and wished them well. The Navy wasn't looking for engagement with any shore-based forces.

The DAP Hawk turned for the carrier about twenty minutes behind the others.

Chapter 8

TRISHA SAT ON THE DECK OF THE AIRCRAFT CARRIER BY her bird. They'd only be here another hour or two, then they'd shuttle back to the *Peleliu*. Most of the other guys had gone into the air-conditioned ready room through the deck-level entry to the carrier's tower.

She sat alone by her bird at the very stern of the flight deck and idly slid her finger in and out of the bullet hole in her flight suit. It was along her ribs, third one up from the bottom. Once she was alone, she'd fished out the bullet, which had flattened against her armor. She'd be black and blue for a week, but it didn't hurt, much, when she breathed so the rib wasn't cracked.

All those years of running on the street, circulating around the edges of the Boston gangs, she'd always managed to not be there when it "went bad." Not chicken, it had just worked out that way. She'd been in plenty of fistfights, even a couple knife fights, but nothing that led to gunfire.

More than once, she'd come back from a week gone to discover she'd missed the death and funeral of someone she'd been laughing and telling lies with just the week before.

When she flew, she'd certainly been shot *at* a lot. But never hit. Even the RPG that had taken down her chopper in the mountains past Mosul, Iraq, hadn't actually hit her chopper. It had exploded right in front of her engine's air intake. The shrapnel had killed the engine, cut off one of her rotor blades, and shaken them hard. The explosion also had been far louder than Fenway Park full of baseball fans filling the bleachers and protesting a bad call against the BoSox.

She'd managed a Mayday before the radios shorted out and then auto-rotated into a narrow valley by the Great Zab River in Kurdistani Iraq. She'd rigged her chopper with a remote detonator, then she and her co-pilot had hunkered down, hiding as well as they could.

Eight hours later, while they were debating the best route to start walking out that night, a squad dressed in poor clothes and AK-47s began investigating the site. She blew up the Little Bird. That, in turn, attracted the attention of the choppers that were out looking for them. Turned into an easy ride back to base rather than trying to walk out of Iraq's northern mountains.

She hadn't mentioned that her hearing had suffered for a week, despite her helmet, from the explosion of that RPG so close to the chopper.

Now she had three holes in her flight suit, and she couldn't stop slipping her finger in the one along her ribs. The hip and thigh shots had bounced off and the bullets were gone, actually leaving little more than small tears in the outer fabric.

But the rib one would have killed her if she hadn't been wearing nonstandard-issue armor under the survival vest.

That close. She rubbed her finger against the flexible material, as if she could find some evidence of where the bullet had pancaked. It must have come in exactly square-on to not skim to the side. She was still able to breathe and was able to join Roland in a full inspection of their bird the moment they had it down— and do it without too much pain to her side. That told her it was a 5.56 mm round, because anything bigger would have broken her ribs even if it hadn't punched through the armor.

In her left hand, she held the bullet. Its head had mushroomed to a couple times its normal width. A hollow-point round. If it had found a seam in the armor, she'd be dead right now.

"Hey, O'Malley."

She clamped her fist shut around the bullet.

"What have you got there?" Billy the SEAL dropped down to sit beside her on the deck.

"Nothing." Trisha slipped it into a pocket on her vest and leaned back against the side of the rocket pod sticking out from the right-hand side of her chopper. Maybe she'd make a necklace out of it. Or just throw it over the side. Or something. Later.

She turned her face toward the stern, watching the phosphorescent wake churned up by the aircraft carrier powering through the night. It felt good to be leaving this behind. She was alive. Damned lucky to be so, but alive.

"Something's up."

Trisha turned back to face Billy. "You don't know me."

"No," he admitted slowly. "But something's up."

She studied his face by the red lights washing the nighttime deck. The red allowed pilots and deck crew to retain most of their night vision, as long as they looked away when a jet was taking off. The intense white of a jet engine's exhaust could blot out your night vision for eight to ten minutes.

At the moment, SOAR's helicopters parked along the port edge of the carrier's deck were the only flight operations. The deck was quiet. The night crews were hanging out wherever they usually did while waiting for an action call. Probably spreading more gray paint on every surface they could find.

By the red light, Billy's face didn't look demonic like some people's did. His skin was dark enough, tanned by living and fighting outdoors, that it looked warm and friendly.

She saw his eyes widen and suddenly he leaned right up to her as if studying her face.

"You were shot!"

"No!" She shoved back against his chest, but he didn't even waver.

It was in that moment that she realized just how strong he was. She hadn't pushed softly.

"No." She said it again, but it didn't sound very convincing, even to her.

He began inspecting her with probing hands like he was a surgeon and she was on a stretcher instead of sitting quietly minding her own damn business.

Trisha slapped his hands away, just as he probed her right rib cage. Her hiss of pain stopped him cold.

"How bad? Are you bleeding?"

"Will you get your damn hands off me?"

He didn't. "How bad, Patricia?"

Had his voice been one bit angrier or if he'd used her last name or her rank, she'd have brushed him off.

But he hadn't. He'd used the perfect tone to calm her.

"No one calls me Patricia except my parents. No blood. No broken bones."

He probed a little more gently for a moment.

"Dragon Skin. Good armor."

"It's the most protection I can wear and still fly."

"Good. I'm glad you do."

"No one calls me Patricia." Yet it hadn't sounded awful when he said it. "Where did you get that idea?"

"Then what do they call you?" He probed a bit more, studying her face as he did so. He was surprisingly gentle, and she only winced a couple of times. "Not broken or cracked."

"Trisha. Everyone calls me Trisha."

"Except Michael."

She started to laugh, but it came out rough for reasons she didn't want to know. Her emotions were a mess tonight. Probably something to do with getting shot. Or with the way it felt to have his hands on her, even on the opposite side of her armor.

"Michael probably gave you rank and serial number along with it. He'd never dare use that name to my face."

Billy eased back until he too sat with his back against the rocket pod.

She missed how his hands had held her, even if they had been merely probing for wounds.

"Name, rank, serial number, and a threat to kick my ass." His voice held such deep chagrin that she couldn't resist patting him on the arm in sympathy.

"Don't worry," she told him. "If I ever get pissed at you, I'll be sure not to leave anything for him to kick. So you're safe from that."

Billy the SEAL groaned. "Great, just what I need. A woman who wants to kick my ass."

"It's a nice ass."

He turned to look at her with narrowed eyes.

Trisha bit her lower lip. She wasn't sure if she was doing it to keep from laughing at him or from leaning into him, which would be much too easy at the moment. She would really not mind if he wanted to just hold her for a moment, but there wasn't a chance in hell she was going to let that happen. Instead she turned to look along the carrier deck and out over the dark ocean.

He did have a nice ass, but she couldn't believe she'd just said that. Even for her, that was a wild statement. Good thing he was in a whole other branch of the service. So, harassment wasn't likely to be thrown at her. In the current state of the U.S. military, wouldn't that be the ultimate joke? A woman accused of harassing the man. Might even be a first.

Her emotions were indeed all over the place.

Again she rubbed her finger along her ribs.

~~~

Bill sat in the dark and watched Patricia, no, Trisha O'Malley's profile in the red nighttime lights of the carrier's deck. The red deck lights turned her red hair black, making her fair skin even starker white.

He knew he had a good ass. It was something he'd been told often enough by his lovers over the years. One of the many side benefits of training a minimum of eight hours a day, year in and year out.

But he'd certainly never been told that by a fellow soldier, male or female. Well, there had been Garvey, but he was always razzing everybody in the squad about something. He'd done a whole riff on Bill's backside on one really horrid watch where they didn't dare sleep.

Garvey had kept them all awake by keeping them laughing, which they didn't dare do aloud. They'd all laughed silently until they wept at the pain in their sides. Garvey was also the guy who would be right beside you when it all went to hell.

He missed his team and wondered what mess they were getting into right now. Three months in-country and now assigned to Operation Heavy Hand, he was completely out of touch with what was going on in SEAL Team Nine. Instead, he was sitting in the red-lit darkness with a SOAR pilot.

Bill couldn't figure O'Malley out at all. She was a crazy mix of skills and wild, of serious and sass, of breeding and street. He couldn't pigeonhole her one bit.

He glanced aft to see where she was looking. Just out into the darkness. The red deck lights were bright enough that the stars were hard to see. No moon. The only real light was the phosphorescent green lifted in slow, lazy waves by the carrier's passage. This ship could actually throw a rooster tail when she was in a real hurry, but a thousand feet of ship weighing a hundred thousand tons rarely needed to race along at forty miles per hour. Tonight she was moseying along at maybe ten, not really going anywhere, just staying in constant motion as any carrier should.

It was a beautiful night, but he'd bet Trisha O'Malley wasn't seeing it much.

He'd seen soldiers go shocky when they were shot. Some were still so high on adrenaline that they didn't even know they'd been hit. But you could see in their eyes that some part of them knew.

One in fifty of the two and a half million who had served

in Iraq and Afghanistan had been physically wounded, aside from traumatic brain injury. The TBI rate was estimated at one in eight and came from being blown up without being actually wounded or killed in the process.

While Trisha's injury was marginal for a wound, and he knew a lot of soldiers who didn't bother reporting such injuries, getting shot wasn't all that common. One in fifty wounded in Afghanistan. Drop that ratio for wounds by improvised explosive devices and other types of mine shrapnel, crashes, bombs, stupid-ass drunken brawls, flat-out accidents, and so on. Maybe one in a hundred and fifty was actually shot, perhaps one in two hundred.

He had been shot three times, once before and twice since joining the Navy. You didn't get used to it, but after a while it didn't change your worldview much. You just woke up in pain being damn glad you could wake up at all.

Then he looked back at her. She was so absolutely still. It seemed that if he touched her she'd break.

"First time, huh?"

She nodded sharply, once. Like a mechanical doll. She was holding herself together by sheer force of will. The woman was so damn strong it was amazing. It would almost be easier to deal with her if she'd just cry. Not that he was any good with a weeping woman. But she was wound so tight.

If he did touch her, she wouldn't break, she'd shatter. And for reasons he wasn't going to think about right now, he cared a great deal that she didn't.

He leaned back and looked away from her, giving her a bit of privacy.

"I was fourteen the first time I was shot." He kept his voice low and soothing. He also did his best to not remember how that long-ago night looked, tasted, felt.

Nothing. No sound. No movement. He didn't watch her out of the corner of his eye because even if she didn't know he was watching, she'd feel it.

But both of their backs rested against either end of the two-hundred-pound, seven-rocket launcher hanging from the Little Bird's hardpoint. He'd feel it across his shoulders if she so much as wiggled a muscle, but she didn't.

"Buddy and I were working a con, a confidence game. We were both fourteen and so damn smart and so convinced that we were indestructible that we decided to take on Ralph. No last name, like he was some runway supermodel or something, just Ralph."

Even now he could feel the heat of that July night. Detroit wasn't like the Arabian Sea. Here, even when it was hot, it was achingly dry. Three months in Somalia, and from the very first day he wanted to lie all day in a pool trying to rehydrate his flesh. Even when the temperature fell below eighty, Somalia still leached the moisture right out of you.

"Detroit was sticky with heat. This was over fifteen years ago, and trust me when I say the city was even worse then. It stank of desperation and we reeked of it."

The con was supposed to take minutes, but it had taken seconds. Only seconds to go completely wrong.

"Old Ralph saw through us so fast that we didn't even have time to blink. We'd both worn white. We thought it looked sharp and cool when we swung into his black-lit club that night. What it did was make us easy targets as we sprinted down the back alley at midnight."

He closed his eyes against it, but the image was there anyway.

"Buddy always followed along with all my stupid ideas. That night it got him killed. I was hit first. But just before the bullet got me, I stumbled on a pile of broken garbage bags from some restaurant. What should have gone through my back went through my arm as I fell and flailed, landing right in the garbage. I just rolled under, dragging the bags over me. Soy sauce, sesame oil, sticky rice all dripping on me."

He didn't know he'd been hit and had peeked out to see what happened to Buddy—just in time to see his heart explode out the front of his chest as the bullet passed through him from behind. Must have been a hollow-point to do that kind of damage. A big one.

"Buddy didn't make it. I heard Old Ralph curse about 'damn amateur punks' before he went back into his club."

He'd also come up and put another round into the back of Buddy's head and hunted for Bill, finally kicking the garbage bag that was over Bill's chest in frustration before giving up. If Bill hadn't been holding on to it in sheer panic, he'd have been exposed and died that night as well.

"I got away. Mom patched me up."

"What did she say to you?" Trisha still hadn't moved a muscle, but she'd spoken.

"She told me to be more careful."

"Be more careful?" The strain still filled her voice.

"Yeah. There wasn't a whole lot of her left by that point. She always did honest work, but you don't get far without even a high school diploma. The income on a couple part-time, minimum-wage jobs in Detroit sucked, even when they did pay her what she was due."

They'd never spoken of what else might have happened to her at those jobs. They'd both been trying just to survive.

"Can't say as she had to tell me. It wasn't being shot that woke me up. That fixed itself well enough after she sewed it up. It was that someone had shot me and there hadn't been a damn thing I could do. In one moment I went from indestructible to wholly powerless. I couldn't save Buddy, though I could have reached out and touched his hand. He'd fallen that close to me. Couldn't help him any more than I could save my mother."

A slight movement of the rocket pod against his shoulders, one he barely registered before a hand rested on his arm. It was a small hand with long, slender fingers. He'd never told anyone any of this. Not even his mother.

"What did you do about Ralph?"

A warrior's question. Deserved a straight answer, though he wondered how she'd take it.

"It took a while. But I made sure he wasn't around to kill anyone else. He'd never seen my face, so I went to work for him. I ran numbers and did other small stuff until he trusted me some. Got him drunk one night and we went for a walk along the train tracks. Seems he stumbled under a freight train."

The small hand squeezed his arm rather than drawing away.

"Not something I'm real proud of, but I'd bet there was one helluva party the next day. Not a soul to miss him. I didn't touch his wallet so that it would look like an accident. But he kept a roll of bills in his pocket that no cop would ever miss. I bought us a fresh start. By the time they found him, Mom and I were on a train from Detroit to the south side of Chicago. Not any different really, but at least no one knew me. Done my best to go straight since."

The words had exhausted him. Why did he think that was a comforting story? It made him feel like shit every time he even thought of it. Saying it aloud for the first time in his life had ripped it right out of his soul.

"Billy?" Her voice was so gentle.

How did women do that—speak like their heart was shared right out in the world?

"Billy the SEAL."

Her voice was stronger. It made him face her.

She was looking right at him, so close that once again she filled his senses with her scent of fire and summer.

"I think you've got that going-straight bit all worked out."

"What do you mean?" He'd never been around a woman who made him feel slow before.

She slapped him upside the head. Not hard, just a friendly cuff that left him blinking in surprise.

"Lieutenant William 'Billy the SEAL' Bruce of the United States Navy, probably decorated a couple times, knowing you. More than a couple, looking at you. Tell me how that isn't overcompensation for your past deeds."

He had to smile at that.

And he'd been the one trying to comfort her.

Chapter 9

They hadn't talked any more. Trisha and Billy simply sat with their backs against the rocket pod and watched the night beyond the stern of the aircraft carrier.

Trisha considered being amused that they were in the same position, both with their feet flat on the deck and their knees up with their arms rested atop them. She'd left her one hand resting lightly on his forearm, and he'd covered her hand with his big, enveloping grasp. They didn't interlace their fingers, but they were holding hands anyway. Not something she did much. Couldn't think of when she ever had.

They shared the quiet for a long time.

She'd have to thank Billy someday. It felt as if she was coming back into her body so that it fit once again. She'd been hit, which had been news to her.

But she hadn't watched friends die.

It wasn't hard to hear the parts that Billy left out. He'd seen Buddy die. He'd executed Ralph. His mother had undoubtedly been… Trisha shivered, trying not to think about it.

Oddly enough, that was how she'd come to run with the street gangs. At thirteen, she'd jumped ship on yet another of her mother's endlessly planned endless parties. She'd set out walking across Boston, any direction that was away.

By the time night fell, and not knowing any better,

she'd wandered into Southie. She had been grabbed and half her clothes torn away before a gang, a rival to the one that had grabbed her, used the distraction to conquer some turf. She hadn't seen the actual deaths, but she'd hidden in her room for a month afterward. But she'd eventually gone back. She wasn't sure why. Maybe to say thanks. Vinny, the gang leader, had given her some clothes and the fare for a ride on the T to get her home.

Once she'd come back, Vinny had showed her many things beyond the reckoning of a girl with a big family home out in Milton. The first place he'd taken her was a tae kwon do dojo he belonged to. There she'd learned to defend herself, though it was on the streets that she'd learned to fight. Their relationship had ended with a very private celebration on her sixteenth birthday. It had been a sweet sixteen indeed.

She was never sure why they'd drifted apart so soon after. Trisha figured that maybe she just didn't like being "someone's girl," even if that someone was Vinny. By seventeen, she rarely saw him. By eighteen, she was heading off for college in New York and had gone to see him one last time before leaving.

Vinny's was another funeral that she'd missed. No one in his gang except Vinny had known how to track her down, so they couldn't find her to tell her. He'd guarded her true identity right to his death. Didn't want her to be treated any differently than if she'd just walked in off the streets. Once he found out who her parents were, he also didn't want her to be at risk for kidnapping and ransom. She'd run enough with Vinny's gang that there was probably no danger for her there, but if another gang got wind of it, she could have been in real danger.

Vinny hadn't even been put in the ground, so there was nowhere to visit him. Cremated, but no ashes to collect. She'd looked it up. There had been ashes, always were, but if no one claimed them, they were just poured into some common grave, typically in a churchyard corner. She wished she could plant them in the orchard out behind the main house, but maybe it was just as well. Vinny wouldn't have known what to do there. He'd never been outside of Boston. Never went to her house even once.

And it didn't matter. Vinny was gone. She went to college and then the Army, never looking back.

With a final squeeze of Billy's arm, she extracted her hand from his. Rising to her feet, which stung bitterly from being so long in the same position.

He loomed up in the night beside her.

"Thanks, Billy."

"Bill." His voice a rough rumble that she could really get to like.

"Sure, Billy."

He grunted but didn't say anything more.

She began going over her chopper again, partly making sure it was okay, partly looking for where the two other bullets had skipped off her armor.

Soon she was explaining the Little Bird's capabilities to Billy. Just what her chopper could and couldn't do in varying conditions. He was an attentive audience, asking intelligent questions that showed a broad knowledge base and often pushing her to find a clear answer. Finding some way to explain what had become instinct.

Trisha found one bullet wedged between the center

console and the windscreen. She managed to recover it with the back edge of her combat knife at a moment when Billy wasn't watching.

She never found the third round.

Chapter 10

A WEEK. FOR SEVEN WHOLE DAYS TRISHA HAD BEEN avoiding him, and Bill wasn't sure why.

She hadn't been obvious about it, so it had taken him a while to notice. She'd take the last open seat at a mostly occupied table at meals. Or be finishing a run on the hangar deck just as he was starting. She'd go straight from briefings to maintaining her machine, often conferring closely with a mechanic.

He'd found her more than once sitting out in the morning sun, discussing the aerodynamics of dragons with the Air Mission Commander's kid. It was as if the girl had acquired a second mother. Kee doted on the girl but was terribly adult about it all. Trisha was different, maybe more like a big sister than a mother. She and Dilya were always laughing together, a wondrous sound that no sane man would interrupt. A child's laughter was not something he'd had much experience with. But when she and Trisha were going at it, it did something to his heart—just the best sound on the planet.

It wasn't as if he'd expected something from Trisha O'Malley, but he'd expected…something.

The nightly missions were nothing much to write home about, even if the team had been allowed to write home about an active operation. Twenty-three vessels of varying sizes and a dozen navies trying to patrol from the Gulf of Aden down to the Seychelles, over fifteen hundred miles south and a thousand east. Even across such an impossible expanse of ocean, attacks were down.

The problem was that ransoms were up. Seven years ago, insurance companies had paid out six million dollars total. Last year, the total had crossed a hundred and fifty mil.

"The average ransom has jumped from half a million to five," Bill told a briefing of the officers during the daily senior staff meeting in Lieutenant Commander Ramis's conference room. "And the individual dangers have risen sharply over that time. Back in the 2000s, the piracy was being run by the fishermen. Due to the lack of any unified government, other nations' vessels arrived and began fishing out the rich Somali waters. Korea, North and South; Japan; and the Taiwanese are the worst offenders, though they aren't alone."

It was hard to believe that he felt empathy for the Somali fishermen, but he did.

"They armed to protect their fishing rights and discovered that it was a lucrative occupation. So they started taking bigger prey. But their rule of the sea, *Uruf Alba'hr*, respects the lives of other mariners, even in hostage situations. Then the inland tribes heard about the money, armed up, and set out upon the sea. Most of this second wave of pirates failed miserably because they knew nothing about the sea. But they learned. They are now not only effective, but often lethal as well. A true criminal class."

Actually Somalia was never that simple, and the more time he spent studying the situation, the more aware of that he became. The fishermen had suffered, their livelihood fished out from under them due to the political squabbles of the combined clans. Then the criminal elements had arrived to take over. And the fourth kingdom of Somalia, if any of it could be called a kingdom, was made of the nomadic tribes who were affected by almost nothing beyond the extent of each year's drought. Somalia was so dry that even a good year was still a drought.

Every day he spent an hour, sometimes two, briefing the officers. But that never included Lieutenant O'Malley.

They'd fly together on different choppers at night on wide-area sweep missions. Occasionally, they'd stop a pirate. Typically with less gunfire than the first crew had demonstrated.

Word was getting out that the patrols were hammering the long coast harder, and the pirates were turning tail more easily. At least the ones they saw. Twice tonight he'd seen Trisha do the same thing. They'd been coming toward each other when she'd abruptly turned and headed in the opposite direction or engaged someone in conversation who Bill was sure had merely been passing by a moment before.

Bill finally descended to guerilla tactics after one particularly long and messy flight along the edge of a growing tropical storm. It had turned into a plain old, though very drawn-out, rescue mission before the idiot pirates drowned themselves in the twenty-foot swells building beneath a thirty-knot wind.

He didn't want to embarrass O'Malley in front of any of the crew, but he was getting pissed about her avoiding him. That, in turn, was starting to mess with his head, which he couldn't afford.

He stripped off his gear, skipped a shower, and switched into civilian clothes. He'd smell of flight suit, but he was past caring about that.

Bill arrived at Trisha's cabin while the water was still running in the shared shower between her and the Maloneys' cabins.

Her cabin door was open. He considered staying out but was annoyed enough to ignore such niceties.

It wasn't much, even if it was private. Bed, chair and small desk, locker and hanging closet. Whole room was a fathom and a half by two. The Navy still thought in six-foot chunks. At nine by twelve feet, it was a very comfortable space, typically reserved for the top dozen officers aboard. But without Marines, Harrier jets, or service squadrons on board, they could afford to be generous.

O'Malley had unpacked into the locker drawers; he could tell because she'd left one open with a pant leg sticking out of it. Her dirty clothes were scattered across the single bunk, which had been made military fashion. He almost wished he had a quarter to see if it bounced when flipped onto the top blanket.

He looked for anything personal.

No pictures of family or, he was cheered to see, any man taped to the small mirror. No jewelry hanging on one of the handy hooks meant for an officer's cap. Not even a "girlie" jacket on any of the mounted hangers. The only thing dangling there other than a thick jacket and a rain slick was a set of immaculate and untouched Army Service dress blues.

He tweaked aside the lapel on the jacket to look at the awards pinned there and tried to suppress a whistle of surprise. Multi-tour Iraq and Afghanistan, sharpshooter, parachutist. Both Commendation and Air Medals with the *V* signifying that the exceptional service had been in battle and the number 5 on the Air Medal indicating this was far from her first one. Weapons specialist in addition to Aviator and Air Assault, which was why she flew the attack version of the Little Bird. Carrier certified, of course. The woman had clearly never hesitated when the call came to join battle.

So why in hell was she avoiding him? Well, he was ready to engage in at least a serious skirmish right now.

The collar device was the single golden bar of a second lieutenant. The sleeve bore Special Ops and Ranger tabs, and a Night Stalkers insignia of a white, sword-wielding, winged centaur beneath a crescent moon.

He still couldn't make any sense of her at all.

"See anything you like?"

He let go of the lapel of her jacket as if he'd been burned and turned to face her.

Damn. The answer to her question was a very definite yes.

Lieutenant Patricia O'Malley in nothing but a towel and a hot temper choked his breath in his chest. Her short hair was still dark red with water. Her shoulders showed muscle, the long lean muscle of fitness, but still looking incredibly feminine with no adornment but her dog tags and some of the creamiest white skin he'd ever seen. And beyond the dark-blue towel a deceptively long length of leg on a woman so short. Either the towel was dangerously short, or her legs were dangerously long. They certainly were seriously good.

"Yep. See a whole lot I like." He aimed a leer in her direction.

She scoffed.

"Do you mind waiting while I get dressed?"

"Not a bit." He settled into the chair in front of the desk, which was barely big enough to fill out a two-page report.

Trisha's glare was intense, and her eyes were incredibly blue with her temper.

"Eyes not turned purple yet. Guess I'm safe for now."

"Don't tempt me, sailor."

He leaned the chair back against the cabin bulkhead behind him and folded his hands over his stomach. "I'm wondering to myself, 'William…' I call myself William when I'm wondering about things. 'William,' I ask, 'is she going to have to drop that towel in order to beat the shit out of you?'"

"What's your answer?" She shifted her weight, cocking a hip in a way that the towel did nothing to hide but also caused the lower edge to ride an interesting inch higher.

"My guess is yes. And my conclusion is that it would definitely be worth the risk considering the potential side benefits."

If he hadn't been expecting it and prepared for it, he'd have been on the floor when she kicked the chair out from under him. Instead of laying him flat on his back, he hung there because he'd braced his feet on the floor and shoulders against the wall as if sitting on air.

"Damn!" She stormed the two steps away that the cabin allowed. He leaned down to retrieve the chair without leaving his "sitting" position. As he relaxed back onto it, he refocused on her legs.

"What are those?"

She looked down at herself, then tugged down the lower edge of the towel. "They're called legs."

"No, I'm talking about the two bruises on your right leg." He narrowed his eyes to inspect them more closely. Mid-thigh, and another just peeking below the lower edge of the towel, a fading yellow edge of what must be a much larger bruise farther up on her hip.

"They're nothing. I bruise easy. Comes with the fair skin you seem so intent on staring at." She gathered some clothes. "I'll get dressed next door since you're such a rude son of a bitch."

"Mom's a nice lady. You'd like her. But I am her son. You got that much right." Now why had he said that? He'd never found a girl worth taking home to meet his mother. Not ever.

Trisha scoffed again and left the room clutching her clothes and her towel.

He'd never stayed long with a girlfriend anyway. They hated that he disappeared on assignment with no notice and never wrote. Never knew what to write even when he thought to. His longest span before a Dear William email had been about six months.

He kept a mixture of prewritten letters and postcards in the hands of his SEAL team adjutant to send to his mother each week when he was on a black ops assignment, like being undercover in Somalia. He never wanted her to worry. For the first time he was thinking that Patricia O'Malley was a woman he wouldn't mind writing home about.

Trisha had two bruises. Almost faded. If they'd started out really intensely black and blue, they would be about a week old, based on the coloration. A chill went down his spine as he imagined the line of them: lower thigh, hip...ribs.

She returned minus the towel, but not looking one bit less fine in khakis and an Army-green T-shirt. Or one bit less pissed. Was it angry or was it defiant?

"You were shot three times, not once."

"So?"

Defiant. Holding hard onto her pride. Bill clunked the chair legs back onto the deck. "Did you think that I'd think less of you because you were in shock over being shot? Never mind three times?"

"Maybe." A slight softening of her expression told him that he'd hit the problem on the head. Or at least part of it. She moved to hang up the towel, then bent down to pull socks out of one of the locker's drawers. Everything in the drawer inspection ready. He'd expected her to have messes instead. Again, that constant contrast versus expectation.

"Shit, O'Malley. I've seen guys who never made it past the sound of the first bullet going by, never mind three hitting them. Have you missed a single mission this week?"

"No." Her voice was soft and she wasn't facing him. Instead she was straightening the dress uniform jacket on its hanger as if by touching it he had soiled it.

"Have you held back or hesitated even the least little bit on a single mission that you've flown since then?"

"Never! I wouldn't do that."

"Didn't think so." He rose to his feet and, taking her by the shoulders, turned her to face him.

She looked up at him with an expression he still

couldn't read. He'd had months of training, like any other SEAL, in reading what another's unspoken thoughts, or at least what their mood, might be. But he couldn't read her and it was frustrating the hell out of him.

"Then why in blazes are you avoiding me?"

"I would think that would be obvious."

He racked his brain again to no avail. "Well, it isn't to me."

———

Trisha looked up at Billy. His narrowed eyes revealed that he was indeed totally perplexed.

It was perfectly clear to her, and she just figured that meant she was too damn stupid to live. She shrugged to herself, feeling the warm weight of his large hands still resting on her shoulders.

Well, stupid is something I'm really good at, she had to admit to herself. With one foot, she shoved the door to her cabin closed until the latch clicked. Then putting a hand on either side of his neck, Trisha pulled his face down to hers.

His hesitation didn't last long, then the kiss became everything she remembered from the first one. Power, heat, strength.

And then it became more. When he folded his arms around her and held her tight against him as they teased each other's lips, she was just gone.

She'd never felt such a thing before. In Billy's arms, Trisha O'Malley felt…safe. As if someone else would take care of the world, just for awhile. That was so foreign, she almost pushed away. Then she changed her mind and leaned closer because it felt so damn good.

Trisha wished she was still wearing the stupid towel, so that she could just let it slide ever so slowly to the floor like some heart-fluttering romance heroine. But she was dressed now, so she went for plan B.

Sliding her hands down to his waist, she tugged Billy's T-shirt free and dragged it off over his head. If she could have shredded it with her teeth, she would have.

When she reached bare skin, rather than throwing herself against it, she hesitated. A desecration of multiple scars ran across one of the most beautiful chests she'd ever seen. Two obvious bullet holes, one by his waist and another terrifyingly near his heart. A third, old one deep on his arm, just below the shoulder—the one Ralph of Detroit had given him. Thin white lines crisscrossed as if he'd been whipped or dragged over rough ground.

And one deep line that matched the scar across his face, as if a knife had been dragged diagonally down from his ear, over his chin, then sliced him from clavicle most of the way down his ribs below one breast.

Trisha looked slowly back up to his eyes, which watched her intently from just inches away.

Awaiting her reaction.

She didn't know what to think. She'd been all freaked out over a bullet that hadn't even penetrated her armor. He appeared to have been tortured and clearly been close to death several times.

At her continued inspection, he shrugged slightly as if to say, "It's who I am."

She watched a shiver ripple over the skin as she stroked a single finger down the long line of the deep knife cut.

Then she leaned in and kissed it. The shiver turned into a soft groan that rippled across his magnificent chest.

It was the last sound they made.

Bill had never made love like this. He'd been with women who couldn't even hack it when he pulled off his shirt. Some had insisted on making love in the dark; some had quickly left. A few had been turned on by his scars, and truth be told, those were the ones that bothered him the most.

Trisha's simple kiss had both acknowledged the pain of earning them as well as what they meant about him. He'd been in harm's way; he would be again. That wasn't going to change.

And she accepted that in him.

By the time his head stopped spinning, she had removed his pants and shoes as well, until he stood naked before her while she remained fully clothed. He wasn't quite sure how that had happened. Or how he felt about that. Naked and exposed, but neither in a bad way. As if his true self was on display for the first time in his life.

In silence, she walked around him in the small room lit painfully bright by the single overhead bulb. Her hand never left his skin as she looked him over. Not like a slab of meat or a greedy lover, but rather like someone who wanted to know who he was. Who understood that he and his scars were not separable, but rather one was a part of the other.

When she returned to stand in front of him, she undressed slowly. Her clothes hadn't deceived. She was as trim as she appeared. Her breasts were small and high, but would have looked wrong on her frame if they were any bigger. Shoulders that showed strength, and a waist that flared to womanly hips that fit his hands perfectly when he rested them there.

She continued undressing until she revealed that her hair color was all natural and her legs really were that long and that amazing.

He swept her up into his arms and laid her upon the bed.

He turned off the glaring overhead.

She switched on the bedside reading lamp. Now she was a pattern of light and shadow, of perfect skin and infinite promise.

He lay down beside her on that Army-tight blanket and slowly traced his hand over her. She was so perfect, as if built of porcelain. But he'd seen her run, he'd seen her fly, and he'd seen her angry. This was definitely no china doll, but a woman.

Her body responded and twitched as he ran his hand over her many shapes. He continued until her body's reflexive moves of unfamiliarity with his touch shifted ever so slowly to moves of pleasure caused by a touch becoming known, then familiar.

He caressed her amazing form until she leaned into or rose against his hand wherever he moved it.

Bill traced a single fingertip over her ribs, outlining the still livid bruise where the bullet had hit her.

That's when he became aware that she was watching him. He'd become so fascinated by her body and her incredible responses to him that he'd just sort of assumed that her eyes had drifted shut.

He leaned down and kissed each eye on the lid so that

she did shut them. Then he shifted his lips onto hers as he cupped his hands between her legs.

She thrust up against him, bruising his lips and straining against his hand.

Even as he drove her upward, she slid a finger along the big scar over his chest. When she came, she dug her short fingernails into his pecs and held on.

No inhibitions, no catty games: she simply gave herself to the sensations and held on to him. Bill wanted to do more, so much more, but he'd neither prepared for nor expected this.

When he finally let her come down, she shifted them around until he was lying on his back.

She reached over to the desk drawer, without leaving the bed or losing contact with him, and pulled out a small string of silvered packets.

He could just kiss her. So he did and she seemed to melt against him as their hands and mouths ranged over each other's bodies.

Trisha sheathed him, caressed him, then straddled him. She took him in, and when he would have thrust upward, she kept him in place with palms braced against his hipbones between her spread legs.

With one of those cool, long-fingered hands of hers, she reached up and brushed his eyes closed. Then she took him in so slowly that it was almost agony, exquisite agony.

All at once she relaxed and let him all the way in. At the same instant she nipped his chest with her teeth. She continued to tease him with her tongue and her hips until he knew he was done for. He placed his hands on her hips and drove up at the same moment she drove down.

The release hammered them both until they could do no more than shudder. Then, like a falling leaf, she slowly collapsed to lie full on his chest, her head nestled below his chin as he stroked her hair and back.

On the softest sigh, she seemed to fall asleep.

He'd never had an experience like this one. As he continued to brush a hand over her wondrous skin, his analytic brain began to kick in. He knew himself well enough to know that if he tried to stop it, his analysis would just kick into high gear. It was a survival mechanism, so he decided it was best to just let it go.

Why had it been so different with Trisha?

It wasn't that she was an amazingly skilled Mata Hari. She had done no more than any another woman might have done. Well, actually, there were a couple of immensely creative things she'd done that had made his eyes cross, but that wasn't what was confusing him.

And he didn't know her well enough for the deeper emotions to be engaged, if he even had any. He'd thought he'd been in love once or twice, but that was when he was ten and Tasha Yar had been on *Star Trek*, not in the real world. Even at ten he knew the difference. And later, the Chicago whore who hadn't been able to pay the cash when he fixed her sink, but had paid him in the flesh for his first several experiences at fourteen. That no one had ever pulled any deeper emotions from him made him suspicious of their existence.

No, there was something different about Trisha O'Malley, and like so much else about her, it eluded him. Then he had it.

It was like the way she ran and the way she flew.

It wasn't practiced at all. She made love as if it were totally natural.

As if what she did came straight from her heart.

—⁓—

It was funny; Trisha could practically hear Billy thinking as she lay upon him. She wondered what was running through his mind, but didn't want to ask. Half afraid he'd make up some line to cover his real thoughts.

Behind his words would be, "Damn! She was a good lay." Or an easy one. Or…

But it hadn't felt that way. It had been life changing, as she somehow had known throughout the long week of mostly sleepless days that it would be. He'd now ruined her for any lesser lover. She hadn't treated men as disposable… Well, not quite. But the few, very few, that she had taken into her bed she certainly hadn't kept for long.

She'd thought Billy the SEAL should be too tall, too arrogant, too self-needy to treat a woman right. Instead, he'd found that perfect mix of gentle but strong, of attentive to her needs rather than first focusing on his own. And the way they fit together, she could lie here on his chest forever.

She opened one eye to study the expanse spread before her. This one shoulder was clean of injury, about the only part of him that was unblemished, front or back. Yet his scars had not made him ugly. Rather, it had made her feel even safer in his arms. As if he had held the world at bay just for her.

His hand slowly ceased stroking her, coming to rest hooked over her shoulder rather than cupping her butt as most men in his position would. His heartbeat slowed against her ear until she knew he slept.

Trisha closed her eyes tightly to keep back sudden tears that threatened to spill.

This one was really going to suck when it all came apart.

Chapter 11

THE STORM HAD GROWN WHILE THEY SLEPT. WHAT had been ugly flying the previous night had become a named tropical storm by mid-afternoon. Their naming system here was ARB for Arabian Sea and a number. But even if it wasn't named Ursula or Betty Boop, this storm was nasty. By the time they awoke in the evening, the storm still wasn't making landfall anywhere. Instead it was just boiling upward from the heart of the Arabian Sea.

Of course, that's when the call came in. An oil tanker, the *Sepeda*, registered out of Jakarta, was being chased by pirates. That meant the tanker crew had about ten minutes, perhaps twenty, before they were boarded.

The *Sepeda* was more than thirty minutes from the nearest help, which was aboard the USS *Peleliu*. Nobody even cleared their meal trays. They bolted from the middle of dinner in the officers' mess and raced up the various ship's ladders. Pilots and crew geared up. Teams hit the decks to untie the choppers. They'd been fully fueled and rearmed after the prior night's flight, so they were ready to go in minutes. There were so few aircraft aboard that they hadn't even had to fold back the rotors for everyone to fit on the flight deck, so there were no delays there.

The rain was pattering against the windscreen as Trisha climbed aboard. She felt loose and ready to go, *thank you, Billy*. Roland slammed in beside her and threw the engine startup switches even as he buckled himself in. Two crewmen came up and quickly hung the doors and swung them shut. That would protect the chopper's electronics when they flew into weather, but suddenly the cockpit felt terribly small. More vulnerable than it did without the doors on.

Once they had the engine moving, Trisha began waking up the electronics: radar, night vision, radio.

Peleliu command was giving a running commentary on status. "…is a quarter-million-ton VLCC traveling laden. She just took on one and a half million barrels of crude. She is not in convoy, but she does have a security force and a citadel. They are attempting to repel boarders and will then retreat if necessary. Crew of about twenty."

Roland looked at her and grimaced before pulling on his helmet and snapping down the visor. He was right; no way this was going to be pretty.

A VLCC was a Very Large Crude Carrier. That meant about a hundred and fifty million dollars of oil on a sixty-million-dollar ship that was a thousand feet long, traveled at twenty miles per hour, and took an hour to make a turn. The ransom on that would be a record-breaker. "Not in convoy" meant she was stupid enough to try running these waters on her own, without military escort.

At least the oil tanker had an armed crew and a citadel.

"Don't get your hopes up," Billy said over the radio from his position on the DAP. He'd clearly heard the last part. "They're now reporting two boats after them and poor visibility in thirty-foot waves. The weather may suck, but it could also be a life-or-drown motivation for the pirates to get aboard. The *Sepeda*'s 'army' is probably four guys with rifles and a couple fire hoses. Two boats probably means thirty to forty pirates with automatic weapons. Even with losses, they will take the deck. And it's a first-generation citadel."

"Crap!" Roland said over the internal intercom.

Ships had taken to fortifying their command bridge. When attacked by pirates, everyone would pile into the citadel, seal the doors, and wait for rescue. Now that the criminal element had taken over piracy, being caught meant beatings, rape, or worse. Recently, one hostage was keel-hauled, a pre-twentieth-century British Navy punishment of running a line under the ship from side to side and then using it to drag some poor soul down one side and back up the other, usually slicing them near to death with the barnacles growing on the hull. When later rescued, the hostages said the pirates had "done it just for fun."

The problem with the first generation of citadels was that the builders didn't think it through. Locking yourself in kept you from being shot—until the pirates targeted the main windows with .50 cal machine guns. Or fed smoke into the air vents or cut the power to your radios, then waited for you to run out of water, or... Armoring ship bridges had become a major industry, just another piece of the seven billion dollars a year that Somali piracy cost the global economy.

So, that meant the SOAR team had to fly through terrible weather and recapture a ship from a large group of desperate criminals before the out-of-date citadel was breached.

"Sounds like fun," she told Roland.

She knew that, despite having his visor down, he was rolling his eyes at her. She glanced up-deck at the other Little Birds. This time the D-boys were climbing aboard, two per side on the benches. That was going to be an ugly ride out in the weather.

Then she saw two figures who couldn't be mistaken for anyone else, notwithstanding the red deck lights and the rain. They walked side by side to the *Merchant*. They moved the same, light on their feet, not one wasted motion. Each carried a long sniper rifle in their hands, a combat rifle across their backs, and more weaponry at their hips and in pouches. One was obviously Michael, trim and average in height, wearing the unique MICH helmet that all D-boys wore. The other loomed over him. Billy the SEAL.

They climbed onto the outside seat of Dennis's chopper and tied themselves in.

Trisha didn't know what to do with that. Her hands continued the preflight preparations, but her heart had not been ready to see Billy ready to jump in on the front lines. She'd never seen him fight, barely seen him run. Her mind had him safe, warm, and dry, tucked away in the back of the DAP Hawk *Vengeance*.

He must have noticed her attention, because he gave a cheery salute. Michael looked at him, then over to her. She had no way to see Michael's expression and decided that was a good thing. She sent back a cheerful wave and turned to focus on the flight.

Which would be far easier if she could just breathe.

Bill was kind of glad that he and Michael didn't have an intercom circuit that only included the two of them. There was the general frequency for the flight and the Delta freq that Michael had provided when Billy volunteered to be on the insertion team.

There was no question about what they'd have to do. The pirates would definitely be aboard by the time they arrived. So they were going to have to take the battle to the deck and hope they beat the pirates to the citadel.

Michael hadn't even blinked at Bill's offer to go. He'd simply given him the frequency and gone back to putting on his gear. Bill was glad he'd drawn a full combat kit from the Quartermaster and was ready in time to walk beside Michael. It felt good to be geared up. The familiar weight of weapons, ammo, and various explosive ordnance was a comfort. He'd selected the FN-SCAR rifle that the Night Stalkers favored rather than the HK416 rifle that Michael chose to wear across his back. He'd chosen a Remington M24 SWS, Sniper Weapon System, rather than the HK-PSG1 the Delta Colonel carried. They didn't need to share a nod to read each other's approval of their weapons selection.

But as they sat shoulder to shoulder on the *Merchant*'s bench seat, it was clear that he and Michael were going to have a talk when they got back to the *Peleliu*. Bill huffed out a breath and almost laughed. Well, no one had promised that anything to do with Trisha O'Malley was going to be simple.

He and Trisha had arrived separately to breakfast and sat apart, just as they had been all week. But he'd never been so aware of someone's position in the room before and of each thing they did, other than a team member or an unfriendly while on a mission. And maybe not even then. Although she sat behind him, each word she spoke, each laugh, had been like an echo locator to place her exactly among all of the people in the crowded mess room.

Her quick wave just before they lifted from the deck of the *Peleliu* had heartened him. It had been so good between them, and it clearly wasn't affecting her on this mission. Not in a hundred years would he have guessed that she was avoiding him because of that first kiss. Well, the second one had sure stamped "Paid" on that one.

They were halfway to the *Sepeda* when word came that the pirates were aboard and the crew was falling back into the citadel. Give the Somalis maybe ten minutes to all get aboard and discover that the crew had locked itself away. That would draw all of their concentration toward the stern conning tower for a little bit, so maybe the pirates wouldn't have guards posted yet by the time the choppers arrived.

A sharp jerk against the belt around his waist drew his attention back to the weather. They were definitely headed into the storm. The rain drummed off his helmet, and visibility was zero. He missed the ADAS gear that projected the images directly to his visor. They'd let him wear it when he'd been aboard the *Vengeance* and spoiled him for life. But it required that he stay wired to the chopper's camera system, and tonight he needed to be mobile. He flipped down the night-vision goggles and toggled them on.

That was little better. In the narrow range of the binocular elements, he could see the night world as a thousand shades of green. The other choppers in the flight cast bright lines, clear enough that he could even make out the figures behind the windows by their body heat. The waves passing fifty feet below them were a roiling mess with little definition. If they had to ditch in that, they'd be in serious trouble. What had been twenty-foot rollers last night were thirty-foot chaos tonight. Not so far below his dangling boots, breakers crashed against each other. High wind ripped spume off the top of every whitecap.

They'd have canceled tonight's patrol, at least in this direction, if it weren't for the *Sepeda*. How much worse did it have to get before they'd call back the choppers? Any outfit other than the Night Stalkers would already have grounded their fleet. The *Peleliu* was turned and driving toward the storm in case a rescue was needed, but in this sea there was little chance of that succeeding.

Trisha's attack Little Bird flew along right beside them, and he took some comfort knowing she was there. Not that she was likely to be much help in tonight's operation.

He was starting to wonder if he should speak up, when Michael's voice sounded calmly over the general frequency. His voice was as steady as if he still sat in the Lieutenant Commander's office aboard the *Peleliu*, rather than being slammed around on a hard wooden seat while rain and wind drove against him at over a hundred miles per hour.

"Okay, here's the plan."

Chapter 12

MERCHANT OF DEATH HAD DROPPED SO CLOSE TO WAVE height that Bill wanted to pull up his feet to keep them dry. The Sepeda was big enough that this storm didn't toss her around much, but they were certainly surrounded by some awful seas.

The bow crested out of the darkness impossibly close, but the pilot must know that. A moment later, *Merchant* popped up over the bow, spinning until he faced into the wind, and came to a hover over the front twenty feet above the oil tanker's deck.

Michael tossed the FRIES descent rope free so that it dangled from a small hanger on the chopper. Even as the two-inch braided rope snaked toward the deck, Michael had wrapped his gloved hands and his boots around it and was sliding out of sight.

Bill counted to three and slid down behind him. He hit the deck at the same moment as the second D-boy from the other side of the helicopter. Michael and the first D-boy were already down in a crouch with their weapons raised.

Bill stepped forward just as the ropes dropped to the deck. *Merchant* had hit the release to shed the ropes and was already disappearing again over the bow. A quick glance with their NVGs as they crested the bow had revealed no forward lookouts yet. Over the sounds of the storm and with the terrible visibility of night and rain, no one should know they were aboard.

The four of them began moving forward as two teams, working down either side of the ship in two-by-two formation. Like a game of leapfrog, one man ran forward while the other covered him from behind, peeking out around a handy pipe or other deck fitting. Alternating sprints, they were able to move at a continuous fast trot. They had a fifth of a mile of deck that was as wide as a football field to clear. They didn't want to end up with anyone behind them when they arrived at the aft superstructure tower where all of the people, both crew and pirates, would be concentrated.

Bill was in the lead when he spotted the first person on board. He dropped to his knee and held up a clenched fist so that Michael wouldn't move yet. With a slicing motion of his flat hand, he indicated the direction of the man he'd spotted.

Through the night-vision gear, Bill could see one man. He ducked low and leaned his head out farther from the hatch he'd taken refuge behind. Two men. Cowering together against the storm at the head of the gangway.

The gangway was a long set of stairs that ran down the side of a ship so that a pilot or service boat could pull alongside. Apparently the *Sepeda*'s captain hadn't even retracted those for the storm or to keep off the pirates. That was bad. It meant the pirates had probably been aboard for ten more minutes than they'd originally estimated.

Thankfully, the first two pirates had their backs to the weather. It wasn't cold, but the rain was driving hard. He waved Michael forward.

The D-boy slid up beside him. With a quick set of hand signals, they made their plan, then they were in motion. They came up so fast that the pirates had no time to react before they were facedown on the hard steel deck. A sharp rap of their heads together had them too dazed to shout before they were bound, gagged, and tied to the stanchion with plastic zip ties. A slap-shot injection would knock them out for a couple hours, so even if someone freed them, it wouldn't be an issue.

Quick inspection revealed no radios. That was good. No one would be calling them to check in.

A flash and a muffled "crack" from the far side of the deck showed that the other team hadn't been quite as successful. Hopefully the flash suppressor had been enough to mask the shot from any other sentries.

Michael waited a full three seconds without moving but nothing else happened from that direction. With a wave, Michael had Bill moving once again toward the stern.

Bill would have to take that back to his unit. No communication. No potentially revealing microphone click, even on an encrypted circuit. Had there been real trouble, the other team would have broken radio silence. But since they hadn't, it must mean the situation was under control.

It was so smooth that Bill felt a stab of envy and a bit clumsy. As if the SEALs weren't quite up to Delta standards. They weren't, no one was, but it didn't help to have direct experience of that, even if the SEALs probably came the closest.

They now had three or four fewer pirates to deal with. But since they didn't know how many there were, that wasn't of much use.

The next round of sentries was more alert. They had deck lights on and were standing in the shadows of the eight-story superstructure. The citadel, which would include the command bridge, perched at the uppermost level where the bridge wings stuck out to either side for visibility when docking.

Bill looked at Michael and tapped a smoke grenade that was hanging from his belt. Michael shook his head and pointed upward. The rain was driving down hard now. It would knock the smoke out of the air too quickly.

Bill had almost forgotten about the weather. He'd spent so much of his life at sea that the rolling of the massive ship had felt natural rather than unbalancing. And he might be wet, but a couple thousand hours as a Navy diver had made that of little consequence as well.

Then Michael took the smoke grenade from Bill, signaling him to stay, and scooted off to mid-deck staying low.

"Now." Michael transmitted the single word, then lofted the smoke grenade up against the middle of the superstructure. The guarded entries were at either side of the tower. The middle expanse of the structure was just blank wall and windows.

With a flash and a sizzle, a billow of bright green smoke erupted and was quickly beaten down by the rain.

But both of the guards turned to face what they thought was a threat.

He and Michael charged them. The pirates were aware of the attack at the last second and managed to get off just one wild shot before they were taken down.

That single shot was like an alarm bell.

———

Trisha watched the *Sepeda*'s superstructure erupt with gunfire from a dozen places. From her position a hundred meters off the port side of the ship and just above deck height, she was as good as invisible, but she could see that the pirates already occupied the first four or five of the stories. They shot out windows and then began firing wildly downward.

The Special Ops Forces knew this was going to happen. Michael's "Now" had launched Phase Two of the plan. At this instant, while all attention was to the front, *Mad Max* would be delivering the four other Delta operators onto the narrow stern of the ship close behind the tower structure.

Per instructions, Trisha unleashed a line of fire from her miniguns close across the front of the superstructure. Her rounds would go harmlessly out to sea, but the stream of bright tracers was intended to attract the startled attention of the pirates. Perhaps even scare them back inside, leaving the D-boys and Billy time to put their part of the plan into action.

The DAP Hawk was doing the same thing just aft of the superstructure. A heavy stream of fire two stories above the deck. Let the pirates think that the entire U.S. Army had landed.

The captain of the *Sepeda* had reported they were still secure within the citadel. Then he'd begun asking an endless stream of questions that no one had time to answer. Trisha turned down that radio frequency to just a murmur. She figured when that frequency went silent, the citadel would have been breached. Now it was her and the *Vengeance*'s mission to keep the pirates distracted so that the hostages stayed safe and the Captain could keep talking.

A round pinged off her windscreen.

Someone had shot wild in hopes of hitting whoever was shooting at them.

Her visor showed a pirate leaning out one of the windows, fourth story up. She'd been ordered to make no direct attacks in Phase Two of the plan, but this was an easy shot.

She shifted sideways until she was exactly flush with the front of the superstructure and fired off a half-second burst. The shooter and his gun disappeared back inside. She couldn't tell if she'd hit him, but at least he'd think twice before leaning back out. A sudden roll of the ship made her accidentally shoot one of the main floodlights on the front of the superstructure. No great loss in the scheme of things.

Bill cursed as a rain of glass showered to the deck around him. He looked for the shooter, but couldn't see one. The main light fixture had blinked out abruptly, plunging their section of the deck into darkness. He had to flip his night-vision goggles back into place and did so barely in time to spot and kill a pirate who was about to shoot him.

That cleared the lower deck and the Special Ops teams began clearing the superstructure, fighting upward deck by deck. It was now simply a race. Could they get to the citadel before it was breached and the pirates had a set of hostages?

It was a close thing. A small group fought hard on the third level but were finally subdued with a flash-bang. At the final standoff on the sixth story, no one had been willing to give way. Bill and Michael had to shoot more than a dozen with their sniper rifles in the tight confines of the ship's ladders before the pirates gave in, dumping their weapons down the companionways with a sharp clatter. Most of them hadn't even set the safeties. It was a wonder that none of the weapons fired randomly as they tumbled down the metal ladders.

There was no way to get a chopper aboard in this weather. So the Night Stalkers returned to the *Peleliu*, and he and the D-boys took turns standing watch over the prisoners. No one was about to trust the four South Africans who had been hired on as security but clearly barely knew which end of a gun to hold. On day three, once the *Sepeda* had driven out of the dying storm, a British cutter was able to come alongside and take off the pirates.

They'd steamed far enough south that only Dusty James's transport Black Hawk had the range to come fetch them. The *Vicious* took a midair refuel each way to get them back aboard the *Peleliu*.

After three days at sea standing back-to-back watches, all Bill wanted was a shower and sleep. Even if Trisha was willing to repeat their intimacy, he wasn't sure he'd have the energy.

When he stepped on the deck, Boyd was waiting for him. Beside him stood an orderly with the duffel bag that the Quartermaster had issued to Bill.

This didn't look good.

The Lieutenant Commander came up and shook his hand, resting the other on Bill's shoulder in a companionable way. "I hear you did really great things on the *Sepeda*. Well done."

"Thanks." Okay, Bill wasn't in trouble. So why was he being shipped out on no notice? Not that it hadn't happened before, but he'd only just started to feel as if he and Michael and the Night Stalkers were becoming an effective team.

"Turns out that *sepeda* means 'bicycle' in Indonesian. Who would name a quarter-of-a-million-ton oil tanker 'Bicycle,' I ask you?"

Bill had known, but didn't care why. Indonesian was one of a half-dozen languages he spoke well enough to be understood, little better than an experienced tourist, but understood.

"Dennis is waiting for you, over in his chopper, to get you out to the aircraft carrier." Boyd looked genuinely upset on Bill's behalf.

"Care to tell me what's going on?"

"Right, sorry. I, uh, have some bad news and feel awful that I'm the one to deliver it. No way to sugar-coat it. Last night we received notice that your mother just died. Didn't want to tell you over the radio. You've been given immediate leave to, uh, go home and take care of things."

Bill staggered to one side as if the *Peleliu* had just slammed into a hurricane. Only Boyd's remaining grasp of his hand kept him on his feet.

"Come on. I'll walk you."

Bill couldn't see, couldn't have walked without the escort. He must not have heard right. Constance Bruce couldn't be dead. But here he was, climbing aboard the Little Bird *Merchant of Death*. A helicopter he'd jumped off just three days before. How goddamn appropriate was that?

If Dennis greeted him, he didn't hear it.

As they lifted, all he could see was the wide empty ocean and the sky scrubbed a painfully bright blue by the passage of the storm.

"Someone's waving you off." Dennis tipped the bird so that Bill could see down on the deck.

A small figure with bright red hair stood there with an arm raised.

He was too numb to return the gesture.

Chapter 13

"O'MALLEY, WALK WITH ME."

Trisha dropped off her tray at the cleaning station of the officers' mess and followed Lola Maloney out the door. Had word gotten out about her and Billy? Not that it seemed to matter. He hadn't even waved back when he left the ship last night, as if he didn't want to acknowledge her. She was still hurt and angry about that, so she shoved it aside for the hundredth time in the last twenty-four hours.

In silence, the Chief Warrant led her up one flight to the helo hangar. In the middle of dinner service there was no one running. The vast, cavernous space echoed with its own silence. It felt as if even a whisper would be trapped here and repeat forever.

They walked in silence until they stood at the wide opening in the starboard side where the aircraft elevator ran. The ceiling lights in the helo hangar were just bright enough that she could make out the crescent moon down near the horizon but no stars.

"What is it, Chief?"

Trisha took the initiative and tried to sound casual about it. She certainly didn't know Lola Maloney well enough to call her by her first name, especially when Trisha didn't know what the hell was going on.

"Pull up your shirt." Maloney's voice was rough, as if she was having trouble getting out the words.

"What the—"

"Just do it!" No questioning the order.

Halfway through tugging the shirt's hem out of her jeans, Trisha finally knew what this was about. No point in playing games. She exposed the black-and-blue mark across her ribs. At Maloney's nod, she dropped the shirt back in place but didn't bother tucking it in.

"Who?"

"Not that it matters, but Kee Stevenson spotted it in the shower. Made some idle remark about it. I didn't think anything more of it until I spotted the new patch on your flight suit. Anyone looked at that?"

"No need." Trisha shrugged it off. "Doesn't hurt anymore." Not even when she and Billy—there was a painful thought she shut down hard.

"When?"

"Last week, first mission with Lieutenant Bruce. Stupid pirates didn't know they were done after I shot off their engine and tagged me as I swung aside."

"You should have overflown them."

"I know that now."

"You should have already known that *and* reported it immedi—" Maloney cut herself off with a deep sigh.

Okay, so Trisha now knew that too. But she hadn't wanted to go see a medico and complete all the paperwork that went with any injury. Or admit to anyone that she'd been shot. How could she have told Billy the jerk SEAL? How could she have done that?

"Shit!" the Chief swore under her breath. "I can't believe this fell to me. Emily should be here."

Trisha guessed that Maloney was talking about Emily Beale, but she'd retired to fly with a firefighting outfit

in Oregon. Something to do with getting pregnant. But
what did Emily have to do with anything? It still wasn't
an association she was going to admit to. She'd succeed
on her own merits, or not succeed at all.

"Okay, O'Malley." Again that puff of a sigh. "I'm
going to say this about half as well as I should, not
something a commanding officer should ever admit."
They'd been standing side by side, facing the night, but
now Maloney turned to face her directly.

"You're a wild card. You're an amazing pilot. No one
denies that. But to fly with the 160th SOAR, you have
to be more than that."

Trisha's heart stopped beating for a moment. There
was something going on here that was going to be a far
bigger blow than Billy flying off without even a word
or a wave.

"On some flights you are exceptional, but on others
you are taking liberties that put yourself or your team at
risk. Missing the third technical in Bosaso and especially
not calling for help to begin with. Getting shot because,
I'm guessing, you didn't trust your gunner's timing or
that *Max* would be in the right position. And shooting
out that deck light when you'd been *ordered* not to engage the structure. The broken glass and unplanned loss
of lighting put the deck-based crew at severe risk."

Trisha opened her mouth to protest that. To explain
about the shooter she'd taken out, or at least chased back
inside. But she stopped when she thought about exactly
who was on the deck at that point. She'd shot out the
light right over Billy and Michael's heads. If her action
might have killed one or both of those men…

Maloney continued in the silence left by Trisha's shock.

"I need team players, not individuals, no matter how good. The Night Stalkers can't use individuals. Exceptional people, brilliant skills, ones with deep intuition, yes. We need every bit of that, and I'm starting to think you have all that. But if you aren't a team player, if you continue flying as a maverick who doesn't also consider the consequences to the rest of the team, we can't use you."

Trisha could only bite her lower lip. The only thing she'd ever wanted to be was to be like Emily Beale. She was the most amazing woman Trisha had ever met. They'd fought side by side through the 101st together. Both of them had done Green Platoon, the first two women to survive it and come out the other side of that brutal month-long test. No way Trisha could have pulled that off if she weren't trying to live up to Beale's standard.

"Shit!" Maloney cursed once more. "I had no idea this would be so hard to do. Emily always made it look so simple." Then the Chief Warrant squared her shoulders, and Trisha shifted into a stance at full attention in response, even though her shirttail still hung out.

"Lieutenant O'Malley. I'm hereby ordering you off this ship for a week of paid leave. Transport will be provided immediately. After a week, you may choose to return to this ship, or return to the 101st Airborne Division with the highest of recommendations. The choice will be yours. Dismissed."

Trisha saluted sharply. She didn't know what else to do. Unable to release it, even after Maloney's answering salute, she remained there until long after Maloney had walked away into the shadows.

She finally was able to drop the salute, and then a bit later found she could still walk upright off the hangar deck, though her world had crashed down around her. Trisha returned to her cabin to pack her duffel. She found Dennis standing there waiting for her.

"You my ride?" She managed to say it without her voice cracking.

He nodded reluctantly.

"And my escort?"

His shrug was even more uncomfortable.

"Glad it's you," she managed before she turned to pack so that she wouldn't have to see whatever his next pained physical response might be. It only took her a minute or two, then they trooped up to his bird.

She didn't touch the flight controls, felt she didn't have the right to. Nor did they speak most of the way to the aircraft carrier. From there she could catch the next C-2A headed…who knew where.

She sure as hell wasn't going home to Mommy and Daddy in Boston. Somehow going to her apartment at Fort Lewis, Washington, the home of the Night Stalkers' Fifth Battalion, didn't sound very cozy at the moment. Hell, she'd only been there long enough after training to drop off a couple boxes of belongings and climb aboard a transport to the Gulf. She hadn't even looked in the bedroom to see if the place came with sheets.

"Where the hell did Billy go?"

"Vermont."

Trisha didn't even know she'd spoken aloud. Of course Dennis would know. He was the one who'd carried Billy off the *Peleliu.*

"What was so damned important in Vermont?" That he had to leave without talking to her or anything.

"His mom died and he went back to Richmond, Vermont, to bury her."

"Oh." She was such an idiot.

God, no wonder he hadn't waved back.

Chapter 14

SHE WAS IN THE GROUND. THAT WAS ALL BILL COULD think to hold himself together. Constance Bruce was finally at rest.

He sat in the afternoon sun on the top of the three stone steps at the front of the Round Church in Richmond, Vermont, staring out across the broad, green field that stretched toward the Winooski River. Most of the town's four thousand people lived across the narrow, two-lane steel bridge, and it felt as if he'd met every single one. Even if it wasn't true, he was tired enough for it to be true.

People had come for the service. Not many, but enough. She'd made friends here. Ones who came up and shook his hand and said kind words about her.

Now she had died here.

There was so much he should be doing, but he didn't even know where to begin. He was baking in the warm sun, but couldn't find the energy to do more than loosen his tie. The jacket was far too much effort.

He closed his eyes and just focused on his breathing. Fresh mown grass, the air thick with the dusty smell of leaves turning their fall colors, the Vermont air reeking of autumn. Most of the flowers were gone, though he'd found some late-season black-eyed Susans to set on his mother's coffin. She'd have appreciated that. She'd always like the sunny yellow blooms.

That was it. As long as he remembered to keep breathing, he could get through this. Somehow.

Constance Bruce would have liked the ceremony, so everyone told him. And how proud she'd been of her only son. God, she'd deserved so much more, but he'd only been able to give her this.

She'd deserved a husband, not a folded flag. She'd deserved a comfortable life, not desperate poverty.

And she certainly didn't deserve to die alone at forty-eight from a cancer she'd never told him about. As if he could have done anything the doctors couldn't.

Well, that was over. Now he had to pack, sell, or give away her meager belongings. He had to be done with this and get out of here before he went any crazier.

He raised his head, though he was too weary to sit up. He wiped at his eyes as he did so and saw that he was not alone.

A lone figure stood in the center of the curving one-lane road that passed in front of the old church. Just clear of the shadows of the maple trees that lined the drive. A lone figure standing hipshot, with a duffel bag over one shoulder and hair that flamed the color of the maple trees in the bright sunlight of the last day of September.

"O'Malley. What the hell are you doing here?" He couldn't sit up, instead hung there in the balance with his elbows braced on his knees.

"Where are your friends? Where are your SEAL buddies? Aren't they supposed to be standing by a comrade-in-arms?"

"I didn't tell them."

"About the funeral?" She crossed the road and came to a stop just a few steps in front of him.

"About my mother." God, Trisha O'Malley was just about the best damn thing he'd ever seen. "Never told anyone about her, except you."

"Oh." She went quiet at that, still leaning against the weight of the duffel bag. Then she brightened. "That's why I'm here. I heard what happened and figured you needed someone beside you."

"Squeezing the bullshit-o-meter there, O'Malley." Didn't know why he said it, but it was true.

She winced, then shrugged merrily. "Can't get squat by you, can I? Won't deny it, but let it stand for now." She relaxed a shoulder, dumping the duffel onto the grass, then stared up at the tall, white church behind him.

He was too tired to argue.

"It's not round."

"What? Oh, the church. That's just its name."

"It's got like sixteen sides or something. Not round. Hexadecahedron?"

"Hexadecagon unless it turned into a geodesic dome since I stepped out of it."

She squinted up at it again, but he didn't have the energy to turn around and make sure it hadn't changed: two-story white church with sixteen sides, sloped roof, and center steeple. It wasn't a church anymore, just a historical landmark. He'd rented it for the ceremony because Constance Bruce had loved it so much. And it was pretty.

"Two hundred years old last year. Maybe the year before."

"It's old."

He didn't even have the energy to nod.

She came to sit beside him on the wide stone steps.

Facing partly away from him into the westering sun, she closed her eyes and sighed.

"Man, this place is so serene it must be phony, like a stage set or something."

He listened to the world around him. Late afternoon in the tiny town of Richmond, not a whole lot was going on. A single car rattling over the steel bridge a couple hundred yards away. A tractor in some field to the west turning the last of the year's hay to dry in the sun before baling.

Birds, he hadn't noticed how many birds were chattering away. Blue ones, red ones, black ones that flew by with their yellow-and-red armbands of rank, the master sergeants of the air. They always looked so proper and serious compared to the little ones that flitted madly about like nattering privates. And cows, he heard them mooing to be milked somewhere off to the south-southwest.

"You're right. This place can't be real. How did you find me?"

"How many people named Bruce had a memorial service in this town today?"

"Okay." He didn't have any words left. The few he'd had were used up at the memorial service when he spoke of the mother they knew, not the one he knew. Carefully editing his few words for her friends.

"Is she buried?" O'Malley's voice was so soft that he barely heard it over the call of some overeager private-first-class chickadee.

He nodded.

"Can I see where?"

"Not yet." He opened his eyes and looked at her

questioning gaze. "Not because of you. For me. Can't go back there yet."

"Okay." Her nod was slow and easy. Not moving at Trisha speed, but rather more in sync with the town, or perhaps with his degree of shock.

"Come on, sailor." She stood before him, though he hadn't seen her rise. The sun had shifted the shadows around her duffel where it still rested on the grass. "Let's get you out of here."

He stood and bent down to pick up her duffel, but she grabbed it first.

"Is the car yours?" She nodded toward the white Toyota parked under the maples. The next closest vehicle was a tractor parked in the field beyond the trees.

He nodded.

"Keys." She held out her hand.

He dug them out and dropped them in her palm. "Where are we going?"

"Just climb aboard and lie back, sailor." She got behind the wheel, shifting the seat way forward.

Past the ability to do more, he collapsed into the passenger seat and shifted it way back.

—⁓—

Trisha drove past the small pizzeria in the tiny row of brick stores that was obviously the center of this nowhere little town. The town looked as idyllic as the churchyard. Probably be a sucky place to grow up, unless you were into farming or something, but otherwise it looked okay. She actually kind of liked the feel of being nowhere at the moment, but she expected that Billy needed to be elsewhere. Her stomach growled, which was a terribly impolite thing to do under the circumstances, so she ignored it.

Billy looked like he'd been shot. He just lay there with his eyes closed, dark circles under them.

Well, you took control, O'Malley. So what comes next? She had no idea. At first, she just let the road take her where it wanted. Then she saw signs for Burlington. It was the closest thing Vermont had to a city, just ten miles away. That's when she knew she had to get him out of Richmond.

Twenty minutes later, the road ended where it ran into Lake Champlain on the far side of Burlington. She turned right along the shore and passed another pizzeria. This one looked old and worn, like it had a lot of good years under its belt, like maybe it was built by the last of the French fur trappers or something and would have more good years to come. They didn't need a campus place or a tourist hangout. They needed a local's pizza pie.

She parked and then shook Billy.

"What?" He jerked upright in the seat.

"You look pretty as a picture, sleeping there, sailor. But you'll wake up a cripple if you nap in that seat much longer. C'mon. Pizza."

"No," his voice was still slurred. "Don't want food."

She punched his arm, as hard as she could sitting beside him in bucket seats. "I'm not talking food. I'm talking pizza. Now dig deep, sailor, and move your ass."

He clawed his way out of the seat and looked a little better when he got his head out into the breeze off the lake. The painful brightness, blue sky hazed soft with windblown dust even out to sea, and sweaty heat of the Gulf had been replaced by a cool fall evening and a blue

sky so rich it looked polished. The dark waters of Lake
Champlain spread before them in stark contrast to the
turquoise tropical waters of the Gulf.

It was going to get cold, especially for her Persian
Gulf–acclimatized blood. But if she took him inside,
he'd be asleep in minutes due to the restaurant's warmth.
A quick poke through their duffel bags in the trunk and
she came up with a jacket for each of them, then led
him to an outside table and a pair of steel chairs where
they could see Lake Champlain and the setting sun shining off its surface. No one else was stupid enough to sit
outside in the crisp fall air.

When the waiter showed up, she ordered a large pizza
with everything on it and a pitcher of stout. Billy looked
at her questioningly.

"Neither of us is getting called up in the next twenty-
four hours. We get to have a drink."

Together they watched a ferry come in. Lake
Champlain was ten miles across and ran forever in each
direction with Vermont on one shore and New York
on the other. This far north there was nothing in New
York except farms and towns almost too tiny to deserve
names. There wasn't that much more here in Vermont,
but someone ran a ferry back and forth anyway.

"Last run of the year," the waiter informed them. At
her look he continued, "Only runs through September.
Tomorrow is October. Until next May you have to drive
around the south or up to Grand Isle crossing. I like it.
Gets quieter."

Trisha tried to imagine this place any quieter, but
just couldn't come up with it. Compared to Boston
or Fort Campbell, where the Screaming Eagles and

SOAR were both based, most things were quieter, but this place was ridiculous.

By the time she poured Billy his second beer, he appeared to have mellowed and woken up a bit. She was barely through half of her first, but she wasn't used to drinking and could already feel it. SOAR pilots were on twenty-four hour call even when they were on vacation. And they followed a twenty-four-hour bottle-to-throttle rule, which didn't make for much opportunity to build up a tolerance for alcohol. As a Screaming Eagle, she generally knew when she'd be off shift for a while, and those parties had been serious. Though even at those, she'd rarely drunk past comfortable. SOAR fliers pretty much didn't drink because of the on-call rule. Family leave was one exception. And her current circumstances were another.

"Why here?" Trisha asked him. Again up to her to carry the conversation, because Billy sure wasn't up to it. "Was your mom from here?"

Billy set his beer down on the ironwork table and stuffed his hands in his jacket pockets, though it was still unzipped. Hers was already zipped to her chin, and she wished she had a sweater rather than a T-shirt underneath it. He gazed out at the lake. New York State was just a hazy shadow in the evening light.

"Right after they married, my folks took a drive through here. Their one and only road trip. They were always dirt-poor. No surviving relations to help out, either. She loved that old round church. Spoke of it often. Turns out there's a good chance that I was conceived in the woods not far from there. After five more years of everything getting worse, he joined the Army. I was eight when he died. They never made it back here, though he'd kept promising her."

The pizza arrived and Trisha dug in, relishing the heat that singed her fingers and scorched the roof of her mouth.

Billy took a bite and worked on it slowly. "On my eighteenth birthday, I took my signing bonus, bought her a bus ticket, and rented her an apartment just in town across the bridge from the church. Sent home most of every paycheck in the twelve years since."

"Holy crap, Lieutenant. You weren't kidding when you said you were a straight arrow."

He smiled softly at that, then offered one of those expressive shrugs of his.

"I blew my signing bonus on one last good drunk," she informed him, which had been lousy. "And a new iPod." Which had been great. "You make me feel like a total loser."

"Loser? Queen of SOAR doesn't get to call herself a loser."

He couldn't have landed that punch more solidly if he'd tried.

—⁘—

"You're white."

Trisha had gone paper white, even compared to how fair-skinned she normally was.

"You okay?" Billy leaned in to inspect her more carefully.

She had a slice of pizza clamped between her teeth, but wasn't biting it off or chewing on it.

He thumped her back sharply and she nearly tumbled

out of the chair, choking a bit as she did so. He prepared to thump her again, ready to move around for a Heimlich if necessary, when she waved him off.

"You don't need to beat on me. I'm fine. Just fine."

He eyed her uncertainly, but her color slowly came back. She slugged back the rest of her beer hard, and her color came back a bit more. He went to refill her glass, but she blocked the gesture.

"No, I'm driving. Rest of that pitcher is yours."

"You trying to get me drunk, girl?"

"Maybe so, sailor. Maybe so. Girl can always hope she'll get lucky, can't she?"

He winked at her and then took another slice.

He tried to remember the last time he'd so enjoyed just sitting with a woman, or with anyone.

No one came to mind.

Chapter 15

BILL HAD TROUBLE REMEMBERING QUITE HOW HE'D gotten here. A bed, a big one, with fresh sheets.

He looked around and spotted the woman in the bed beside him. A short mop of red hair and white skin, and the sheets pulled up so tight around her neck that it looked as if Trisha was trying to choke herself in her sleep.

It wasn't that he'd gotten drunk. He remembered the beer and the pizza clearly. That was a memory wrapped up in all kinds of good. They'd talked long past sunset about almost nothing at all. Missions, stories from their old days surviving on the street, all sorts of things.

She'd even teased him into a slice of apple pie after far too much pizza with some yarn about the definition of a true Yankee and wasn't he a true Yankee after all. His attempts to point out that he was from the Midwest were summarily dismissed as irrelevant.

"To someone outside the U.S., it's someone inside the U.S. To someone inside the U.S., it's someone from north of the Mason-Dixon Line. To someone north of that old Civil War line, it was someone from New England. In New England, it's someone from Vermont. In Vermont, it's someone from the Great Northern Kingdom, which includes us right now. And in the Great Northern Kingdom, it's someone who eats Mom's apple pie. So you gotta have a slice of pie, sailor, or you aren't a Yankee." Against such logic, he'd been unable to argue. And Trisha had made him laugh, actually laugh on the day he'd buried his mother.

That's when it slammed back in and the fuzziness of how he'd gotten here was blasted away. He'd buried his mother yesterday. And now he had to take care of cleaning up the last pieces of her life.

Trisha had offered him a few brief hours of sanity, made sure he ate, and then brought him to a good hotel that wasn't in Richmond. No one here in Burlington knew who he was, or who Constance Bruce might have been. Here he and Trisha were just anonymous people. A gift of immense value.

He'd pitched into bed. Trisha, who had turned into one giant goose bump, which he felt pretty guilty for not having anticipated, wrapped herself around him for warmth, and it was the last thing he remembered.

He slid out of the bed quietly and headed for the shower. There was going to be a ton to get done today, but thanks to Trisha, now maybe he could face it. Maybe.

Bill was getting out of the shower and just starting to dry himself off when Trisha stumbled in. Her eyes were shadowed with sleep. She practically ran into him. She wore panties and a T-shirt that sported a picture of the Milky Way galaxy and a little arrow pointing to an insignificant dot declaring, "You are here."

"Good starting place."

"Huh?"

He pointed at her T-shirt. "In case I'm ever lost, it seems like a good starting place."

"My breasts?" She looked down at her chest for a long moment.

"Well, that too. But I was talking about the T-shirt."

She looked down again. "Yeah, sure. I guess."

Clearly not a morning person and in desperate need of coffee, if she drank coffee. Funny the things he didn't know about her. In some ways he knew more about her than any woman he'd ever slept with, but in most ways he knew far less. Somehow they'd skipped all that getting-to-know-you dating crap and moved straight on to…what?

She turned on the shower and peeled down. It might be rude to watch, but he decided that the view was worth it and leaned against the door frame to enjoy himself. She might be small, but she wasn't delicate like he'd expect for a woman of her size.

Her back was to him as she adjusted the water temperature. He admired the definition of her muscles. Runner's calves, but more than that. Some of the muscle was that of a bicyclist, probably from the foot pedal controls of flying a chopper so much. Like every other soldier, she clearly pumped iron. It was the one exercise that could be done in almost any camp. There was always room for a weight set. Her waist, which he could practically encircle with two hands, built in a taper up to shoulders with exceptional definition and form.

Trisha climbed into the shower, a smooth and graceful motion that was doing really nice things to his blood flow. She slid the glass door closed behind her.

He wrapped the towel around his waist and was turning to order them some breakfast when she called out.

"I'm pissed at you."

"You are? Why?" All he'd done was slept beside her.

"You don't wake me up. You don't ravage me. What's up with that?" Her voice echoed around the bathroom partly muffled by the cascading water.

"You looked too damn comfortable," he called back loud enough to be heard. "And all cute tucked in bed like that."

She slid open the glass door a crack and peered out at him. "I'm not cute." By her tone she'd clearly taken that as a deep insult. Her hair was already plastered to her head and washed partly over one eye.

"You're about the damn cutest thing I've ever seen."

She slapped the door closed on him.

Grinning to himself, he once more turned toward the bedroom and the phone. Then he thought better of it.

Shedding the towel, he went back to the shower and slid open the door. He had one foot in when she slammed it closed. Had it been heavier, it would have hurt. Instead, it just trapped him momentarily off balance, with one foot in the shower and the rest of him balanced on one foot on the slick bathroom floor.

He hopped around until he had his balance back, then shoved sideways on the door. It resisted momentarily as she tried to find some way to brace it in place. Finally giving up, she let go and he stepped under the scorchingly hot water.

"Ow! Crap!"

"Don't touch that or I'm leaving."

He turned it down to merely scalding.

She went to slide open the door at the other end of the tub, despite still being half covered in soap, but he caught the door before it was open wide enough for her to escape.

Giving up, she turned to glare up at him as the water pounded down against his back.

"I'm not cute! I'm beautiful!" Her Irish temper was practically steaming out her ears.

"You're immensely cute."

"You're a jerk, Mr. SEAL. Bloody Scotsman!" She thumped the side of her fist hard against his chest.

"And you're not beautiful, you're gorgeous! You crazy Irishwoman."

In that moment her expression shifted from ire to disbelief.

He laughed. Bill couldn't help himself. The woman was a constant wonder to him. He pulled her into a kiss, their bodies moving slickly together. Without hesitation, her arms slid up around his neck and held on, fingers digging into his hair.

His senses were awash in her. The smooth perfection of her skin. The strength of her kiss. The heady taste of her. The life that practically exploded from her pores. Bill actually had to shift and rest one hip on the shower wall to make sure they remained steady on their feet.

Trisha pulled back and nipped at his shoulder. She paused for a moment and mumbled barely louder than the pounding water.

"I'm not cute."

God, but Trisha loved Billy's laugh. Even when he was laughing at her, it somehow included her. She remembered the laugh of all of the people who had judged her based on her size or her gender or her background or her jumping style of conversation that she was told skittered along like a flat stone on a mud puddle, or any of a hundred other excuses they'd found to belittle her.

That was one of the things Vinny had taught her and

why she'd kept running with his gang whenever she had the chance. He'd taught her how to stand up for being who she was.

And now this big galoot of a sailor was sweeping her feet out from under her just by being himself. She wasn't ready for that. Didn't want that. She wasn't going to let herself be made less of by anyone, even if they didn't intend it.

Then she laid her ear to his chest and wrapped her arms around him, letting the shower water cascade over them. So slowly, so gently for a man of his immense strength, he in turn wrapped his arms around her back and held her tight. He didn't make her feel less than she was; he made her feel more.

And that sent her nerves to skittering. So, she'd go for something that was more familiar.

She slid her hands down to his waist and pulled him tightly against her, his arousal pressing against her belly.

Well, she might not have any protection in the shower, but that didn't mean she was out of ideas. She snagged the bar of soap and, keeping him close, began lathering that nice ass of his.

His sigh, and the combined relaxing of his body and tensing of his hips, was all the answer she needed.

She soaped her chest and breasts and then slid down along him, tracing her tongue along that big scar crossing his chest. Trisha didn't know why that line so intrigued her. Perhaps that he had been so damaged and yet come out whole. It was how she often felt inside—like anything that even started to make sense was always chopped off and shredded, never allowed to come together, never allowed to heal. Like damned

Chief Warrant Maloney and her get-your-shit-together-or-get-out talk. She'd had it together. Trisha had made SOAR and...

Bury it!

Just bury it!

And, with a hard blink, she did. She cast it aside and instead focused on that impossible contradiction of males, that something so hard could be so soft and so sensitive. Rubbing him between her breasts until he moaned aloud was the perfect anodyne for the mess she was inside. This was simple, clear, controllable.

"So, what's with this?" She traced a line of soap down the scar. "Zulu warrior? Crazed Burmese drug lord? An angry Smurf?"

She soaped herself some more and used herself like a human washcloth, rubbing herself over him until he had to brace himself against one of the walls to remain upright.

"The last is actually the closest." His voice hitched with the effort to speak.

"Tell me."

"Later."

"Now, or I stop." She wrapped a leg around him and began rubbing that up and down.

"If you don't stop, I'm not sure I can keep speaking."

"If I stop, I don't restart. Figure it out, sailor."

His eyes rolled in frustration. God, he was so much fun to torture.

"Angry husband."

At that she did stop. Stopped and stared at him. He hadn't seemed like the type to sleep with someone else's wife. Her expression must have been clear on her face.

"I was only nineteen, but I wasn't stupid. She didn't tell me he was a trucker, out of town."

"No ring? No male crap scattered around the house?"

"Neither. Makeup on her ring finger, so not even a shadow. Didn't know it at the time, but we were in her guest bedroom. All his stuff was in the master bed and bath. He surprised us and came at me with a machete." He traced the stroke down.

"Damn! What did you do?"

"Disarmed the son of a bitch. Broke both his wrists and a knee to do so. Actually, it was the wife he ended up pissed at. He was going for her throat with that big blade when I stopped him. Then his wife came at me like it was all my fault." He traced a tiny scar on his left arm. "Point of a nail file. Tied her up with a bedsheet and called 911."

"With a bedsheet, huh?"

"Yeah."

"And?" His grim look had a smile hiding in it somewhere.

"I, uh, tied her to the bedpost with her hands behind her back. Once I told the cops what was going on and the ambulance crew was working on the husband and me, they just kind of left her tied there a good while. Stark naked. She wasn't real pleased about that or her injured husband screaming for a lawyer so he could divorce her sorry ass as soon as he could sign a paper again."

Trisha ran her hand down the scar once more. It didn't change how it felt. A slice like that and he hadn't killed the man. As always, Billy did right by everyone he met.

"Tell me about this one?" She traced the bullet hole so near his heart.

"That one was a Smurf."

She took a soapy hand and massaged him right between the legs.

"Okay. Okay." His groan was deep and shook him. "It was a crazed Burmese drug lord, except he was Argentine and dealing in Russian arms."

Trisha led him across the road map of his body, scar by scar, wound to wound, teasing and taunting him until he shook with need.

There was a thrill to having such a strong man so wholly under her control. One of the nation's best trained warriors was almost whimpering at what she could do to him.

She kissed Billy as he came in a rocket-hot jet against her palm, with a massive groan of release and joy that lodged in places far deeper than any scar.

When Trisha tried to slide free in the shower, Bill wrapped an arm about her, keeping her in place.

All he could think… He couldn't think. All he could do… He thought of several things he could do. He tipped his head back into the water that continued to sheet over them to clear his brain.

As soon as he was steady enough to do so, he pushed her back half a step and looked down into those sparkling blue eyes made even more so by all of the water drops caught on her darkened lashes.

Ever so slowly, he turned her around, until her back was facing him. She glared at him, but finally submitted. Then he lifted her hands and placed them against the shower wall. Again the resistance until he leaned in and whispered into her ear, "Trust me."

"Like I'm going to do that." But she did turn to the wall, bracing her hands high.

"Close your eyes."

She gave an exasperated groan, but he hoped she did so.

Then he poured a squirt of shampoo on her bright red hair and began working it in.

Her startled gasp was all he needed. She'd clearly expected something else. He liked surprising her, keeping her guessing. As he worked his strong fingers into her scalp, she began relaxing until she truly did need those hands on the shower wall to hold herself up.

Taking up the soap, he began massaging her neck and shoulders. He dug into muscles until they gave way and she moaned as they loosened. He worked down her incredible body, learning each curve, investigating and memorizing every shape.

When he reached her feet, he turned her around and began working his way back up her glorious form.

She simply lay back against the wall and dug her fingers into his own hair, not to massage, but merely to hold on as he continued his investigation with soap and touch, with tongue and teeth.

By the time he'd worked his way back up to kiss her on the mouth, she was frenzied for release and finally let go rubbing against him. Now he knew each of her muscles as well as he knew any weapon he'd ever carried. Perhaps better, for he knew he'd never forget a single curve of Trisha's incredible body. He could feel every shift and change ripple through her slender frame as she heated past reason. Bill could feel the pulse of each wave as it traveled

from one muscle to the next up her body to where
their lips met.

He had kept his eyes open to watch the wonder of it
shimmer up her length.

What he hadn't been ready for was seeing the tears
that flowed from under her closed eyes.

Chapter 16

IT HAD BEEN A LONG COUPLE OF DAYS.

The meetings had been endless, and if not for Trisha's infinite aplomb and good manners, Bill would have probably made enemies of everyone in the town of Richmond, Vermont—and been a wreck besides. Instead, Trisha had taken the lead, applying breeding—that still didn't fit with her stories and the charm that flowed from her naturally, in sharp contrast to her normal irascible self—with everyone they had to deal with.

Most of Constance's belongings had gone to the thrift store that also hosted the local food bank, so they took her kitchen supplies too. One box of shared memories remained to be sealed and sent off to his storage locker at Little Creek Naval in Virginia. There was so little in it that it was almost impossible to believe. He'd moved them both here from Chicago in two suitcases and then he'd gone to the Navy, sleeping on the couch of her one-bedroom whenever he got leave.

But after a decade, it shouldn't be so little. Some photos, a deck of cards, and the backgammon board they used to play on. A small framed picture of her and his father at their wedding and a month later standing in front of the Round Church, not yet knowing they had just conceived a child. Totally unaware of the hardships to come. A folded flag, which showed the worn spots of the desperate clutch of a woman who had lost her

one true love twenty years before. A woman with few
enough skills for being in the world on her own, saddled
with a very angry eight-year-old boy.

He barely recalled Trisha finally removing the box from
his lap, sealing it, and taking it away to the post office.

They paid off the coroner, canceled the apartment rental,
and paid someone else to come in and clean the place after
they were gone. The to-do list had seemed endless.

In the apartment, he'd uncovered her will. Simplest
damn document, almost made him cry because it was
just like her. Even with the lawyerese, it had only covered two pages. At its core it simply said, "To my son."
The attorney that Trisha scared up assured Bill that he'd
take care of filing it, not that there was anything much
left to matter.

Constance Bruce must have harbored every paycheck
Bill had sent her as if it were gold. Not only was there
a very tidy sum in their joint bank account, joint so that
he could deposit his pay there, but she'd taken out a life
insurance policy in his name years before. And, as far as
he could tell, she'd spent almost nothing else. The VA
had covered most of her medical. She'd been content to
join the local church and work at the grocery. Her big
evenings out were apparently going to the Grange on
Family Night to help out.

He sat on the couch now, in an apartment empty
of everything that might have been hers. It had been
a cheery place with bright yellow walls and some
local farmers' market watercolors and weavings that
had made it quite pleasant. With nothing remaining
on them, the walls were now overbright, especially
where the missing art had shadowed the paint from the

years of sunlight fading the rest of the wall. His mother wasn't here anymore.

He'd have slept right here the last two nights if O'Malley hadn't kept dragging him back to Burlington or wherever. She'd made sure he ate room service before she tucked him in. Bless her. They hadn't even had sex, at least not that he remembered. He rather assumed he'd remember sex with Patricia O'Malley, no matter what state he was in. Not the kind of thing any man was likely to forget.

There appeared to be no man around to remember his mother, and few enough others. She'd left such a small impression upon the world.

"I knew Mom was a simple woman with simple needs," he told Trisha who sat opposite him in the lone armchair. "Just never quite realized how true that was."

"Everyone we spoke to liked her a lot."

He nodded. He'd heard that too. It was about all that had sustained him beyond Trisha's endless reservoir of ability to deal with things. If he had to do one more thing on the list, though, he'd scream.

"C'mon, sailor."

"Where to now?" Maybe he'd scream now and save the trouble later.

Trisha came up and pulled on his arm, finally dragging him to his feet before he could go fetal right there on the couch. "You aren't fit for service, so we're going to see what we can do about that."

"How?"

"Just shut up."

He let himself be led out. It was a relief when she placed the apartment keys on the kitchen counter and pulled the door closed, locking it behind them. So, done with that. Trisha practically manhandled him into the car. Womanhandled. Done with some skill and some force.

Right. He reminded himself of what Michael Gibson had warned him. *Don't mess with Patricia O'Malley.* He was starting to realize that hadn't just been some overprotective idle warning. If nothing else, the woman was tenacious as hell.

Trisha hoped this place was as good as the clerk at the post office had said. She knew what Billy needed; now she just had to find it.

After heading through the two blocks of downtown, they drove across the steel bridge. At the Old Round Church she took a right. In a hundred yards at most they were among farms, with actual cows, plowed fields, and a farmer on a tractor who actually waved as she drove by.

"What happened?" Trisha stared back at the farmer in her mirror. "Did we fall off the edge of the Earth here or something?"

"No. Vermont is just like this. Haven't you ever lived in small towns?"

"The only time I touch nature is on training exercises, and even then I'm usually flying over it." Again that sharp pinch, again she shoved it aside. No matter what CW3 Lola Maloney thought, CW2 Trisha O'Malley was going to be flying. It was the best thing she'd ever done, kicking ass across the sky.

They wound along a two-lane blacktop past streets with names that had "Pine" and "Hill" and "Crest" in them. Streets! Dirt tracks she'd want a Humvee for, rather than a Toyota rent-a-car.

Three miles out and she was on the edge of despair and ready to turn back when the road hit a T. Well, not really, but she was getting desperate and the post office boy had said it was like that.

"It's kind of a T but isn't one," he'd told her, a cute kid who kept trying to not stare at her chest. He mostly succeeded. It wasn't all that much to stare at, though Billy appeared to like it. "You'll be facing a big field, I think the Jansens have beets going in." As if she'd have any idea what that might look like. "Dugway Road cuts back to your left."

There was indeed a road cutting back to her left, paved, thank God, though the sign was covered by yet some other tree, this one with white bark and leaves gone all golden. Kinda pretty, actually. Dugway was an even smaller two-lane that rapidly dwindled to such a tiny width that the trees met overhead, blocking the afternoon sun.

She spotted the river and knew they were most of the way there, despite their entry into the forest primeval.

Sure enough, right when she thought she was going to be lost forever—come spring, they'd find her and Billy the SEAL's corpses in a white rental car buried under great mounds of picturesque red-and-gold leaves gone brown with winter—the road widened to include a shoulder parking area just as the kid said it would. And not another car in the whole strip. They'd be alone. Excellent.

"We're here!"

"Where?"

"Stop whining, Billy, and get out of the car. This should be good."

Fingers crossed, she led him down the footpath at the farthest end of the pull-off strip. A sign warned against swimming in the upper falls on pain of death and then listed more than a dozen names of people who had achieved that glory.

"Those fallen in the name of being stupid."

Trisha didn't get him to laugh, but she did get a grunt of agreement.

They descended a steep little path fifty feet through the trees, and then she knew it was perfect. The sound of rushing water blocked out all else. Even a sparrow singing on a bush not far away could barely make her song heard.

A tiered waterfall almost thirty feet high poured over layers of worn rocks. From here they could see most of the cascading waterfall.

"The water is low this time of year." The Huntington River was only twenty feet wide in the autumn and swift but not deep. "My undercover informant said it would still be pretty."

"It's great, O'Malley." Billy just stood there, his face up toward the cool mist rolling off the fall.

A broad pool spread before them at the base of the lowest fall, clearly the swimming hole the kid had mentioned. There was room for a dozen or more people to splash about comfortably, the last little tier of the falls feeding one end, and a stream draining the other. She considered suggesting that Billy take a go in there, but the water looked cold.

What the hell. She sidled up behind him and gave him a quick shove.

As he fell, he spun and grabbed her. His reflexes were so fast that he succeeded in catching hold and they both plunged in.

She was wrong. It wasn't cold. It was freezing. She surfaced sputtering and surged for shore.

His arm snaked about her waist and pulled her farther into the pool.

She got a mouthful of water and spit a stream at his face.

He planted a hand atop her head and shoved her under.

The water was about four feet deep at this part of the pool. She let herself be driven down until she could grab his ankles. Then she tucked into a squat and drove herself back to the surface with all of the strength of her powerful legs. With the help of the water partly floating his body, she managed to flip him into deeper water.

A fast crawl almost got her to shore again, but trying to outswim a SEAL had clearly been a waste of effort. Billy clamped a hand around her ankle. Rather than kicking against it, she used it as leverage to double over and grab his wrist with both hands. Then using a nerve pinch to free her leg, she did a flip she'd seen on the wrestling channel and scissored her legs around his throat, locking her ankles behind his neck.

He got a hand on her face and shoved her under.

Trisha considered biting his hand, but thought better of it and nibbled on his thumb instead.

He let her pop up to the surface, and when she did, he was laughing.

She was still hanging with her legs about his neck like an overlong scarf, her back floating in the water.

She squeezed his throat a bit with her knee, just enough to choke off his laughter.

Casually as could be, he reached up and dug a finger into the mid-thigh nerve junction. Not hard, just enough to make her want to let go really badly to avoid a severe charley horse. He gave her legs a push over his head after she eased up and she did a backflip into the water, landing with her feet on the bottom facing him.

"What were you laughing about?"

"Michael was right. Messing with you could be dangerous."

"You bet, sailor." She splashed a palm's worth of water in his general direction just as he was trying to inhale, leaving him sputtering and wiping his eyes.

"You look like you're freezing."

"I'm not a big hunk of meat like you." The water that practically reached her shoulders barely washed around the middle of his chest. His T-shirt clung to every curve of muscle. "God, Lieutenant. You're gorgeous."

"And you're damned cute, Irish."

She cocked an arm back to fire another load of water in his face, but he was too quick and grabbed her. She didn't even put up a struggle as he dragged her against him and kissed her hard. Trisha wrapped her legs about his waist so that she couldn't float away.

Billy walked them to shore without breaking the kiss or showing any sign that he was carrying an extra person.

Then he lowered her to the water-smooth, sun-warmed rock and had his way with her. His need so desperate that his emotions battered at her. His hands, his big powerful hands, dug and kneaded and grasped and held. When at last he drove into her, he roared like a wounded beast. The sound echoed along the rocky walls and deep inside her.

Chapter 17

WHEN THEY WOKE IN EACH OTHER'S ARMS, THE AFTER-noon had cooled around them. They were gentle with each other. Kind. Bill pulled on his cold, wet pants with only a minor shiver of disgust and returned with fresh clothes from their duffels in the car. They rode in comfortable silence, hadn't spoken since they had woken.

Trisha once again took care of him, getting him in the passenger seat. He felt better, but worse. He felt… *Yeah, another lousy start to another lousy sentence he'd never know how to finish.*

At the edge of Richmond, just crossing the bridge, she broke the silence.

"Where is she?"

Crap! No question who Trisha was asking about. "Tenacious" was an understatement for this woman. Well, he knew by now that arguing was pointless. He waved east along Main Street and collapsed back into the passenger seat as she drove. No need for further directions—the cemetery was only a quarter mile or so out of town.

Three days earlier he'd been there. They'd held the memorial at the Congregational Church in town, placed the urn of her ashes into the ground here at Riverview Cemetery, then held the reception at the Round Church. The woman pastor at the Congregational had been great, and with the assistance of some of the church ladies, she'd taken care of most everything. He'd given them a big donation, not because of how well they'd treated his mother over the years, or that it was expected or perhaps even appropriate. He did it because if it motivated them to help even one more soul as lost as he was, it would be money well spent.

He pointed out where to turn, where to park. An unmarked grave. He'd ordered the gravestone but couldn't remember when it would be installed. After he was back on deployment probably. Didn't matter. There wouldn't be anyone to care or visit the grave or bring flowers. Crap, he hadn't even brought flowers.

Trisha parked under yet more maple trees gone the colors of the season. Reds, golds, and yellows spangled the hills in every direction. The leaves had finally started falling, losing little of their color as they landed on the grass and clumped. Some, caught in the gentle breezes, scurried across the ground like the squirrels collecting their winter's nuts. O'Malley dug into the backseat and fished out a piece of paper that she slipped into her back pocket. She took his hand, which gave him the strength to lead her between the gravestones toward his mother's final resting place.

It was a good spot, as far as cemeteries went. He'd thought of burying her in Arlington so that she could be beside her husband, but it didn't feel right. Here she had a view of the river winding through the Vermont hills and trees. He didn't know if she'd been particularly happy here, but he knew that she hadn't been sad. And she'd been at peace. For the twelve years since he'd brought her here, she'd known peace.

He almost walked past her grave, then had to blink to

make sure it was there. Sod now covered the raw earth
and looked almost natural. The small gravestone was in
place, already. "Constance Bruce, beloved of husband
and son," and then a span of far too few years.

"I asked the engraver to kind of hustle because you
were needed back overseas."

Yet another thing she'd taken care of. Trisha went
to pull her hand away, but he clamped down on it hard.
This was one place he certainly didn't want to be left
alone with his thoughts.

"Ow! Ease up, Billy. That hurts."

He let go, but she didn't leave his side. Instead she
dug into her back pocket.

"She liked wildflowers, right?"

"Yeah. Why?"

She handed him a small paper packet labeled
"Wildflower Variety Pack" that had a picture of dozens
of cheery flowers, including black-eyed Susans.

"I figured if you scattered them around the grave, I
mean I know it's the wrong season for planting and all,
but if you scattered them, some might make it. I don't
know how soon you'll be back here and I'll bet you
don't, either. Now you won't have to feel bad about it.
You know, if you can't come."

He looked at the little packet of seeds for the longest
time, trying to understand the gift that had somehow
come to him in this pint-sized redhead.

"What do I do?"

She knelt down, pulling him to kneel beside her.
Together they scraped finger-deep furrows for several
inches all around the stone.

He tore open the packet and sprinkled the tiny seeds

into each one until they were all gone. Then Trisha smoothed the soil back over them and patted it into place. She took the packet from his numb fingers, folded it in half, then dug his wallet out of his pocket and slipped the packet into one of the deep corners.

Bill wrapped an arm about her and, still kneeling, looked down at what they'd done.

"I wish she could have met you."

Then he did something he hadn't done since an eight-year-old boy lost his father. He folded his arms around Trisha O'Malley and wept.

Chapter 18

"COULDN'T YOU HAVE FLOWN TO BURLINGTON OR Montreal or something and rented your car there? Why did you have to fly into Boston?"

"C'mon, O'Malley. What are you griping about? It's the USS *Constitution*." Billy waved at the masts and ropes and hull like it was something too incredible for words. "I've always wanted to see her. What's your problem?"

"Don't like Boston. And never was much of a history buff." Though Trisha had to admit to herself that "Old Ironsides" was a pretty amazing ship. The thing that was really incredible was that George Washington had commissioned her and mostly likely walked her decks while president, and she was still in incredible shape. The black-and-white-painted hull was immaculate. Even the curlicue numbers climbing up her sides to show the keel depth were shining white.

Trisha had wandered all over it as a kid, though she'd be the last to admit that to Billy. Street kids didn't care about such things or waste money on touring a big, old ship. Coming to the ship was one of the few tolerable family outings they'd ever had, perhaps the only one she ever looked forward to.

She and Billy climbed the gangplank together. The deck was burnished within an inch of its life. Fresh-painted cannon lined either gunwale, each with its rope harness in perfect shape. All image-perfect right down to a small pile of cannonballs and a tamping stick. Such a show for the tourists.

"O'Malley, even an Army grunt like you has to appreciate this boat. She's the third vessel ever specifically built for the U.S. Navy. She defeated four different British ships of the line during the War of 1812. No one had ever done that. It was a massive blow to the ego of the British Navy, who ruled the world at that time. For the first time in their navy's history, they were vulnerable, and this ship is the one who proved that to the world. It was the beginning of the end of the British Empire, which claimed a full third of the world's land-mass at its peak."

He led her back among the moseying tourists and covered hatchways to the big, spoked double-wheel of the ship. The wheels were as tall as she was and would allow four men to simultaneously steer the ship if a storm or combat maneuvering required it.

Billy placed his hands on the wheel for a moment, and she could see him belonging there. One of the great white masts, bigger around than he was, soared toward the blue sky. Twenty different hanks of big hemp rope, prickly on the hands, dangled from the pin rail and led up to adjust the dozens of sails the crew could place aloft on that one mast alone.

The air would be so thick with gunpowder smoke that he wouldn't be able to see a ship that was close alongside and would have to rely on shouts from the lone sailor in the crow's nest high above. The shattering roar of fusillades of the *Constitution*'s monstrous thirty-two pounders, ginormous for the time. The enemy's twenty-fours

bouncing off the two-foot-thick oaken sides of Old
Ironsides. And Captain Billy ordering men aloft to swing
down on boarding ropes to attack the British cads.

She pulled his face down to kiss him because he was
just too damned handsome. He actually made her toes
curl inside her sneakers. Who knew such a thing was
possible? Then she let him go back to his dreams of
steering a ship almost as old as their country.

Bill stared forward in wonder. This was the original ship
of the line. In many ways she and her deeds were the
start of the United States Navy.

"Do you know they had more crew on this little four-
deck boat than we have on the *Peleliu* right now?"

Trisha looked up at the rigging high above them.
"Wouldn't want to try landing a helicopter here."

God, she made him laugh.

Without really thinking about it, he saluted a woman
in period garb with the rank of lieutenant commander
on her collar. The salute came right back with a trained
snap. Billy straightened up in shock.

"Sorry, sir. I thought it was a costume." She was a
tall black woman. She wore a long black coat with tails,
doubled brass buttons down the front, and gold piping.
White pants, buffed boots, and one of those cocked bi-
corne hats that stuck out fore and aft.

"At ease, sailor. We get that all the time. LC Deborah
Reynolds at your service." Her voice was rich with Alabama.

"Lieutenant William Bruce of SEAL Team Nine
at yours. And this interloper is Lieutenant Patricia
O'Malley of the Army's 160th SOAR."

Trisha snapped a sharp salute and then grimaced at him. "Trisha. And this one is called Billy the SEAL by those who know him and Mud by everyone else. What is a real officer doing here?"

"Welcome aboard. Well, Trisha of the Army…" She had a good smile to go with her pleasant attitude. "This ship is still on the active-duty roster, and as long as she is, she'll have a professional crew to see that she's in top form. That's how we do it here in the Navy anyway."

Bill loved the way they were teasing each other.

"When our stuff gets old, we throw it out."

Bill spotted the light of combat growing in O'Malley's eyes and interrupted the next round. "Please forgive her, Commander, she's in heli-aviation. They barely go back to World War II and have no sense of history. They're all absolute heathens with no sense of tradition or propriety."

The two women laughed together and shook hands, the tiny redhead in a tight T-shirt from a Styx concert and an elegant officer in clothes and on a ship two hundred years behind the times.

The Lieutenant Commander offered another salute and Bill returned it smartly.

"Just let me know if there's anything you want to see that's roped off. We'll be glad to take a SEAL anywhere they want to go, whether or not their name is Mud. Can even bring along this Army brat if you feel so inclined."

She turned to leave, then paused and looked back at them.

"Patricia O'Malley?"

"Trisha."

"You're the spitting image of Shawna O'Malley. Are you her daughter?"

Bill didn't miss how impossibly still Trisha became, though the Lieutenant Commander appeared not to catch it.

"Yes." The word was bitten off hard.

"Oh splendid." Deborah rolled right on, missing the warning signs that Bill didn't know how to interpret. "We were so sorry that you couldn't be here for the ceremony. It's a pleasure to meet you at last. You're just the spitting image of her."

There was an awkward silence that Bill quickly filled with, "Ceremony?"

LC Reynolds had now caught the note that something was off. Bill hadn't filled in fast enough, and his own voice had been rough with surprise.

"Yes." She glanced at Trisha and then, picking a safer target, answered Bill instead. "The O'Malley family just sponsored a major fundraiser for improvements to the Museum." She indicated the big, two-story stone building at the head of the pier. "Shawna O'Malley joined the Board of Trustees of the Museum as well. We're, ah, very honored to have you both aboard." Again they saluted, and like a wise commander, the LC retired rapidly from the field of pending battle.

Bill turned very slowly to face Trisha.

She appeared to be studying the deck.

"Shawna O'Malley."

"Yeah."

"Board of Trustees."

She shrugged but didn't look up.

He reached out and took her chin to make her look at him.

She slapped his hand aside but did glare up at him. "So?"

So? Well, that explained her upper-crust accent, but it sure didn't explain anything else. All her talk about "the street" and her pals in Southie.

"Is any of it true?"

"How can you ask that?"

"How can I—" He started as a roar, but managed to pull it back under control when several tourists edged abruptly away in alarm. He grabbed her arm and dragged her down the ship to the stern. She struggled against him, but he didn't care. She should just be damn glad he didn't toss her overboard. He stepped over the sign that said something about "No Tourists" and hauled her right along with him. At the aft rail he let her go, shoving her a couple steps away.

She reached for him, but he raised his palms to fend her off. She dropped her arms to her sides and hung her head once more.

"Is. Any. Of. It. True?" He had to grind through it word by word to get it out.

"I never told a lie."

"You never—" "Not a li—" What the hell was he supposed to do with that? He crashed a fist down on the polished taffrail so that he didn't hit anything else, like himself for being stupid enough to buy her whole act.

"I didn't tell the whole truth, but I never told you a lie, Billy." Now she was looking up at him and pleading.

"Like growing up living on the street?"

"I never said that." When he went to protest, she held up a hand to stop him. "Your childhood sucked. I have no idea how bad. Mine wasn't any joyride. Living with my parents was a kind of extreme hell that you'd never believe because it is just too damn foreign to your experiences.

"Your mother loved you. Mine?" She flapped a hand clearly unable to find the words. "My father checked out and my mother saw me as a carbon copy of herself who would never be good enough. I ran on the street for years because I had friends there. My friends. Real friends."

A fire came back into her eyes, and she crowded him back against one of the cannons until he was trapped in the corner between the barrel and the rail.

"They were friends *I* made, that *I* earned." She thumped bunched fingers against the center of her chest hard enough for him to wince in empathy. "Not ones bought and paid for by my family's status or money. I could have officered in. I could have stayed out and married Mister Easy-and-rich. God knows my sainted mother wanted to sell me off at the first chance. 'Go to Smith, dear. That will help you find the right sort of man.' Shit! I earned every penny to take myself to NYU. I enlisted, and I fought for every goddamn thing I ever got. It didn't come from Mommy or Daddy, and it didn't come from you."

He watched her cheeks flaming as hot as her hair. Her finger stabbing toward his chest. He cocked one eyebrow at the finger and she lowered it.

"Uh, sorry about that last comment. You didn't deserve that. You've been one of the best things to happen to me in a long time. I was just kind of on a roll. Sorry." She turned to face the Charles River, rested her folded hands on the taffrail, and rested her forehead on those.

He let his breath out slowly. This would take some

thinking to readjust. O'Malley with the high-and-mighty Boston breeding, which finally fit her accent and the smooth efficiency with all things bureaucratic she'd shown in Vermont. Who'd also fought on the streets of Southie, which fit her fighting skills and general battering of the English language.

He wondered if Michael knew this about his friend, but Bill would guess that he didn't. That no one did, just as he'd never told anyone of the sad, quiet woman who was his mother. All Trisha ever showed anyone was the cocky outer bravado. That slap-you-in-your-face power she carried, all of that energy and heart and hurt.

But she'd showed him more. He'd seen the woman who'd been shot for the first time. She'd helped him bury his mother more assuredly than the ladies of the Congregational Church. And he'd seen her when they made love. Trisha O'Malley couldn't fake any of that. All those myriad facets of this woman came straight out of her with no games. At long last, all of the pieces of her fit together. Now she made sense to him.

The one thing they could never teach a SEAL team was the absolute trust learned in your first battle together. Not even BUD/S or Hell Week did that. Lieutenant Patricia O'Malley had stood right beside him through his own personal battle. He couldn't help but trust her because he knew all the way to his core that he could.

The problem, he decided, was that she couldn't trust herself.

Well, he straightened up, that was a battle he knew how to fight.

"Where are your parents?"

"Milton," was the mumbled response. She waved

Chapter 19

"THIS IS SO STUPID!"

"We're here now." Billy sounded so damn calm that Trisha could hit him.

"I don't want to be here now."

"But you should be."

This time she did hit him.

He didn't even have the decency to blink when her fist bounced off his arm.

"But why?"

"Because I'm smarter than you, at least at the moment."

She'd give him "smart" right between the eyes. He'd stopped at the head of the O'Malley estate driveway to give her a moment, though she'd had an hour of rush-hour traffic to bitch about it on the way from the *Constitution*.

"Maybe they're not home. You said they have a place in Boston too, right?"

"They're home. The condo is only for when they're in the city late for the symphony or something. I used it way more than they did." This was like a death sentence.

The long stone wall had been erected by the first O'Malley who homesteaded here back in the 1700s. What had started as a cow fence was now a privacy bastion eight feet high, covered in ivy and overshadowed by tall trees. The iron gate that now stood open had showed up in the early 1800s, along with the massive Tudor-style house that had grown through the 1900s with additions here and a guest cottage there. It was now one of those places that lead the list on annual home and garden tours.

Trisha could see her dad's Jaguar pulled into the old carriage house. Definitely home.

"Do we have to?"

"They're your parents. Flight back isn't until day after tomorrow."

"We could just go to an airport motel and have sex for two days?" Trisha didn't bother to listen for a reply. She'd gotten nowhere with that offer several times on the drive out.

She glared up at the big house almost lost among the towering oaks and white pines that masked much of it from the road. Lights were on in the living room, kitchen, and study. Dad, senior partner of a major law firm, would be in his home office, Mom harassing the kitchen help, and the living room lit so they could pretend they were together there.

"If you tell me what nice people they are, I'm going to have to kill you." It had been a disease of her youth. She'd tell stories about how horrid her parents were, then she'd bring home a friend and her parents would flip into host and hostess mode and charm them no end. She'd stopped bringing friends home before she was out of junior high.

"Why? Are they that nasty?" Billy was eyeing her curiously. He'd just buried his mother, who sounded great, and Trisha wished she'd met the woman. Hers was alive and well, and Trisha didn't want to see her for a single, solitary second. She still wasn't sure quite how this was happening. It was as if Billy had slipped her a Mickey Finn and she'd woken up in Hell, with the capital *H*.

"Nasty? Oh no." Trisha held up her hands to fend off the possibility that anything she said could be taken wrong. "Not ever. They would never give offense. Especially never to a house guest, nor to their only daughter who"—she folded her hands neatly in her lap and fluttered her eyelids as if fighting off tears—"had so much potential, but…" Then she released a tiny sigh with a little shrug of her shoulders.

Billy laughed.

It was only years of training in restraint that kept her from cleaning his clock.

He put the car back in gear, drove up the circular gravel drive, and parked in front of the double front door with stained-glass upper panels installed in God-only-knew which century.

"You really came from this?"

"Trust me, the street is way more real than this place. Everything here is a sham."

Billy came around to open her door, like the place was already infecting him. She ignored that, swung herself out before he could get there, almost whacking him with the car door, and stormed up to the front entry. She threw it open and stepped into the main hall.

"Hi, Mom, Dad. I'm home."

Her shout elicited an oath from the man just exiting his office to see who had driven up, and a loud crash resounded from the kitchen.

She whispered to Billy who stood close behind her, "Sounds like Mom will have to buy a new serving platter."

—~~—

"Can't we just leave?"

Bill looked down at her sprawled across a twin bed with carved head and foot boards nicer than any he'd seen, even in a hotel. He still couldn't believe it, even if he was seeing it.

Trisha's third-floor childhood bedroom had clearly remained untouched, like a museum or something. And it was as big as his mother's one-bedroom apartment; it even included its own bathroom. Wood paneling that must go back a hundred years was covered with decade-old rock-and-roll posters held up with rammed-in pushpins.

A third-degree tae kwon do black belt and a red kung fu belt with a black band were draped over a brocaded wingback armchair. Several weapons hung from the walls, including a fighting staff, a well-worn set of *tonfa* blocks, and a very battered Japanese *bokken*, the wooden practice sword.

No wonder Michael wasn't worried about O'Malley's ability to protect herself. Martial arts competition awards were piled haphazardly across many surfaces. Only the dresser was clear. The old, oaken six-drawer had a sheet of glass on top. Carefully preserved beneath the glass were O'Malley's first pilot's license, her Army induction form as an E-1—she hadn't even taken advantage of starting three pay grades higher because of a college education—and her chief warrant's commission actually signed by the President. She had worked her way up the hard way before going officer.

"We serve at the pleasure of..." he whispered half

to himself. He had a similar letter as an officer of the SEALs.

At the very center was a letter signed by Major Emily Beale, inviting her to apply for the 160th SOAR. Damn! He'd heard about Beale; everyone had. The first woman of SOAR was a bloody legend in the Special Operations Forces. She had saved the President's life, stopped a war, and who knew what else. And she had invited Trisha into the reclusive and elite 160th.

No matter what else was going with Trisha O'Malley, Bill knew one thing for certain—she'd earned it the hard way.

"O'Malley." He turned to face her where she still sprawled on the chenille bedspread like a pouty teenager.

"What?"

"You did all this shit." He waved a hand to indicate the room's contents. "And you're scared of those two people downstairs? What the hell is up with that?"

She opened her mouth to protest. It hung there a long time. Finally she closed it with a snap and flopped over on her back to stare at the ceiling.

He waited her out.

"That isn't fair," she finally stated, then tipped her head back to look at him upside down.

"What isn't?"

"A Scotsman being right about things. That's just not supposed to happen."

"Why not?"

She stuck her tongue out at him and he felt much better. She'd stood for him through three days of hell; now he could give some back.

—∼—

Trisha really did try. Bill could see her doing it. And her
parents were desperately struggling to be pleasant about
being in the same room with their daughter. But it was
as if they were waiting for a bomb to go off but were
too polite to say so and too afraid to run in case even
that set it off.

Bill allowed himself to be a welcome distraction
for all of them at first, answering questions over some
of the best roast beef and winter vegetables he'd ever
had. He recounted how he'd come to join the Navy and
the SEALs and, no, his team wasn't part of the raid on
Osama bin Laden's compound. That was now the number one question of anyone to whom he admitted he was
a SEAL. He mentioned nothing of his upbringing, other
than his father dying in the Army when he was a boy and
his mother having just passed from cancer.

By halfway through the dinner, conversation was lag-
ging, and he couldn't recall the last time he'd talked so
much. Trisha had settled some, but her parents hadn't.

Dylan O'Malley was a lawyer and clearly a power
broker of some sort. Bill had worked with JAG a couple
of times, and the Judge Advocate General's office had
nothing in common with Trisha's father. He had quickly
qualified, then classified Bill as poor background, limited connections, and therefore of little interest.

Trisha's father had then gone on to inform Bill that
he'd been an NCAA Division I swimmer in college a
couple decades ago and boast about his half-Olympic-
sized pool out back, and how he'd still go and turn laps
in it every morning before work.

Trisha's one volley about Lieutenant Bruce being a professional U.S. Navy swimmer hadn't even dented Dylan's tales of his final swimming matches. He'd have gladly spent the rest of the evening talking about himself if Shawna O'Malley hadn't been the perfect hostess she was.

They were an interesting counterpoint as a couple. Dylan, at five-ten and weighing around two-ten, showed the evidence of too many power lunches, despite his daily swimming. He showed his fifty-odd years pretty clearly.

Shawna could have been Trisha's older sister who was clearly trying to look like her younger one. It was obvious where Trisha had gotten her size, coloring, and stunning good looks. Her mother's hair was the same rich red, but flowed to her shoulders over the tasteful dark-blue jacket she'd selected for dinner. She wore a dark green stone hanging at her throat from a gold chain that was so elegant, Bill would have to get one for Trisha someday.

He blinked hard at that thought, wondering where the heck it had come from. She'd probably lose it anyway, even if he could afford it.

Trisha, on the other hand, had pulled on a tattered pair of jeans she'd unearthed from the large closet and a T-shirt in black with a painfully bright, orange lightning bolt that said, "Let's Spark It Up." Maybe some band he'd never heard of, maybe something sexual, but either way, carefully selected to tick off her parents. He'd considered requiring her to change but was afraid that whatever else she unearthed might be even worse.

He'd brought nothing formal except the one suit for his mother's funeral, and that didn't seem appropriate.

He wore the white dress shirt open at the collar, but not far enough to show the continuation of his scar, and a pair of clean jeans.

No matter how Bill tried to deflect Shawna O'Malley, she couldn't help picking at her daughter as if she were twelve. It was clearly a knee-jerk reaction to who Shawna thought her daughter still was.

"You know, dear..." Almost every sentence was phrased that way.

"Sit up, dear." Trisha normally had amazing posture, like a dancer's augmented with military fitness and training, something he'd always enjoyed watching. Clearly she was slouching to piss off her mom. Trisha shrugged at a scowl from Bill, but did sit up straighter after that.

"You remember Zachary Stein, don't you, dear? Well, he just went through this horrible divorce and..."

"I don't want to marry Zachary Stein, Mom. He was a jerk in high school and probably still is. I'm surprised it took Bethany so long to get rid of him."

Long awkward pause.

"Did you know that Dennis O'Leary still hasn't settled down?"

"That's because he's gay and hasn't admitted it to himself yet."

Bill wondered if he'd become invisible. Trisha had already made it clear that Bill was staying in her room, which hadn't gone over well. He'd tried to offer to stay in the guest house, but Trisha had shut that down hard. Once he began to understand what was going on, he decided that maybe it would be better if he stayed near Trisha when she was around her parents. If only so that it might give him the opportunity to avert murder, in either direction.

Clearly Lieutenant William Bruce was not a viable candidate for their only daughter. He wondered what precedent he was following, what other men Trisha had brought home in the past, perhaps specifically chosen to tick off her parents. Was he innately unacceptable or merely unworthy because he'd been selected by Trisha herself? He suspected that the answer to both was yes.

And had those men who came before him been as consistently uncomfortable as he was, sitting here trying to pay attention to his slice of apple pie and scoop of vanilla ice cream? Didn't her parents see how far she'd gone to get their attention, until she felt that pissing them off was her only avenue of expression?

"You know, dear, as soon as you're done with that flying nonsense—"

"I am done with it." Trisha's sudden snarl drew Bill's attention back to the conversation he'd been mostly ignoring as he simply watched the dynamics around him.

"You're what?" Bill managed the words in the sudden silence brought on by Trisha's acid tone.

She shot to her feet, knocking the heavy armchair over backward with a crash that rattled the silverware, and glared across the table at him. She chucked her napkin down onto her food.

"I've been thrown out of SOAR. The only thing I've ever really loved." Then she turned to face her parents. "Your daughter is a fuckup, just like you've always told her she was. Break out the bubbly. The good stuff. You should be celebrating. Not sitting there with your jaws down like a couple of stuffed sheep."

He saw the tears streaming down her face as she

stood there. He knew she was unaware of them. Then she turned and ran.

He froze.

Bill never froze.

It had been trained out of his brain and out of his reflexes. He never acted rashly, not even under fire, and he never froze. For five beats of his heart after she was gone, Bill simply couldn't move.

By the time he shook loose, her parents had started asking him what all that meant. He didn't bother listening. Instead he replayed the other sounds his brain had recorded during those five slow heartbeats. Running feet. No stairs. A door to the left, another beyond it.

The table was too long to waste time going around. He placed a palm in the middle and vaulted across. He moved fast and quiet, careful to not mask further sounds Trisha might make in her flight with his own. Through the kitchen door, past a startled cook who gave a small cry as he raced through her domain.

Back door. But even as he reached for it, he knew that was wrong. He'd heard a rattle that would have been the old brass knob, but nothing that matched the glass-paned door being slammed. It had been a heavier door, farther away, that he'd heard as he'd entered the kitchen of shining tile and steel.

He cut right into a long back hall. The change of sound in his footfalls as he shifted from linoleum to old wood was right. There were a half-dozen doors, rooms, cellars, servants' quarters, but it was the second to last door on the left. A floor mat in front of the door had been skidded sideways. He was out the back door and knew he was no more than fifty feet behind his quarry.

But full night had fallen and he was on unscouted terrain.

To his right, one of those inflatable pool domes, clearly accessed by the last door in the long hall. To his left, a formal garden. Straight ahead would be her direction. He blinked hard several times to force more blood to his eyes so they'd adapt from light to dark faster—which never seemed to help much, but he did it anyway—and cocked his head to watch out of the corner of his eyes to make the best use of the heightened light sensitivity of peripheral vision.

The night was quiet. A bat flitted by on its night patrol. Cars along a distant road. Dylan O'Malley had mentioned how they still held sixty acres of the original farmstead, making this one of the largest properties remaining in all of Milton, other than the city park that had been donated to the town by an earlier generation of O'Malleys as a tax write-off.

Bill dropped down a steep grassy slope and pulled to a halt along the verge of an orchard that filled what appeared to be a small, bowl-shaped valley. Houses perched along the upper edge, but no lights reached here. It was pitch black under the trees. Looking up, he could see a hint of the sky through some of the highest branches. The leaves had started to drop, so he listened.

Ahead and to the left he heard a soft rustle of running footsteps. Fast and light, but not silent.

Bill followed in starts and stops, moving quietly, then waiting to hear the next sign of where Trisha might have gone.

Even without being able to see the stars, he could tell that she was circling. She must know he was there.

"Stop following me!" He heard the result of the

sobs that had ripped at her throat as she shouted at him through the darkness.

Thirty yards at two o'clock.

"Damn you, Billy! Just leave me alone."

Twenty-five at three o'clock. "What do you mean SOAR threw you out?" He kept his voice soft and faced to his left so that he'd sound farther away and in a slightly different direction.

"I don't want to talk about it. Can't you figure that out inside that thick SEAL head of yours?" It had worked and she'd made a wrong turn. Now fifteen yards to his right.

"That's why you showed up in Vermont." He lowered his voice's pitch as much as he could to decrease its directionality, this time speaking in another direction.

"Well, I sure as hell wasn't going to come here. I can't believe you brought me here."

Let her blame him, if that made it easier for her.

He took a gamble. He ducked his head behind a particularly thick tree trunk and spoke toward what would be her left. The tree would block the sound of his voice except to one side, making her think he was much farther in that direction.

"I'm glad you showed up for whatever reason." Then he moved quickly in the opposite direction. Walking silently through dead leaves wasn't the easiest thing in the world, but SEALs weren't trained only in how to do easy tasks.

Twenty yards, he should be past where she would move to continue away from his voice. Then he leaned against a tree trunk and waited in the darkest part of the shadow. He held his breath. The night had gotten cold, and he didn't want a hint of the white vapor he'd exhale to give him away.

"I was glad to be there for you." Trisha was speaking to herself in little more than a whisper. She passed not three feet from his hiding place, heading deeper into the orchard.

"I couldn't have done it without you." He too kept his voice a whisper.

"Shit!" She jumped about two feet straight up, then stopped moving and turned to face him, her white face the barest outline in the darkness. "Damn you, Billy." She thumped a fist on his chest, but it didn't have any real energy behind it.

He smoothed a hand down her shoulder, partly to reassure her and partly so he could grab her if she jackrabbited away again when he asked his question.

"Now what's this about being tossed out of SOAR?"

———⁓———

Trisha wished she could cut out her tongue. She'd also like to know how Billy had found her. She'd been so sure he was headed north. She'd half hoped to lead him into the small marsh there. Maybe he'd get slowed down in the mud and lose track of her. Maybe he'd become mired and never find her again.

Instead he stood there at the center of the orchard, leaning against the old oak she'd been planning to climb into. She'd spent hundreds, probably thousands, of hours up that tree as a kid, reading books, listening to music, whatever. The center tree in the old untended cherry orchard had been her haven throughout her youth, the ground beneath its spreading branches stamped clear of any growth by unending hours of martial arts and weapons practice.

And somehow Billy had known exactly where to find her.

"I oughta pelt you with pinecones or something." She kicked the ground, hoping to find some even though it was a cherry orchard. Not even any acorns. The gray squirrels had already collected those for the winter.

"No, what you 'oughta' do is answer my question."

She rubbed at her arms. "I'm freezing."

"No dice. I don't have a jacket either, and I'm not giving you my shirt. If we go back to the house, you'll find some other thing to delay answering. So, you stand here and freeze until you've answered the damn question."

Trisha scrubbed at her face and resisted the urge to scream. It wouldn't help. Neither would running. She might know her way around these woods better than she did around her Little Bird, but she'd never lose a SEAL. She folded her arms tightly across her chest and hugged herself for warmth.

And she'd be damned if she was going to cry in front of him. If she did, he would probably see it in the dark with whatever special, top secret, X-ray vision trick they'd taught him that had let him find her on her home ground. No help for it, so she said it fast, hoping that would make it hurt less.

"I'm not a team player. Lola Maloney says she can't use someone who doesn't play all nice by her cute little rules." Saying it made it hurt even more.

"Okay, now what did she really say?" Rather than being cold or commanding or pissed like she deserved, Billy's voice was actually tinged with humor. It kind of shamed her because he'd always played straight arrow with her.

"You aren't supposed to know me that well."

His shadow might have shrugged. Her eyes were slowly adapting to the pitch dark. His outline was as solid as the tree he leaned against.

"She gave me a week off duty to consider whether I wanted to return to SOAR and play her way or get tossed back to the Screaming Eagles. Highest recommendations, of course." Like that mattered. Everyone would know she couldn't hack SOAR. Including Emily Beale. Even though she was out of the Army now, Emily would find out, and Trisha didn't know if she could live with that. But she didn't know if she could hack SOAR, either.

Billy settled to sit down under the tree. She copied him, a scant yard between them, pulling her knees to her chest and wrapping her arms around them for warmth.

"You always ran with the same gang?"

Not a question she'd been expecting. "With Vinny's crew, yeah, until he screwed up and a Chinese Tong burned him down. I guess I was mostly out by then anyway, though I kept up the martial arts he'd started me in."

"But you could leave whenever you wanted, come here to this place? This tree?"

She could. Damn, he knew her too well. She didn't bother to answer.

"You missed something." Billy's voice warmed the night a tiny bit. "Something I'd looked for in Detroit, then Chicago. You missed really belonging to something."

"I belong to the Army."

"No."

His single word felt like he'd slapped her with it, though he'd said it quietly. Her cheeks flared with the heat of anger. But his calm voice cut her off before she could think of what to do with the fiery heat.

"I think that the Army has been a game to you. A good one. Great training that you clearly thrive on and gobble up whole. Cool toys like that chopper of yours that you fly so damn well. Getting back at your parents was probably your initial reason to join, but it's served you well. A game that went real for the first time when you were shot."

"Damn, Dr. William, what do I owe you for this session?"

"Straight answers."

A different heat roared to her cheeks. She didn't trust her voice, so she just nodded once, hoping he could see it.

"You've got to know what you're fighting for. You're a goddamn magician in the Little Bird. Everyone agrees. One of the best soldiers on the planet thinks you are truly exceptional, while I can barely win his acknowledgment."

"No!" Trisha cut him off. "No, don't think that. I've never seen Michael so impressed with another soldier. He's certainly never let anyone else in on an otherwise Delta-only mission before, at least not that I've seen. I mean, there were forty seasoned U.S. Rangers from the 75th Airborne aboard and you're the one he took on the mission. He talks even less than you do, but he thinks you're something special. Really."

Billy was quiet for a while, digesting that. She'd learned to appreciate and understand his silences. She'd found it irritating at first, but finally relabeled it "processing internally" in her head. That seemed to fit and give her the patience to accept it.

"That aside."

Processing completed. She smiled to herself in the dark.

"The subject here is you. Why do you think the BUD/S course takes twenty-four weeks? They're not teaching us to be a team. They're making it so that we can't be anything else. Every person who fails, other than during the first four weeks who just can't hack the physical challenge, fails because they can't accept their place in a team."

"So, I have to give up who I am and play nice?" Even though she tried to make it sound funny, it didn't.

"Do you think that's all I've done?"

It wasn't all Billy had done. It wasn't anything he'd done in the least. Lieutenant William Bruce was the most amazing man she'd ever met. More unique and individual than anyone she'd ever known. And yet he'd blended into Michael's team that rainy night on the oil tanker as if it was the most natural thing in the world. It didn't make him any less Billy the SEAL.

Now that she thought of it, she tried to imagine the other women she'd flown with in some sort of Army cookie-cutter form. Emily Beale and Lola, Kee and Connie, Amy Patterson and Claudia Casperson coming up through training now. She'd flown with incredible women who all somehow managed to fit in where they were.

But how was she supposed to do that?

"What the hell are we doing here?" A bare whisper was all she could manage, and even that raked at her aching throat.

"We don't know yet." Billy's voice was soft in the night, filled with sympathy and a confidence she'd completely lost somewhere in the dark.

Chapter 20

TRISHA'S DAD HAD STOPPED AFTER TWENTY LAPS, HALF a mile. The broad plastic canopy allowed the morning sunlight to wash over the pool but held the cool autumn morning at bay.

Trisha had pushed herself to fifty laps before dragging herself out to dangle her legs in the pool while they burned with the lactic acid buildup of such a long swim. It's what she deserved for trying to keep up with a SEAL for the first twenty laps.

And he was still out there. A hundred laps would get him three miles, and he showed little sign of slowing before then.

"He's good." Her father settled beside her, dipping his own feet in beside her.

She wanted to say, "Navy SEAL, Dad. Duh!" But instead she said, "He is," and left it at that. He'd taken care of her last night, carrying her back to the house after she'd wept herself sick. And he'd been there in the morning, sleeping on the carpet beside her bed. Leaving her to sleep alone when she'd been too vulnerable and wrecked to make any rational choices.

She and her father sat side by side watching Billy do another couple of laps in silence. The broad, inflatable dome of tan-and blue-patterned vinyl arcing above the pool was almost completely unlike an artificial sky. At least the fall sunshine filtered through the material,

making a nice, even light. The wide border of concrete
sported lounge chairs, an "outdoor" shower, and even a
small changing cabana, well stocked with fresh robes,
towels, and sunscreen. Though she'd never understood
the last as the dome was supposed to be UV opaque.

"He treating you well?"

She glanced over at her father but couldn't read
his expression. He was staring out at the water, not in
Billy's direction, just up the empty lane before them, the
smooth surface broken by the ripples of Billy's passage.

"We actually haven't been together very long, but,
yeah, he is." Together. Were they together? Team Billy
and Trisha? How long before she blew that up too?
Well, she hadn't killed it last night despite her best efforts. Though it was pretty clear that she'd have to play
it straight with Billy forever more or he was gone.

Again a couple laps of silence. Her father was such a
weird contrast, so gregarious in business, yet he almost
never spoke at home. Processing internally like Billy?
Or maybe trying to build up courage to deal with his
hyper-reactive daughter?

"What's your question, Dad?"

He waited another half lap before responding. "That
thing you said last night. About failing out. Is that true?
It doesn't sound like you."

The bitter response she had locked and loaded for fire
died at that last comment. "What do you mean, it doesn't
sound like me?"

"Well, you do everything you set out to do. I've
talked to other parents, both clients and friends. No one
else's kid has so many trophies they can't even fit them
in their room, no matter what sport."

Trisha didn't even know he'd noticed.

"Most of them are just following in their father's foot-steps or totally screwing up their lives, like we thought you were in Southie, or getting quietly married."

"Like Mom wants me to do."

"She's just afraid."

"Afraid?"

Her father actually laughed aloud at Trisha's shock. He looked good laughing. She could see for a moment the handsome man with the easy smile that seemed to be everyone's friend but hers. That his mother always claimed to love so much.

"Okay, you're in your twenties now."

"Twenty-eight."

"Fine, you should be old enough to understand this. Pretend that you have a kid who insists on doing the ab-solute scariest thing you can imagine, every single time you turn around. Do you remember when you were five and we took you skiing?"

"Sure, the black diamond trail up at Stowe. You've told that story so many times at so many parties that I don't know if it's my memory or not."

"What you don't know is that it was only your third time skiing. We were on the beginner Toll Road Trail and you turned down Hayride before I could stop you. You tumbled and rolled down half the slope. I thought you'd be broken or dead at the bottom by the time I got there. I dug you out of the snowbank that had finally stopped you, and you asked, in that little girl's voice of yours, to go again because you didn't get it right yet. You were the most terrifying child I can imagine."

That was a new spin on it compared to, "She was

skiing black diamond slopes by the time she was five. Surprised she didn't kill herself." Especially as she'd always seen it as a comment on how incompetent she was as a teen. What a disappointment she'd become after such a promising start.

For herself, she'd never been pleased with her skiing skill. Not even in her teens was she as good as others going by her, even though she often skied the double black diamond slopes by that point. The family didn't go often enough for her to get really good, but she'd always taken it as her not being good enough.

"Waterskiing, horse jumping, that gang in Southie, even the detective I hired couldn't keep up with them"—first she'd heard of that—"all of those martial arts competitions, helicopters, the Army... You are more than your mother knows what to do with. Or me. Every bad match she tries to make for you is just a desperate lifeline she's throwing out to try and keep you safe. It's a habit she had to form from the moment you crawled right off edge of the front porch, and now she can't break it. So, I'll ask you for her sake since she can't phrase the question in a way you can stand to hear. Are you being safe?"

Trisha thought about the three black-and-blue marks from being shot, only now faded enough to not draw a comment, and the technical that had had her chopper in its sights.

"Not as safe as I should be. That's what's got me in trouble."

"That's what scares us so much."

~m~

Trisha watched Billy sitting on the bottom of the pool. Her father had left for work before Billy had finished his laps, the last one down and back, fifty meters entirely underwater. Then he'd swum out to the deep end and treaded water while he hyperventilated before sinking out of sight.

The surface water slowly settled across the pool. With no wind to stir it, it was soon glassy smooth.

She could see him now. Sitting on the bottom, his left arm raised in front of him where she knew he wore his big diver's watch, though she couldn't quite make it out through ten feet of water.

Counting her heartbeats, she kept track of the time going by, fifty-seven beats per minute at rest. Two minutes. Three. No bubbles.

She tried to imagine not serving alongside people like Billy and Michael and all the others.

And she didn't like it one bit. Whatever trade-offs she had to make, she knew that much.

Billy rose out of the water so quietly that she barely heard the drops of water plinking from his hair down into the water. He surfaced after four minutes and fifteen seconds not two feet beyond her knees. He pulled in a slow, deep breath and let it out just as silently despite how his lungs must be burning.

"What are you thinking there, hotshot?"

She leaned forward to brush a thumb over the scar down his cheek.

"I'm thinking I know why we came. I'm ready to go back."

He did nothing big. No acknowledgment beyond a simple nod at such a big decision. Then he pulled her down into the water beside him and kissed her.

Chapter 21

TRISHA SPOTTED LOLA MALONEY ON THE DECK OF THE *Peleliu* as soon as she stepped off Dennis's chopper. Billy nodded to her and turned for his quarters. Trisha thanked Dennis and met Maloney halfway across the deck.

"Hot as a bitch here, Chief," she called out when they were close enough. After New England, it was scorching. They traded salutes.

"You're back?" Maloney came up to her.

"Yes, sir."

Maloney held out her hand and Trisha shook it, the relief coursing through her body. Hoping this was going to work, though how she still wasn't totally clear, she'd rather feared this moment. Lola gave her hand another squeeze before letting go, making it okay.

"I'm glad. You know, you're even more of a pain in the ass than I was, and that's saying something."

"You were?" Trisha suddenly felt out of balance. Lola Maloney was a company leader for a significant and important operation. Air Mission Commander Archie Stevenson might be a captain, but he was in command only during flight operations. The company aboard the *Peleliu* belonged to Maloney.

"Yep! Beale reamed my backside but good. Did the same to Kee and Connie, truth be told. I guess you count too, now that I passed on that tradition. Sorry you never knew her. She was incredible."

Trisha had sworn Billy to secrecy on that point, threatened him with blood and murder and withholding sex. But she felt as if, by stepping back on this deck beneath the blazing Gulf sun, it no longer mattered so much how she got here. What mattered was that she was here.

"We spent two years together," she told Lola. "In the same company with the Screaming Eagles. Busted asses together through Green Platoon. She…" Trisha looked back up at the achingly blue sky and blinked hard. "She's the one who made me who I am. She's how I got here."

Lola shook her shoulder in a friendly fashion. "She'd say that you're the one who made you who you are. But I know exactly what you mean."

Trisha couldn't speak and just nodded her head.

Lola stepped back and snapped a salute. "Welcome back aboard, Lieutenant O'Malley."

Trisha returned the salute at rigid attention despite her civilian clothes. "Glad to be here, sir."

Then they both smiled and Trisha shouldered her duffel. When she stood, Lola tucked her hand through Trisha's arm, much to her surprise, and they headed toward the down ladder together.

Lola leaned in and half whispered, "All any of us got from Beale was a bloody distant nod of acknowledgment. I thought welcoming you back might be better."

Trisha tried to process what she was feeling, but it was too big and it wasn't working, neither externally nor internally. So she kept it simple.

"It is better."

And it was.

"We didn't have much to work with."

Trisha couldn't get her jaw working. They had bombed her quarters on the *Peleliu*. Connie, Kee, and even little Dilya stood in the small space between the foot of her bed and the closet.

"It's amazing!" Stars were cut out of light green and pink Navy requisition forms and taped all over the walls. Paper plates, bearing drawings of helicopters with dragon wings and spitting fire, dangled from threads that had been duct-taped to the ceiling. A cleaning bucket filled with ice and sodas sat on the desk, along with bags of chips and a stack of cookies. "But why?"

"Well, each of us has been through the 'Emily talk.'" Connie actually shuddered, her soft brunette hair fluttering.

"And"—Kee took Trisha's duffel and chucked it into the bottom of the closet as if it didn't weigh much at all—"we'd all stepped back up to the plate, so we figured you would. Though none of us took a damned week to do so."

"I…" Trisha still could believe what she was seeing. No way was she going to cry, but she might start giggling at any moment. "I had some things to work out."

"Tell me about it!" Lola sounded totally disgusted as she took a Dr Pepper and a bag of peanuts before dropping down on the bed. "So, tell us a Beale story from before."

Connie and Kee looked a bit startled at the comment.

"I flew with her for two years. We did Green Platoon together."

Connie whistled in surprise and settled with a soda and a cookie on the desk chair. "No wonder she wouldn't go near you during Assessment Week and left it to me to do your interview."

Kee just nodded. "That explains why you're such a goddamn good pilot. I should have seen it, but you're too different. She was a rock."

"Whereas I'm a nutcase?"

Kee grabbed a Diet Coke and toasted her with it. "Absolutely. Welcome to the club." She sat on the floor beside Dilya, who was drawing another dragon-chopper.

"She's good," Trisha complimented Dilya, but she was too busy drawing to notice. The thing looked like it could actually exist.

Kee nodded. "So give."

Trisha shrugged. She didn't really know how to act in a room full of women. She'd been an outcast in Catholic school. And at NYU she'd never been much of a joiner. She'd run with Vinny's gang, but the girls there were even tougher than the guys in some ways. And regular Army was mostly men. Beale had been her only female friend. Ever.

Kee grimaced at Trisha's hesitation. "Either a Beale story or…" She looked at the others as if eliciting support. "Or you can start with that handsome hunk of a SEAL. You know we'll get to him sooner or later."

The others all nodded in agreement. Trisha settled on the bed beside Lola Maloney and leaned back against the wall.

"Well, there was a time in Sri Lanka when Emily and I—"

Chapter 22

THE TIME-ZONE JUMP WORKED OUT. FLIPPING BACK from daytime living to nighttime flying, Trisha slept that day and flew that night.

Sweep patrols. Nothing special. But she flew. And rather than jumping ahead of the flight line, she told Dennis and Max how she did it, and now they all surged ahead in unison. Many nights they sat in the ready room for hours, all dressed up with nowhere to go as the drones swept over the endless sea. Other nights they worked back and forth around the Horn of Africa checking dozens of boats, some of which were indeed those of night fishermen. Others had heard enough about the patrols to throw their weapons overboard rather than risk having their engine shot off and their leader killed. "Oh no, we're just innocent Somali fishermen who happen to be carrying AK-47s and grappling gear for boarding large ships."

For an entire week Trisha behaved, flew in formation, and chatted pleasantly at meals. Sometimes she ate with Billy and Michael and LC Ramis, sometimes with the Little Bird crews, and more than a couple of times with the three other women. They were getting to know each other and it was becoming comfortable. Another place she belonged. She and Dilya actually got into the dragon-chopper drawings. They started doing technical designs, recruiting Connie on the tricky parts. The kid had a real flair for it.

And by the end of that week, she wanted to hit something…really, really, really hard. Not that she had a whole lot of options about where to express her frustrations.

No way to take it to Lola. The Chief Warrant was too damn pleased with her first attempt to step into Beale's shoes in the fine art of breaking women to the SOAR team. Trisha knew intellectually that wasn't what was going down, but she couldn't stop the feelings.

Trisha didn't want to disappoint Kee and Connie. They'd become friends and wouldn't understand that she still had doubts and fears and frustrations. Especially frustrations.

Roland, Dennis, Max? Not so much. Instead, Trisha simply flew and fumed and didn't show it to anyone though it festered deep inside until it actually hurt, leaving her stomach in knots for hours after a flight.

She needed to tell someone, but even when she tried to say something to Billy, it just choked off. She'd lie awake after Billy had fallen asleep and they'd each sated their apparently bottomless need and joy for the other. She'd review every maneuver from that night's flight in the Little Bird, wondering if she'd messed up a flight somehow or let down a team member or judged something wrong or who the hell knew what. Constantly second-guessing herself took the joy out of flying.

No question that Billy would assume that she could just fit in now. They were a group, a team of f'ing homies. That was his idea of comfort. It was her idea of a garrote about to be cinched tight around her throat.

"What is it?"

"What is what?" Trisha had thought Billy was once again safely asleep.

"Whatever is keeping you awake and fussing these last nights."

"Nothing."

Billy went silent at that.

Didn't the man know when a woman wanted to be prodded for information? *C'mon, Billy, save me from myself here.*

"You sure?" That was his idea of prodding? How lame was he?

"Yeah." How lame was she? He'd given her an opening, a weak-ass lame one, but an opening. And she turned it down anyway. "God, we're a pair, aren't we?"

"I just figured you'd say what you had to say when you were ready to say it."

"Oh, like you talk so much." She tapped a finger lightly where the scar crossed over his sternum.

His shrug was eloquent.

"Don't you get sick of doing what everyone says to do?" Maybe if she came at it sideways.

"But I don't."

"Tell me one single time that you didn't follow the rules. I'm not talking about jumping aboard a Delta mission to rescue an oil tanker from pirates, even if you did great. Tell me about one time that Lieutenant Billy the SEAL did one thing that wasn't for the good of the team but rather for the good of himself." Trisha didn't know where the heat was coming from, but she couldn't keep it from her body or her voice. She sat up and looked down at the naked man still sprawled half-covered on her narrow bunk.

Billy went silent for a while, staring so intently at the plain gray steel of the ceiling that she actually glanced up to see if there was a spider or a stray thermonuclear device that had somehow caught all of his attention.

"Can't come up with one, huh?"

"I'm thinking."

"What are you thinking?"

"I'm thinking of telling you to mind your own damned business."

Trisha felt the slap as surely as if he'd actually struck her. She'd never told anyone the things that Billy knew about her. Even Emily Beale didn't know about her parents. Chief Maloney had the decency to tell no one other than Kee and Connie, not even Dennis who had taken Trisha off the ship, why she'd gone on an emergency sabbatical. But Billy knew. And now he was…

She climbed over him out of the bed and began dragging on her clothes.

"Where are you going?"

Trisha yanked down her green T-shirt with "ARMY" emblazoned across it. She could take strength from that. "Looks as if I'm boldly going nowhere, just like us." And she stormed out of the room.

She heard him scrabbling for clothes before following her, so she headed off fast and light toward a section of the ship she'd never explored. Across the empty mid-shift mess room and out the other side.

How had she ended up in this place? Aboard a Navy ship so thick with Navy regulations that they disapproved of the arrogance of the U.S. Rangers and the "mavericks" of SOAR. Stuck in a Night Stalkers company where she'd be in trouble if she colored the least little bit outside the lines. Her lover, a Navy SEAL for crying out loud, was the biggest conformist of them all.

And now where was she supposed to go on a ship barely eight hundred feet long? There was a big lummox of a SEAL swimming between her sheets so her cabin was off limits. Go for yet another run in the helo hangar? He'd definitely find her there. Explore yet some other lost corner of this empty, echoing ship carrying a quarter of its normal crew and sounding just that way? A thousand or so Marines on board and she'd be able to find some interesting way to get into trouble. Without them, the ship's emptiness was immense indeed.

So, it was the middle of the day, which was supposed to be the middle of her night, and she was wide awake and roaming the corridors.

She nearly ran down the girl when she turned a corner into one of the bunk rooms at the aft end of the ship.

Dilya stood there with her ever-present e-tablet tucked in her arms, staring up at the tiers of bunks in the empty room. The room was the width of the ship by eighty feet long. Bunks rose in stacks three and four high. Each one had its mattress rolled up and tied at the foot of the steel springs.

"Where are all the people?"

"We, uh, don't need them for this trip." It was a little spooky, like a ghost ship, or at least this part of it was. The *Peleliu* had forty or fifty years' worth of ghosts. Trisha didn't think they'd seen any major action, but she wasn't sure. Wherever the men were who had filled these racks, they weren't here now.

"Even Dragonriders get their own rooms, mostly. And they're much nicer than this."

Trisha didn't remember the stories of Pern that well. She'd just been helping to design dragon-copters.

"Except for the holdless. They had to live out of doors despite the thread falling from the skies." Then she turned those green eyes on Trisha, made even more shocking by her dark hair and complexion. "If there were dragons, would they be more powerful than helicopters?"

"Uh, they're kind of different. Dragons can throw flame, but just a little way. With helicopters we can throw our... We can throw them a long way."

Dilya nodded as if filing away that information for future usage. Then she perched on the edge of the lowest bunk. So, for lack of anything better to do, Trisha did the same across the aisle. Their knees didn't quite touch.

Trisha continued. "Helicopters are faster than dragons but we can't go between to other—"

"You kill peoples?"

"Uh," Trisha scrambled to shift gears. No point in lying to the kid. "People, sometimes. When it's needed." And she sure wasn't going to debate with a kid when death was needed and who decided. Either they were shooting at her, which was an automatic black mark in her book, or someone in command had decided that a certain target had to go down.

"So does the Kee. I don't do that anymore."

"Anymore?"

Dilya answered her with silence. The kid was like what, twelve maybe? And she no longer killed people? That meant she had. What a hell of a life. That set Trisha to remembering Vinny's gang as they ran through Southie. Death was rare among the gangs, rare enough that it was always a shock, frequent enough that it felt as if it never stopped. And it certainly wasn't done by ten-year-old kids, at least not in Vinny's gang. Or that she'd ever seen. Bill had at least been fourteen, as if that made it all okay.

"Why?"

"Why what?" Trisha really hoped that the kid wasn't asking what she thought was being asked.

"Why do you kill peoples? People."

"I never thought about it that way."

Dilya looked at her as if Trisha were the idiot child.

"I don't just go out and do it. There are a lot of bad people out there, and it is my job to go out and do my best to stop them."

"Even if it means making them dead?"

"Even if it means making them dead." How in the world had she ended up in this conversation? And in such a surreal setting? Fifteen hundred U.S. Marines had been stationed on the *Peleliu* at any one time. They had fought in Iraq and Afghanistan. They'd evacuated people from volcanic eruptions in the Philippines and helped out at Hurricane Sandy with rescue efforts after New York was slammed. The *Peleliu* had even been here in Somalia twenty years before during Operation Restore Hope, the minor success before the disastrous Operation Gothic Serpent and the Battle of Mogadishu.

And somehow she was the one that the kid had to ask.

"I fly to help people, to help keep them safe. To help keep you safe."

"The Kee already do that when she kill Dog One and Dog Two."

Clearly some story Trisha knew nothing about, and Dilya wasn't elaborating so she dropped it. The problem with the platitudes was that they didn't sound like platitudes.

Sure, Trisha had begun fighting because it's just what she did. She could even see now that it was in reaction to who her parents were.

Had her father really meant that about Trisha scaring her mother to death? Maybe she had. In retrospect, so much of what Trisha had done was fighting back against a past she didn't want any part of. If all her life to date had been built on reaction against something, maybe it was time she started acting on her own behalf.

And her first step was that she'd better find Billy and apologize for storming out. He was definitely someone that she wanted to keep around for a while. How long? She had no idea, but a while anyway, which was a step forward for her.

"Thanks, kid."

Except Dilya was gone. Trisha sat alone in the bunk space. How long had she been snarled up in her own thoughts? Had the kid even been here? Yes, Trisha decided. Either Dilya had been there or Trisha was really losing it.

—◊◊◊—

Halfway back to her cabin, she ran into Roland headed the other way at a narrow hatchway where one of them had to give way.

"You going to the show?" Roland asked her as he passed.

"What show?" She hadn't heard anything about a show.

"Rangers vs. Navy. They cleared a wrestling gym down on fourth deck, forward. Put some matting down in one of the empty bomb storage lockers. It should be good fun to watch."

"Young-buck Rangers and old-hand Navy defending their own ship." A passing fuelie, Navy flight-deck service guy, stopped to join the conversation.

"Hey, Sly," Trisha teased him, "almost didn't recognize a grape without his jumpsuit. Does it come with booties?" When on the flight deck, all Navy personnel wore color-coded clothing. Because he worked with fueling aircraft, Sly wore a bright purple vest, hence the "grape" nickname. You'd think red meant fuel, but that prize went to the munitions guys.

"And a little flap door in the back. You betcha, O'Malley." They both knew that no matter how hot the weather was, he spent his working shift in a full-body Nomex fire-retardant suit, just like a smokejumper. "We're gonna be putting some Ranger face into the mats tonight."

"Going to be doing that personally?"

"Might be. Might be." He was a big guy and Trisha saw that he moved well. Powerful, even dangerous, but too heavy on his heels.

"Maybe I'll come watch that." But she wanted to find Billy first.

The grape headed down ladder. At a signal from Roland she waited. Once Sly was gone, Roland turned back to her, keeping his voice low.

"Don't wanna intrude, but if you're looking for that SEAL, I just saw him. He headed down as soon as I told him about the matchup."

Without even searching the ship from stem to stern looking for her.

"He looked some kinda frustrated when he asked if I'd seen you. Didn't make a big deal of it. Wouldn't have thought anything of it, the way he did it, but since I knew you two were…" Roland shrugged.

Trisha thought she and Billy had been a bit more subtle than that. The women hadn't thought so, and neither had Roland. She glanced at her watch. Three hours. It had been that long since she'd stormed out of the cabin. Long enough for her to cool down. And, she made a wager with herself, probably just enough time for Billy's slow temper to heat up. Good thing they didn't both flash hot at the same rate, or they'd murder each other one of these nights.

Roland was watching her.

"Thanks, I'll…" She looked down at her clothes. Loose sweats with nothing underneath, sneakers, Army T-shirt but no bra. Where the hell had her brain been that she'd gone out on a Navy ship without a sports bra? "Sure. What the hell, I'll be down in a few."

⁓

Bill stood along the port bulkhead of the ammo storage room. It still smelled strongly of cleaning fluid and fresh paint. Munitions storage spaces were always kept immaculate. Minimum number of ways to spark something you didn't want sparked, and maximum visibility to see if something was leaking that shouldn't be.

Other than its smell, the room was wholly unremarkable. The bomb racks had been pulled along with the bombs since there were no Harrier jets aboard to use them and the *Peleliu* was destined for decommissioning after this operation. A couple-ton elevator filled one corner, big enough for a pair of bomb carts. Three different access hatches, each with a fire hose coiled close beside it. Matching ones would be out in the hall in case the crew had to fight their way into the room. The two big drains in the floor were buried under the mats. Incandescent lights in glass shields and steel cages lit the room brightly, lending it a yellowish cast.

And, he almost wished Trisha were here to remark on it, unremitting gray. After a couple hours of searching the ship for her, including their haunt on the afterdeck, he started thinking about accessing the shipwide paging system, which would be a really bad idea. When he'd heard about this matchup, he figured she'd be here and had come looking. Just as well that she wasn't. Who knew what he'd do to her in his present state of mind.

The space was crowded despite its size. Maybe forty-foot square, with about a hundred guys pressed into the room. One of the chief petty officers was acting as the referee over a blond ensign Bill recognized and a bald Ranger that he didn't. They were both stripped to their pants and barefoot, going for it on the mat. Side bets were trading hands despite the CPO forbidding them when he started.

The senior officers had made themselves scarce, allowing the men a chance to defuse and burn off some of the energy at being cooped up shipboard.

Wrestling for now, but there was room in here for some serious sparring. Maybe he'd bring O'Malley down here and pound some sense into her.

He grimaced. Bill could feel the heat of his emotions and knew that was a bad sign. He needed to be careful, calm down, and find the center of his anger so that he could let it go. Control the emotion before it controlled him. Maybe he should bring Trisha down here to pound some sense into him.

Someone sidled up beside him, moving so smoothly and quietly that he almost didn't notice. He didn't even have to turn and see.

Michael.

They exchanged nods and continued to watch the crowd.

"Blond guy," Bill said quietly, watching the two wrestlers shoulder to shoulder, both grappling for a hold that would knock the other over onto his back.

"If the bald Ranger shifted his left foot back about six inches, he'd have him."

Billy studied their positions and then nodded. It would be an unconventional move, based on his own weight distribution, but it would absolutely unbalance his blond opponent. Would he think to do it himself? Maybe, hard to judge a fight without being in it yourself.

The bald guy shifted in the opposite direction and moments later found himself slammed to the mat, both shoulders pinned for the crucial moment before the kneeling ref slapped the mat to declare the victor.

"You giving it a go?" Michael asked after another Ranger had come forward and squared off against the winning ensign.

Billy had been assessing the crowd. There were some guys bigger than him, but watching them move showed they were no real threat. There were a couple of Navy seamen first class, a petty officer or two, and one Ranger master sergeant that would be a good challenge, but as long as he kept his head, none of them worried him.

With a single grunt, a slam, and a groan from the

gathered Rangers, their comrade was slammed into the mat and pinned on the first move.

"Doesn't seem fair for me to play. Maybe if Navy gets backed into a corner, I'll give it a go."

After that it went back and forth for a while. The blond guy made it through four matches before a fellow Navy man took him down. A Ranger planted him down hard in the longest match yet, lasting well over a minute.

The space was heating up and starting to smell of sweat and anticipation. A bloody nose that was apologized for and shrugged off as unimportant added a coppery bite to the air.

One of the Navy petty officers came forward, a lifer rather than some young punk. Several of the younger Rangers, not being smart enough to know they were beaten before they stepped on the mat, went at him one by one. Bill had been right. He was good. Damn good. He even cleared off the Ranger Master Sergeant. That pretty well put paid on Bill having to join the fray. Go Navy!

The Navy PO second class, having won boasting rights and a pretty massive adrenaline rush, stood barefoot in the center of mat. His fists bunched and held low in front of him as he pumped up his shoulders. He roared like the Incredible Hulk. A crow of well-deserved victory that elicited rounds of cheers and laughter and an answering roar from the rest of the Navy contingent. They shouted out his name, Sly Stowell, then broke into another round of "Go Navy!"

With hardly a ripple in the crowd, the man beside Bill was moving forward. Michael had shed shirt, shoes, and belt without even Bill noticing. No one saw him until he was well past the front edge of the crowd and standing near the Petty Officer.

The room went quiet. The senior Delta Force operator was about half the size of the Petty Officer.

Bill tried to understand what he was doing. If there was a "no contest" in the room, it would be against Colonel Michael Gibson.

They squared off, the Navy PO pumping himself up, knowing that putting in a good showing was the best he could hope for. Even as the ref raised a hand, ready to start the match, Bill figured it out.

He didn't even bother to watch the Navy man go down.

Bill just bent down to remove his own shoes and socks.

Billy was gone and hadn't made her bed. Trisha decided to shower and make her bunk before changing into more appropriate clothes. She'd known the wrestling match would probably be going on a long while yet. She'd thought to go down and cheer on a few friends while they burned off some testosterone. It was a common enough game, one the commanders were wise to turn a blind eye to. It also let any inter-crew tensions be worked out safely in a controlled environment.

She entered the room about twenty minutes after she'd left Roland in the corridor. She had to squeeze in among the wall of bodies that blocked any visibility into the center of the room.

It had the same low ceiling that the other decks did, but it wasn't Smurf-high. She'd have to remember to harass Billy about that, a good tool to show him that she was over being mad at him. Mostly.

The shouting in the steel chamber made her ears actually hurt. She wished she had earplugs. Cheers of "Rangers lead the way!" and "Go Navy!" echoed back and forth with all of the power of cannon broadsides.

And she couldn't see shit. Most of these guys' shoulders were higher than her head, never mind her eyes.

She shoved and struggled and pushed toward the front as all the Rangers groaned and Navy cheered even more loudly. She spotted a couple of Night Stalkers shouting for the Army Rangers as she worked her way forward.

The room went silent the moment she came up against a final barricade. Two guys blocked her view, both shirtless and sweaty. A blond Navy guy almost as big as Billy and a shaved-bald Ranger who each showed the bright red of palm prints on their skin from having been in a wrestling ring. Moments before, they'd been showing how hoarse they'd become from cheering the matches.

And now they both stood stone still.

In the moment of slack silence, she managed to wedge between the two big guys without getting too much of their sweat on her.

Then she saw why the silence had fallen. Sly stood in the center of the ring, the fuelie she'd chatted with about twenty minutes earlier. Now Sly was clearly the man to beat. And he was facing a guy about half his size.

Michael.

Michael wasn't as scarred up as Billy, but as she knew, his body had definitely seen its own share of hard wear and tear.

The Navy guy slowly chose his spot, made a show of testing that there was no sweat under where he'd planted his feet on the mat. Assuring himself that he'd have good traction for his first move. Then he half crouched and waited. Michael stood opposite him, one foot slightly back, his knees bent.

The referee looked intently at his Navy comrade, clearly ready to call off the match before it started. A slight shake of the combatant's head, then he turned to concentrate fully on Michael.

The referee shrugged, took a deep breath, and raised his hand high. Then he sliced it down between the opponents and jumped back to clear the melee.

Mr. Navy decided that to close fast and grapple was a good strategy. Leverage his size and strength against the smaller D-boy. Not a bad choice, and probably his only good one.

Michael stepped underneath Sly's swinging arm and, turning aside, tapped him on the shoulder as he went by.

Sly spun and missed grabbing Michael by mere inches.

Michael ducked low inside the curve of Sly's arm. Close to the ground he hooked a knee under Sly's barely raised foot and rocketed to his feet. Sly slammed to the ground as Michael continued to use the leg as a lever. It only took a moment, but Sly's shoulders were pinned past any recovery.

Less than five seconds and the referee slapped the mat, looking relieved to do so.

The echo of that slap could be heard easily coming back off the room's walls. There wasn't another sound in the packed room.

Michael reached out a hand to help up Sly. Once they were both on their feet, Michael grabbed Sly's wrist and raised his arm high, indicating Sly as the victor. Clearly he wasn't of this match, but Michael was giving him the honor due the best man in the room other than himself.

When she began to applaud the gesture, the slap of Trisha's palms was the only sound in the room. But within seconds, as if she'd unleashed an entire artillery barrage, the guys—Rangers and Navy both—went wild. Hoots, cheers, applause.

The two men in the center shook hands and did that manly half-hug, hard-slap-on-the-back, while-leaning-over-the-handshake thing.

Why had Michael even bothered to enter the ring? There wasn't a soul in the room who could beat him.

That's when she spotted Billy pushing his way into the ring from off to her right. He too had stripped down to just his pants. And the heat so sated just a few hours before roared back into her body. He looked magnificent in a room that contained many partly clothed, exceptional men.

Then she thought about who he was facing and she wanted to tell him not to be such an idiot. But the applause was dying and the room quieting as they saw the next matchup.

Billy saw her and offered one of his scowls, one of the ones with heat behind it. "Couldn't find her when he wanted to, but now he'd found her when he didn't want her here" was how she read it.

Well, tough. This was bound to be a spectacle and she didn't want to miss it.

The room finally settled. Aboard the entire ship, these were the two odd men out. More so than SOAR. Even more than the most senior officers versus the enlisted crew.

The D-Boy and the SEAL, both top-flight operators. Tier One assets is what they'd be called in the terrorist world, those prime targets that you really, really wanted to take out. Even Rangers who harassed every non-Ranger on the planet, including Delta operators, didn't have the balls to mess with Colonel Michael Gibson or Lieutenant William Bruce. Mostly everyone just went silent when the two of them were around.

What was it like living that way? You might belong to a team, but it would be a very small one. Even in the current Operation Heavy Hand, the camaraderie broke down around these two men. She and the Captain were among the few who broke "party" lines to sit with them. Most others left a clear perimeter. At a number of meals she'd seen the two of them sitting at a corner table, and the three tables around them left empty except for the other D-boys and the occasional Night Stalker.

Now the two of them stood in the center of a circle of a hundred men, so silent that all you could hear was their breathing.

The referee sidled into position, but Billy waved him back. The man looked glad to go. Though he joined the front row and stood with his big arms crossed over his chest, still ready to intervene if he deemed it necessary.

For a long minute neither Michael nor Billy moved. A questioning buzz built slowly in the room, reinforced, made far louder than it was, by the close space and the gray metal walls. The two of them hadn't moved, except for their eyes.

Trisha felt like a voyeur. One of these men had been her lover for a brief time and the other was now. She knew both of the bodies very well, and she could feel the tension sliding back and forth between them.

Billy increased the weight on his right foot without much moving his hip. Michael shifted his left hand forward about two inches and Billy settled back. Move and countermove. They both knew what could come next and decided it wouldn't work.

Michael leaned forward an inch at most. Billy dug his toes into the mat, which responded with a sound between a squeak and a groan. Again, they both relaxed.

With no warning she could see, like the moment a gun fired when you didn't quite know the trigger's break point, Billy dove and rolled himself at Michael's feet. Michael jumped up to clear Billy's back. But just as Billy rolled onto his face, he shoved down with hands and feet and sprung upward. His back caught Michael's knees and sent him tumbling through the air. As he fell, Michael planted a single hand on the mat. He used that to push off as his tumble continued, now twisting his fall into a backward somersault. He stuck the landing, standing dead still even as Billy rolled up to land on his feet.

The room gave a collective gasp at the suddenness and power of the moves.

Again the interminable stand and stare. An epic battle by two men who knew the true battle was mental and who could anticipate each move, the countermove, and the strike after that, and… And not find an opening that either felt would provide an advantage worth exploiting. It was much more a chess match played a dozen moves ahead in the mind than a wrestling match.

Ignoring the slow buildup of the hecklers who didn't see what was going on, the two of them did their shift-and-flex dance for almost five minutes. The crowd began stamping feet and clapping hands, at first sporadically, but rapidly coordinating its efforts into a common rhythm. All of it built until it was a solid wave of sound that shook the room.

Again, without any warning that she could spot, Michael exploded into a whirlwind of moves, stunning the room into sudden silence. He moved so fast that Trisha couldn't even see it though she'd been watching for it.

But Billy did, or his body was so in tune with Michael's that his nervous system reacted for him. The spinning strike, wholly out of place in a wrestling match, but appropriate for these two men, got within an inch of Billy's temple before he was able to avert it. He turned it into a grapple that should have locked up Michael's arm in a painful backward bend, possibly snapping the elbow backward or dislocating a shoulder if followed through.

Instead Michael slithered to the mat, his legs and arms wrapped around Billy's knees. Billy was strong enough to step, despite Michael's weight and keep his momentary stagger from turning into a fall. Then Billy knelt down, hard and fast, and Trisha was half afraid that he'd crush the Colonel.

Michael managed to move clear of Billy's descending knees, which made a loud slap when he hit the mat. Michael fired out a straight-edge finger strike that he stopped against Billy's abdomen. Not at the sternum, but a little lower, just an inch.

Trisha had heard about the move on the street, but never heard of anyone actually doing it. A "heart grabber" was supposed to be literally that. Strike up and in so hard that you actually break the skin and drive your hand up behind your opponent's ribs, grab their heart, and rip it out for them to see as they die. If Michael made the move, that meant it was technically possible, which she'd always wondered.

Billy had stopped his massive palm a half-inch from the Colonel's nose. If he'd finished the stroke, he'd not only shatter Michael's nose, but probably kill him when the bones and cartilage were driven into the Delta operator's brain. If they followed through, they'd have died together.

They each held the pose for a half moment, and then released.

There was dead silence as they helped each other to their feet; then deafening applause exploded around the room.

The crowd thought they'd seen a show. A spectacle put on for their behalf. A show of something to aspire to in the U.S. military, as if Michael and Bill were the Thunderbirds doing an aerobatic stunt over Boston Harbor on July Fourth.

Trisha had seen two of the men she cared most about in the world come within inches of killing each other.

She turned and forced her way back out through the bodies, her ears gone deaf to the stupid cheers. If it was what she thought it was, she just might kill both of them.

Chapter 23

TRISHA COULDN'T FIGURE OUT IF SHE WAS CHICKEN OR pissed. And being in that undecided state, she decided it was best to simply steer clear of Billy, mostly because she had no idea what she'd say and what she wouldn't be able to take back later if she changed her mind. Once her head cleared, once her temper had eased enough to think rationally, then she'd be safe. Until then she was as stable as century-old TNT dripping with nitroglycerin.

Stupid Navy didn't put locks on the doors. If it was valuable, you had a small lockbox, but that was all that was private in the military. That and your thoughts, which she couldn't seem to get away from.

So, after the following night's flight, she grabbed a couple sandwiches and a water bottle, then disappeared back to that sprawling empty bunk room where she'd run into Dilya. Selecting a top bunk in the rear starboard corner, difficult to spot because of the structural elements of the room, she unstrapped the mattress and rolled it out. Climbing up into her eagle's aerie close below the ceiling of the next deck, she ate a quiet and unsatisfying meal. Should have grabbed a cookie. Like that would make a difference.

Then she set her watch for an hour before the nightly flight briefing and crashed back into a dreamless sleep. At least that was the plan.

Trisha didn't think they were fighting over her. It

just didn't make sense. Besides, she could take care of her own damn self. In her current mood, she wouldn't mind getting Billy the SEAL on that wrestling mat and hurting him. But her head space sure wasn't right for a friendly screw to clear the air.

God, even that sounded awful. "Queen of SOAR?" Billy had called her. "Queen Bitch!" would be way closer.

Option two, Billy working out some frustration over her fight with him? Reject. Not the kind of game he'd play with Michael.

So rather than dwell on how furious she'd be with Trisha O'Malley if she were him, she reassessed the fight for about the hundredth time. The chance to watch two such masters… It was almost better than flying with Emily Beale. What did it say about her that she'd seen different ways to take them on? She wouldn't know if her ideas would work until she tried them, but short of the killing stroke, there were definite possibilities.

And why hadn't Billy answered her question last night in bed? Was he really such a straight arrow? Former street kid turned angel didn't play any better than Billy and Michael having a spat about one Patricia O'Malley in front of most of the crew. If Michael was really pissed on her behalf, he'd probably come to her first to make sure of his facts. If he was angrier than that, Billy simply wouldn't come back alive from some mission.

So, whatever was between them definitely wasn't about her. Which left her once again contemplating her exceptional taste in fighting men and the fact that Billy didn't feel they were close enough for him to tell her something bad he'd done.

That's what really hurt. It's when she thought of that fact that her vision blurred with frustration, even rage… and bitter disappointment.

She'd trusted him, but he didn't appear to trust her.

—∙∙∙—

That night's flight wasn't totally routine, which was a relief. They'd spooked a pirate mother ship. That's when pirates managed to capture a small vessel, one bigger than their own tiny boats. Then they'd use that to chase an even bigger vessel that traveled farther out to sea, dragging along their smaller boats for the final attack.

It started when Trisha overflew a life raft with a mixed crew aboard. Everyone went on high alert while Trisha and Roland circled down on them. No sign of guns or RPGs. A raft was unusual as well, and neither she nor Roland had seen them dumping an engine at the chopper's approach. They simply didn't have an engine at all. Still, she slid up cautiously. Roland made sure the *May*'s weapons stayed trained on the small raft, ready to tear it to shreds.

They were the crew off a Korean fishing vessel. The fact that they were far inside the Somalia territorial waters was typical. Some militias' regimes had financed themselves with "special licenses" to the very ships they were supposed to be stopping, who then brought in the heavy trawling and bottom-dredging gear that decimated both fish and their reef habitat.

The Korean trawler hadn't had a citadel or enough weapons to repel boarders. They also hadn't radioed for help, probably because they were illegally in these waters. Nine hours. The Somali pirates had a nine-hour head start, placing them anywhere within a hundred and fifty miles, about an hour's flying time.

Unusually, the captain on the raft insisted that the entire crew was on the raft safely with him. "We told them the captain was dead and none of us knew where we were or how to run the boat. They grew so tired of our whining that they put us all overboard." He appeared very proud of his stratagem.

They were lucky they hadn't simply been shot as a nuisance. Very unusual not to take them as hostages; the pirates must have been hot on the trail of that bigger quarry. The captain gave the Night Stalkers a direction that the trawler had headed and the chase was on.

It was after the third refueling of the night, just a few hours before dawn, that *Max* spooked up the Korean trawler. They put up a heavy battle, right up until Kee, Michael, and Billy, all working from the cargo bay door of Maloney's DAP Hawk *Vengeance,* demonstrated exactly what American snipers could do with their rifles. Every pirate who attempted to shift into the clear to shoot at the choppers was shot. When a half dozen of them were sprawled about the deck, dead or dying, some survivor cut the trawler's engine and came out with his hands up.

Dusty, who had brought a team of Rangers along in his transport Black Hawk, dropped them on the boat. The medic set to work on the survivors even before the rest of the team finished clearing the boat and pronounced it secure.

After medevacing the two worst ones into Dusty's chopper, the Rangers turned the trawler back toward the carrier group, where the Korean crew should now safely be. Free to return once again to their illegal fishing activities. Trisha popped up a few thousand feet and spotted a ship not more than ten miles ahead. Under high magnification she could see that it was a container ship. Insider information this time. Someone had clearly fed the ship's position to the Somali crew, maybe some native Somali working at the London shipping company. Or even worse at EU NAVFOR, the European Union-led international effort to stop piracy in the Gulf.

That's why these pirates didn't care about taking the Korean hostages with them. They'd known exactly where their next batch of hostages were; they simply hadn't gotten there in time.

Back on the *Peleliu*, as the first predawn light washed over the sea and ended the too-long night, Chief Warrant Maloney pulled Trisha aside. "You're going crazy, aren't you?"

Trisha considered denying it or making excuses, but finally, mostly out of sheer weariness with it all, she gave up the façade and felt nothing but relief at doing so, damn the consequences. She leaned back against the nose of her chopper and opened the front seam of her flight suit down to her gym shorts.

"Completely bugfuck borderline psychotic, sir. What did I do wrong this time, and what do I need to do to fix it?"

Lola Maloney laughed. "Thought so."

"You're laughing at me?" Trisha expected to get angry, but just felt tired instead. Tired with the situation and tired of herself.

"Yep. You are trying so damn hard to behave that I bet y'all are staying up nights rethinking your flights."

"Uh, how did you know?"

"This gal wasn't born just yesterday, hon. I'm from N'Orleans. I know shit." She was clearly laying it on a bit thick to have fun at Trisha's expense, as she normally spoke accentless English. Or at least accentless American.

Trisha dragged off the upper part of her flight suit and tied the arms around her waist. Even just past sunrise, the air was getting warm. Soon she'd be wishing she could lose the T-shirt and sports bra as well. Another scorcher of a day in the Gulf. No surprise there, at least. But a definite surprise from her commander for certain. She still didn't know what to say.

"What I do know is that you'll never be all you can be as long as you keep holding on so tight."

"Any suggestions?" And she'd thought she was doing such a good job of hiding it all.

"Yep. Y'all come to the forward briefing room on the 02 deck right after we eat. The 'boys'"—she placed air quotes around the word—"have a special mission they want to run. Though they aren't telling me what yet. I'm thinking that the one-off operation is your true strength. And flying those will let you be more patient with the routine stuff."

"Maybe." Trisha kind of liked the sound of that. If she could bust out once in a while, the mundane missions would be far more tolerable.

Lola gave her a cocky salute and then headed down below.

Trisha felt calmer than she had in weeks. A special mission, doing something where she could just do what needed doing. That sounded good to her. She waited in the morning light, enjoying the shifting colors of the sky

as straight above shifted from hard blue toward crystalline, the horizon going from orange to gold and finally
from purplish haze to bluish haze.

And nowhere on that horizon did Billy wander up.
Guess she deserved that.

Chapter 24

"THANKS FOR COMING," MICHAEL GREETED HER EASILY when she entered the briefing room just behind Lola Maloney. Okay, didn't seem to be any problem there.

Billy looked at her and offered one of his carefully neutral nods. The two trays of dirty plates near him and Michael showed that he hadn't been avoiding her at the meal as well. Or at least not only avoiding her. Clearly they'd been doing a lot of planning, Mr. D-boy and Mr. SEAL.

A large electronic map was on a big wall screen. Galkayo. That was a bad sign right there. Galkayo was one of the most powerful pirate strongholds, despite being a hundred miles inland.

At Michael's nod, Trisha closed the door, just the four of them. She and Maloney traded a questioning glance, then sat down across from the "boys." Then Michael indicated for Billy to speak.

"There are presently six ships and fifty-three hostages being held by the Somali pirates. The longest holding period of these is two years, the newest, three weeks. Present demands for combined ransom are well over fifty million dollars U.S."

Trisha had to swallow hard. Somalia was rated as the most dangerous and most corrupt country in the world. Not a good place to be a hostage. And Billy had walked in there undercover.

"We know that at least four of these ships and forty-two of the hostages are either held by the northern pirate lords of Galkayo or others under their direct control. This includes the ship of the hostages we rescued last month. Two of the ships and the other hostages are being held by southern pirates that we know less about."

Michael zoomed the image back and pointed to the small red triangles along the coast south of Mogadishu near Kismayo.

"These two southern ships are being held by a totally different clan than the others. We feel that we can set an operation here in the north without causing further problems in the south because the clans hate each other and would never cooperate in anything. Command concurs."

Command. So they'd already sent their idea up to the Pentagon for approval and gotten it back. This was no idle planning session; a live operation was being proposed here.

Michael pointed to the four triangles located along the northern coast.

"We feel that if we can strip the prisoners and ships from these northern pirate lords in a single strike, their position will be sufficiently weakened so that growing pressure from domestic governments as well as clan elders may significantly curb future activities."

The four northern triangles representing captured ships that were spread across six hundred kilometers. Farthest north, the idiot son's sightseeing yacht was still parked in Bosaso. A small coastal merchant ship at Eyl lay anchored at a seaside hamlet partway down the coast. Both were controlled by Garowe. This despite the Darod clan, which controlled the northern province of Puntland, insisting they had eradicated piracy from their shores.

The last two, a small tanker and a midsized container ship, were anchored close ashore to Hobyo near the middle of the Somali coast. It was on the part of the coast closest to the inland city of Galkayo where the Hawiye clan made no such claims of altruism.

A lot of problems spread out over four hundred miles of coastline, not even counting the Kismayo ships. That's when Trisha figured out what was going on. They weren't talking about prevention. Until now, the patrols had only been concerned with what happened out at sea, preventing more piracy by driving potential ship-nappers back to shore or carting them off to an Ethiopian or Ugandan jail. Or burial if they resisted.

"You're talking about rescue."

Maloney looked up at her, startled. She hadn't caught on just yet.

Michael merely nodded. "Sharp as ever, Trisha. That's exactly the mission that we've been authorized to research. The problem is that we need to get better intelligence on the ground than we've had to date. We were able to rescue the hostages in Bosaso only because of Lieutenant Bruce's willingness to go undercover and find out that information."

"You're not going back in!" Her blood ran cold as she faced Billy. "Being nearly killed once in Somalia wasn't enough for you? Forget about it. You can't go." She had a personal stake in him now. He was important to her, even though she wasn't quite sure in what way. Didn't matter. She was putting her foot down.

Billy gave one of those soft smiles that always melted

her and she fought against it, rising back to her feet to do so.

Then he said, "I'm not going alone, and you're the one taking us." And she fell back into her chair when her knees let go.

—⁓—

Trisha still couldn't believe she was doing this as she swung in from the northwest of Galkayo. She'd circled far and wide to be clear of the city. And she was flying alone to conserve weight. At least alone in the cabin.

Back on the *Peleliu*, the crew chiefs had done a quick change on the *May*. Pulled off her rockets and miniguns. The two big ammo cans that normally sat behind Trisha's seat were replaced with an interior fuel tank for extended range. Her only weapons would be her handgun and her FN-SCAR rifle, neither of which she'd have a free hand to use unless she wound up on the ground. And if that happened, things would have gone seriously wrong.

A special rig had been hung from the anchor point for the munitions struts and the skids. On either side of the chopper, their big knobby tires exactly even with her skids, now hung a pair of 250 cc dirt bikes that looked like they were one-twenty-fives. They were beat, battered, disreputable, and might once have been of Russian or Indian manufacture. That was before the Special Ops mechanics began tinkering with the engines. They were now highly geared, tough-as-hell racing motorcycles that only *looked* like crap.

"Two minutes," she called to Michael and Billy over the headsets. Two minutes until the scheduled

2:00 a.m. drop in central goddamn nowhere a dozen miles northeast of Galkayo. They'd found a very distinct pillar of stone in the desert not far from a road, really a dirt track, which was what described most roads in this country. She would be coming in behind the pillar, masking vision and sound from the road, just in case there was someone on this remote stretch at this late hour.

Ten thousand feet above, Lola and her crew flew the *Vengeance* as both spotter and serious weapons backup if trouble occurred. It felt good knowing *Vengeance* was up there, especially with all the heavy weapons stripped off the *May*.

Trisha glanced back at Billy, who sat astride his motorcycle on the pilot's side of her chopper. He'd pulled off his helmet and hung it inside the chopper's passenger area. Now he wore a bandana and special sunglasses that looked mirrored on the outside to hide what his eyes were doing but offered a clear view from inside, even though it was dark out.

He again wore his battered M-16 and Russian handgun. She'd helped him strap both on just a few hours ago in the privacy of her cabin. He looked just like the battered mercenary she'd rescued from central Bosaso a month before. But now she knew him so well that it was as if he'd become a part of her when she wasn't paying attention.

Last night, after the long strategy session had finally wound down and no one could think of any additions to the plan, she and Billy had returned to her cabin in silence. Neither of them had spoken. She hadn't asked any of her thousand questions, figuring the man had enough on his mind. Billy kept his own counsel, as he was inclined to do.

They had made slow, gentle love, the kind two people make when they're each afraid that they'll never see each other again. Yet another thing not to talk about. They had lain awake and unmoving through the long day, her head on his shoulder, her leg across his hips. Billy spoke as night approached once again.

"I have to go. I don't have a choice."

Nine words. Nine words, and Trisha's only option was to accept them at face value. She'd finally nodded, acknowledging that whatever else was true, she had no words to fight with. And no desire to do so.

He and Michael were no longer wired into the helicopter's intercom, so she couldn't give them the ten-second warning. If she had a copilot, she could remove a hand from the cyclic long enough to flash a "1-0" signal—one finger, then closed fist—out the door for him to see, but flying solo she needed both hands and both feet. A moment later, exactly on time even without the signal, she could feel the chopper wiggle side to side as the two men jammed down hard on their kick-starters.

The dirt bike engines roared awake loud enough to be heard over the rotors and turbine noise of her engine. Billy and Michael revved them once, twice, then her skids touched the ground.

Heads ducked low over their handle bars so that they were well below her spinning rotors, Billy and Michael were beating dust trails to the south before the Little Bird even fully settled. The sudden loss of load popped the chopper back into the air, and she pulled up on the collective to continue the climb. Time on Somali soil… under one second.

Just after they cleared the edge of her rotors, Billy raised his hand in salute, then he was gone.

Rolling right and staying low, she was gone as well.

―――

Three nights now, Trisha had sat behind the rock pillar in the Somali desert. Three nights in a row from 2:00 a.m. to 4:00 a.m., she'd squatted northwest of Galkayo, wondering if Michael and Billy were coming back tonight. If they were alive to do so. There had been no transmissions, nor were any planned. They did have radios embedded in their bikes' structure, but would only use those in a dire emergency.

Had their ploy worked? They'd certainly rehearsed it enough.

She and Lola had listened while Billy gave the pitch they'd been working on for a day or so. Maybe if she hadn't bugged out after their sparring match down in the ship's hold, she would have distracted Billy and all this wouldn't be happening. He and Michael wouldn't have had time to bond over this crazy idea. But instead, Billy had his mercenary act down smooth. Even convincing her that he was already someone else, mostly, though they'd been sitting in the *Peleliu* briefing room.

"If I can track down the pirate leader at his home in Galkayo, my story to him will go something like this: Yeah. I was, uh, busy, you know, with a lady friend, when those choppers came through. Real sorry to have missed that show. Maybe if I'd been in on it, it all

woulda come out differently. Anyway, after I saw the
mess they left behind, I decided the best idea was to bug
the hell out of Bosaso.

"But I wanted to hook back up with whoever sponsored that crew. We were doing just fine up there until
those choppers showed. I want another shot at them.
Hunting around Garowe, I ran into an old buddy of mine
from the Congo days." It was one of the places both
Billy and Michael had served, though on different missions, so they could both talk convincingly about fighting there. It was also a notorious tour for mercenaries.
"Name's Mickey. We didn't have much luck in Garowe,
so we came down to Galkayo hoping to find ya."

Somehow his voice and manners had shifted. He'd
looked less "Billy the SEAL" and more "Bill the
Mercenary" who just might be a little wired on the
ubiquitous Somali drug khat and might be a low-lifer,
but had seen so many battles that he would be eager to
find another. Just another adrenaline junkie hooked on
war. Even Michael managed to shift from his quiet, calm
self to a slightly dumb and nasty-looking piece of work,
despite not saying anything. Just a change of attitude
and body language.

And Billy was far safer with Michael along than if
he were traveling by himself. But no matter how many
times Trisha assured herself of that, she was still sitting
here in the desert suffering over it.

And what if something more did happen between her
and Billy? Without defining what "more" might be, it
was pretty clear that nothing long term would work. One
reassignment and they might never see each other again.
Honestly, they were just hooking up for Operation Heavy

Hand and then he'd swim off to another SEAL mission or she'd be SOARing into the Colombian jungle. That kept it light and easy. Which was good.

It just didn't feel good.

She stewed on that a while, as the clock moved from 03:07 to 03:15. Damn, how time dragged when you were having fun sitting by yourself in a shutdown chopper on a cold desert night.

The problem was, they had left "light and easy" behind the day she chose to show up for his mother's funeral. And they'd traveled a long way further since then.

Her radio crackled. "Vehicles headed your direction."

"Roger." Without more information from Lola hovering ten thousand feet overhead, there was no way to know what to do. This had now happened four times over the last three nights. Someone traveling the road at night, three vehicles from the north and one from Galkayo in the south. Individual vehicles were rare outside the cities in Somalia, but they happened. Pirates or drug bosses, among others, traveled in groups, usually with a technical somewhere in the mix ready to shoot whoever might be stupid enough to bother them.

Waiting in silence, she only kept power to the radios. But now, with traffic approaching, she powered up the other systems so she'd be ready to start the engines quickly if necessary. If the traffic just went by, she'd power back down and keep waiting.

"Go hot!" The command came down from Lola, and Trisha had the turbine spinning up before Lola even got out the next word. "We've got a pair of motorcycles running at high speed. A squad of three vehicles coming fast behind, half a mile back. Can't tell if it's a chase or if they're rushing to Garowe. On your position in four minutes."

It was pitch dark and the moon had long since set. Trisha's night-vision gear came up, covering the inside of her visor with its detailed gray images revealing the few bushes and the dry rolling landscape. She wouldn't be able to see the road until she was in the air and out from behind her rock where she'd been hiding the Little Bird.

The main rotor began spinning faster and making noise. Yes, the *May* was a stealth chopper, but she was far from silent.

And did they want a pickup, or were they just in the lead of the other vehicles? She didn't want to be "blowing" Billy's cover again. They already had enough reasons to be pissed at each other.

"I'm going to give them the option," she informed the *Vengeance*. "I'll park ahead and either they'll board or blow by."

"Roger. Descending to five thousand for cover." That would put the convoy just marginally in range of the *Vengeance*'s miniguns. But it also placed them under a dozen seconds from joining the fray up close and personal if things went ugly.

Trisha had the *May* aloft while the vehicles were still two minutes out. She flew thirty seconds in their direction, then turned facing north and settled right in the middle of the lane just past a small rise in the road. She kept the rotors spinning at full speed, but dead flat. They wouldn't stir up any more dust that way. And between the dust her landing had stirred and the bluff, no one would see the disk of sparks made by the dust and sand as it pinged off the rotors.

She had less than a hundred yards of visibility aft because of the rise in the road, so all she could do was wait.

"Fifteen seconds," Lola informed her.

Trisha tried not to watch the clock in the corner of her visor or count the seconds, but her whole body was so tensed and ready for action that she could practically see each second drawn out as its own piece of reality. She had the dial on her ADAS camera spun to show the aft view along one side of her visor.

An impossibly long time later, the two motorcycles crested the rise, actually catching a little air in the process. She was glad she'd parked the extra hundred yards downslope so that they didn't loft into her spinning blades.

She blinked on her running lights, the white stern beacon and the red and green sidelights, so they'd see her.

The motorcycles split to race to either side of her.

Would they speed by and then she'd have to bug out fast, or would they—

The bikes slammed into the side carriers still moving so fast that she didn't know why the riders didn't go over the handlebars. Their impetus actually shoved the chopper forward several inches.

She didn't need Billy's shout of "Go!" to get gone. She doused the running lights and yanked up on the collective. Before she was a dozen feet up, she heard a hand slap against the chopper's skin, first on one side, then the other. They'd latched the bikes in and she could safely maneuver now. Back down to five feet above the sand and scrub brush, she banked to the right hoping that the dark would cover her dust trail departing the roadway.

"Convoy crossing your point of departure in

forty-five seconds," Lola announced as if she were at
a country fair.

They were three thousand yards out when Lola called
down, "They're cresting the rise… And… Three cheers
for the home team. Ground vehicles past your pickup
position and continuing north."

Trisha aimed for the coast as Billy came on the intercom. He must have his helmet on.

"Go back to the road, ahead of the convoy by ten
miles, and find a bad spot in the road."

She wanted to ask, but Billy's voice indicated he was
still in full-on mission mode. So, against her better in-
stincts, she informed *Vengeance* of the course change as
she curved off her beeline for the coast and headed back
toward the road at an angle to the north.

It was harder estimating what was ten miles ahead
of the moving convoy than it was finding a bad spot in
the road. The roads of Somali were rarely paved and,
outside of cities, required four-wheel drive and a strong
spine to navigate. Out here, there was more pothole than
road in some places. She found a dry river wash down
in a small valley. The bigger boulders had been cleared
to the side, so a bike would probably have to be walked
over the remaining cobbles to be safe.

"Do you have any demolition charges?" Michael
this time.

"Just the ones to destroy the chopper in case it goes
down in bad territory." Every SOAR chopper was not
only a valuable asset, but also a dangerous one. Even
if it could no longer fly, its sophisticated weapons and
controls would have immense value on the black market,
and facing a jury-rigged minigun mounted on a technical

wasn't something any pilot wanted to contemplate. So they all flew with enough explosives to demolish the chopper if needed. And every pilot was trained to do just that as an option of last resort.

Michael came forward, inching along the skid and holding tightly onto the door frame. She compensated with the cyclic for the shift of his weight. He leaned in through the copilot's door, his eyes asking her the question.

"Lower left side of console and just behind my head against the ceiling." The former explosive was big enough to take care of the electronics and any weapons in the forward part of the compartment. The latter would blow the turbine and rotor mechanisms to smithereens. If she'd had the heavy weapons out on the hardpoints, there'd be two more smaller charges embedded in the pylons, one to either side, to destroy those.

Michael reached down and pulled the block of C4 off the console and the one over her head as well. It felt slightly odd for them to be gone. She could see trying to explain the problem to her parents, being uncomfortable because she now had one less way to blow herself up in case she crashed. No way to make a civilian understand that.

"Detonators and remote control are in my right thigh pouch."

As soon as Michael slid back into position, Billy moved forward along the skid on his side. He pulled the detonators and remote, squeezed her thigh reassuringly, and was gone again.

"Hover twenty feet up over the rocks about thirty feet from the road."

She slid into place and waited five seconds.

"Okay, tip your nose down hard."

When she did, the two motorcycles shot forward off their mounts and tumbled toward the rocks below. She almost screamed, but caught herself when she saw there were no bodies. She'd expected they were dumping something to explode, but hadn't had time to think of what. Of course it would have to be the bikes. Each bike also still had a machine gun resting across the handlebars, sure evidence the drivers had been there if they chose to inspect the fire, but not too closely.

Then she fully understood the scenario they were building and turned down the arroyo to the east. When she was fifty yards gone, they detonated the bikes. At the last second, she remembered to warn the *Vengeance*.

"Fire in the hole!" The explosion sent a fireball skyward. Even at her present distance and increasing, they were peppered with small gravel and bits of bike pinging loudly off the chopper's skin. She hoped none hit her two passengers clinging to the chopper out on the skids. The extra fuel tank would allow them only the smallest part of the rear cargo space to let them lean in and shield themselves.

A glance backward in the ADAS revealed that the bikes burned furiously, sending a pillar of fire into the night sky that would be easily visible to the approaching convoy, now barely two miles distant. Hopefully it would still be burning badly enough that the people in the convoy wouldn't look overly hard for bodies. The departure of the black stealth helicopter running fast to the east in the bottom of the arroyo would be invisible.

Michael and Billy had apparently been leading the

convoy but wanted to appear dead by accident. Crashing and burning the bikes in the rocks just to the side of the road—as if they'd missed the arroyo's proper crossing point in the darkness—was a great ploy.

Trisha didn't ease up on the controls, keeping it right at maximum throttle the whole way to the coast. So low that she had to dodge the taller bushes and the occasional tree. She couldn't even risk a glance to look back at Billy, though he'd be clinging to the chopper only a few feet behind her.

"Hi, guys." Trisha greeted them over the intercom.

"Thanks for the ride." Michael.

"Hey, O'Malley." Billy. She thought she detected a private warmth in the way he said it. If anyone else said anything, she didn't hear it because she had to concentrate on the nap-of-the-earth flying without any copilot to feed her engine and position status.

When the *Peleliu* came into sight, Trisha knew two things. First, she loved this kind of flying, right out on the edge of the envelope. And second, no matter how much she didn't want to be involved with Billy, she was.

Her chopper hadn't been the only thing that flew so fast tonight.

Her heart did too.

Chapter 25

BILL FELT LIKE HE'D BEEN STRUCK BY A MAELSTROM from the moment they hit the *Peleliu*'s deck.

Trisha had given him a welcome-back kiss the minute they were off the chopper. Even as the *Vengeance* settled beside them and Michael came around from the other side, she hadn't let up.

"Hi," she'd finally said when she freed his lips.

"Hi," was all he could think to reply. He couldn't believe how much he'd thought about her on the mission and how much better she tasted and felt in real life than in his imagination.

"That's twice now."

"What's twice now?" He breathed her in, the best smell in days.

"Twice I've saved your ass."

"Appreciated." She'd done it perfectly too.

"At least you're thanking me this time."

And that was the last word they spoke in private for the next ten hours. The priority first was the debrief and the next plan. Phase Two.

They took over the big briefing room. No one even left to go to the officers' mess. Instead, sandwiches were delivered. Bill dumped water over a napkin and scrubbed at his face, removing at least a little of three days and nights of Somali grime. Rather than the one screen in the planning room, the briefing room sported three massive wall screens. He brought up the map of Somalia on one side and set close-ups of the four captured ships in the north on the other. In the center, he put up a split screen of Galkayo and Garowe.

Everyone had arrived long before he had a chance to finish his second hamburger, and he barely remembered eating the first one, it had gone down so fast. The room's perimeter chairs were filled with SOAR and Delta crews. The SOAR crew leads were at the main table: O'Malley, Lola Maloney, and Air Mission Commander Archie Stevenson. Also at the table were Lieutenant Commander Boyd Ramis; the head of the Ranger team, Lieutenant Clint Barstowe; and Petty Officer Sly Stowell.

"I was only slumming by pumping fuel with the grapes," Sly addressed Michael as the leader, clearly speaking one warrior to another. "My normal job is running the landing craft. I'm senior man on the crew, so they sent me to answer any questions if there's a 'by sea' element to your plans."

Even the little girl showed up. No one commented on it as she sat in a seat by her mother, so he figured it wasn't up to him to chase her out. And he wasn't terribly interested in getting on the wrong side of the country's top marksman anyway.

Michael indicated that Bill should take the lead once everyone had gathered.

"Okay." Bill took a big bite of his burger before setting it aside. They'd eaten well by Somali standards, and it had really sucked. He and Michael had entertained the pirates by comparing Somalia with their other "mercenary" tours. Amazing how he'd forgotten in his short

month aboard ship to appreciate that the Navy at sea ate
really well. He chewed fast and swallowed.

"Sorry if I'm covering common ground for some
of you, but I want us all on the same chart here." He
grabbed a couple of fries and shoved his plate aside.

"I spent three months in Somalia trying to locate who
the power players were among the pirates. That is easier
said than done. Half of my leads led to the old fisherman pirates who are no longer in power. They just want
to sit around chewing khat and talking about the good
old days when the ships weren't armed and the pickings
were lush. There were times they had a dozen or more
ships up for ransom and no one was trying to kill them
over it. That the ransoms were a tenth what they are
today was only grounds for envy."

He went to the map of the whole country, an upside-
down L-shape around the Horn of Africa, so that he
could point out his route. "I came into the Mog in
the south along with the Ugandan reinforcements for
ANISOM. Then I detached myself and began working
my way north. Al-Shabaab terrorists are operating in the
south and they're outside my mandate."

"And outside the realm of reasonable survivability,"
O'Malley filled in.

"True." He actually appreciated the interruption
and gave her a nod of thanks. It was often hard, due
to standard military training, to shift from briefing to
brainstorming. But with the caliber of people in this
room, they wouldn't need much more encouragement
than that. O'Malley had just broken the ice for them.
Though he still had more to say before they began the
brainstorming of Phase Two.

"It took me three months to work my way into the Galkayo teams. The Bosaso thing was a fluke. Those guys were beginners and weren't expected to catch anything, then they nabbed that pleasure yacht. Any self-respecting merchant marine with a flare pistol could have chased those guys off. A fellow named Hassan Abdullah Abdi sent me—as a test, I assume—to oversee and advise them, along with a fellow named Abshir. That's the guy O'Malley shot while saving my ass."

Got him a bit of a laugh, though Trisha looked grim. She'd shot many more than that when she took out the building and the technicals, though that hadn't been one on one with a rifle. Or maybe it was recalling his stubbornness. That particular trait was something they both had a serious dose of, and it wasn't helping them a bit personally. He'd have to work on that.

"Michael and I were not only able to get back in touch with Abdi, but Michael was able to convince him that the U.S. incursion was just a first attack and that the fleet would be hitting Garowe next. My best information said that Garowe was where a third of the present hostages from the other three ships are being held. Our convoy was a rush job to the north to extract those hostages before the supposed U.S. attack."

Trisha burst out laughing. Damn, but the woman was sharp.

He exchanged a glance with Michael who simply nodded. They'd slept as little as possible the last three days, standing watch-and-watch in case their identity slipped somehow. In the darkest hour of the second night, they'd started talking about Trisha.

It had taken a bit for Bill to catch on that she and

Michael had been more than just friends at one time; not that he actually said so. No wonder the man was so bloody protective of her. But that hadn't turned out to be the issue. Michael really did respect and care about her that much.

This time he didn't have to state the message as baldly, but that night it became very clear that Michael had a close eye on one Lieutenant William Bruce. That's what the fight in the bowels of the ship had been, a one-on-one test of skill as well as a worthiness test for someone Michael cared about. Was Bill good enough for fighting with on a team, and was he good enough for Trisha? That latter one was tough to answer.

Her quick perception of the game they'd played on Abdi was one more proof that all of that speed she had wasn't just physical. It was mental as well. Damn, but he liked being around this woman.

"You tricked them into getting all of the hostages together so that we'd be able to extract them in a single snatch." Trisha practically crowed it out with delight.

"Two locations. Inland at Galkayo is one and the other lies along the coast at Hobyo where two of the ships are anchored. Abdi had been looking for an excuse to take down the Garowe leader for a while anyway. We were riding lead as the most expendable muscle if we hit any bad checkpoints. Don't think they would have liked two white guys on motorcycles much when we arrived, so we really appreciated you giving us a lift."

"We've been keeping a UAV on the convoy," AMC Stevenson reported. "They had three Range Rovers and six technicals. They spent under a minute checking out your demise at the arroyo, not even going close enough to see if you guys were hurt."

"Yeah, about what we hoped. Abdi isn't long on sympathy for the dead. Probably saw it as a neat way to deal with the problem of whether or not to trust us." Bill was even more thankful for Trisha's neat flying skills than he had been.

"We were able to track them," Stevenson continued. "They had a brief but ferocious gun battle in southwest Garowe. They are now proceeding back toward the highway with two Rovers, five technicals, and a big van that could hold about a dozen people, more if they're packed tight, but with the surviving Range Rovers, that might not have been necessary. We do have time to launch and intercept in the desert if we depart in the next thirty minutes."

Half the room went electric, but Bill patted his hands downward and they calmed slowly.

"If we hit them, we'll never see the bulk of the hostages again. This is only a third of them and Hassan Abdi was not traveling with us. There were only fifteen in Garowe. We're better off hitting them at a collection point, even if they will be more heavily protected."

"I agree." Michael's first words at the briefing confirmed Bill's plan. The people who had been ready to leap into action moments before settled uneasily into their chairs. It was hard to let a present opportunity pass in favor of a possible future one. Bill could feel the need for action, but it would be premature at this moment.

He and Michael had agreed on a timeline and the rough outlines of a plan, just not how to pull it off.

"The problem," Michael continued, "is we estimate

that once they're back in Galkayo tonight, they'll hunker down through the day."

"But if they were smart," Trisha picked up the thought, "I'd bet they'll redistribute the hostages as soon as the moon sets after dark tonight."

"Exactly! We have"—Michael checked his watch—"about sixteen hours to form and execute a plan or we'll lose this second opportunity as well."

—∿∿—

Trisha hadn't been down to the well deck of the *Peleliu* before. Somehow it hadn't been a part of her "welcome aboard" tour. Actually her tour had been the "there's your bunk" tour. She'd crashed into it for twenty hours after the forty-hour trip from Tacoma, Washington.

They all followed Petty Officer Sly Stowell down two more decks than the level of her quarters and the officers' mess. It felt as if they were descending into the bowels of the ship or perhaps to the center of the earth.

"You said there were Smurfs here," she teased Billy who was following close behind.

"Nah, they prefer sunshine and daisies and all of that."

"Oh, that's a great comfort." She could feel the thirty thousand tons of steel squeezing in on her. It was one of those odd conundrums. She spent her flying hours in a space smaller than the reach of her arms, surrounded by the best technology America could provide. More than twenty distinct systems were available at her fingertips—from weapons to satellite communications. Sometimes she felt she was half cyborg. Here she was, free to move around in a massive steel ship a thousand times safer from attack, and she felt as if the steel walls were about to collapse in on her.

And when they reached the well deck, she felt even more anxious seeing the ocean wash through the rear half of the hull. The entire stern of the ship lay open right at water level. Several inches of water washed lazily from side to side. A wooden landing deck shimmered just below the surface. A seaman came around handing out heavy sound muffs.

"The well deck can be lowered and flooded deeper so that low-draft landing craft can be driven right into the ship." Sly sounded entirely too pleased and proud to have the ocean washing through the belly of his ship.

At the head of the landing craft well, a steep ramp led up into the heart of the ship. At the next level up was parking space for dozens of Humvees, APCs—armored personnel carriers, and even tanks.

At present all the *Peleliu* carried was a dozen APCs and two amphibious landing craft. The echoing emptiness of the helo hangar several decks above pervaded here as well.

"Watch this." Sly stopped them all halfway down the ramp, as if they were on the last bank of some cozy beach made of corrugated steel in the dark guts of the ship. He pointed out the wide open stern.

While they'd been in the planning session, morning had come to the Arabian Ocean. The golden glow still clinging to the horizon said that it was just dawn, while shadows across the open stern showed that they were facing south at the moment.

A small black dot appeared on the horizon. Trisha tried blinking, but it didn't disappear from her vision.

Billy, who'd come to stand close beside her, also was blinking and turning his head as he looked out. So they were both seeing it.

The well deck acted like a giant amplifier. The tiny splashing of the waves echoed about the space. But the open space was focused toward whatever was approaching. At first she heard a high buzzing that rapidly grew to a throaty roar as the black dot expanded into a low rectangle.

"Muffs," Sly shouted out.

She pulled hers on, which muted most of the noise, but it continued to build.

Then the approaching object resolved itself. She'd never seen one up close, not even in training. The LCAC, Landing Craft Air Cushion, was a hovercraft and it was heading their way fast.

"What's its speed?" It was growing larger fast. She had to shout over the focused roar as it was getting close now and showing no sign of slowing.

"Right now? She's running at about seventy knots. Not really pushing it much and she's lightly laden. She'll carry a dozen Humvees, a main battle tank, or about four hundred troops and their gear. Can still crack forty pretty easily then." Sly had to really shout the last of it to be heard.

Several of the people were stumbling backward, but Sly, Billy, and Michael were standing fast, so she stood with them, though she was desperately cringing inside.

In the last moments, the roar slackening not one bit, the LCAC zoomed up until it filled the expanse of the stern gate and blocked most of the morning light. It felt as if the landing craft was about to ram the ship, but then the LCAC cut her power abruptly. The large twin fans at her stern that had driven her forward now reversed. She slowed abruptly and nosed into the well deck dead center at an easy walking pace.

The craft moseyed up until she touched the base of the ramp and towered above them. The roar of her fans was almost painful despite the muffs. Then, with a sigh as her lift fans eased, she settled to the deck.

The tall front rubber bladder, looking ever so much like an angry child holding a mouthful of breath right before she screamed, abruptly deflated. The front of the ship, a tall steel wall, tilted toward them and landed with a clang on the well deck ramp not ten feet from them.

The thing was overwhelmingly huge. As it went silent, Sly pulled off his head muffs and waved them forward.

"There was no way to adequately explain this vehicle. I thought it better to show what it could do so that you could decide on its utility in this operation."

She estimated the width carefully. "I could land a Little Bird on this thing."

Sly nodded. "By about two feet to your rotor tips. Actually you could land one fore and one aft; she's long enough. But if you hit the least little wave you'd bang the side, and I'm not willing, nor is my precious baby certified, to allow you to scuff up my ship. I had something else in mind." Then he pulled out a piece of chalk and began sketching on the ship's deck plating.

Chapter 26

BILLY PITCHED INTO TRISHA'S BUNK, THE POOR MAN positively weaving. He lay there like the dead while Trisha leaned on the door frame and watched him.

Damn the man for screwing up her personal life. He was making her feel things she didn't appreciate. She'd never before cared if a guy shared his past with her or not. She'd actually preferred not. This time Trisha was pissed at him because he wasn't telling her all of his past.

And she'd long since accepted that there could be nothing long term with any guy as long as she was in the service, because her life was mission based. If she wasn't in Somalia or some other hellhole, she'd be off on training assignments.

There was a reason that most of her relationships didn't survive more than a few weeks. She'd never understood the guys who married a civilian. That always seemed downright cruel to her. The wife never knowing if her husband was still alive, because Special Ops missions were often planned and performed under communication blackouts. Maybe the women liked being alone, but Trisha didn't think so. It was a hard road that way. No wonder so few of the families survived.

Some made it work. Hell, there were three couples in SOAR right now. Lola had Tim Maloney who flew with Dusty. Connie and Big John, Dusty's other mechanic. Kee Stevenson not only had her Air Mission Commander husband, but even had her adopted daughter along most of the time because as AMC, Archie didn't fly on the front line during missions anymore.

But what place could she and Billy have, even if they did want something longer term? Once this assignment ended, they were in different branches of the service. Even their limited vacation time probably wouldn't overlap. Once, maybe twice a year they could get together for a good tumble between the sheets, which with any other man would be enough. Not with Billy the SEAL.

She'd thought he was asleep, but he lazily raised a hand and waved her toward him. Trisha wouldn't join him since it would just increase the hurt when this ended. Which was inevitable.

That resolve lasted about three seconds, then she stepped over and curled up beside him. They sighed with relief in unison.

Fully clothed, they lay together, and it was the closest she'd ever felt to anyone, far closer than naked sex. His hand brushed up and down her back, his heart loud against her ear. Despite their difference in stature, they fit together so well. How could she ever resist that?

"I shouldn't have said that before," his voice rumbled in his chest beneath her arm.

"What?" Though she knew. Normally would have been glad to toss it back in his face. But now a new and different Trisha had slipped into her skin, and pretending that she hadn't been hurt by his withholding from her somehow made it so that she truly was less hurt. It was his past and his business; they weren't tied at the hip.

"You're a goofball, Irish." He knew exactly what she was doing.

"And proud of it."

His low chuckle was a wonderful sound.

"I don't like talking about Somalia. My dad died there."

"You told me. During the Battle of Mogadishu in 1993. I remember." It was a day that was also burned into the brain of every SOAR pilot on the planet. Two forty-million-dollar Black Hawks had been knocked out of the sky by rocket-propelled grenades worth only a couple hundred dollars each. And in that moment, a thirty-minute operation within moments of successful completion became an eighteen-hour disaster of epic proportions.

Five pilots and crew chiefs had died and had their bodies dragged around the streets. Another had been held in captivity for ten days despite a desperate need for medical attention. Six Deltas and an equal number of Rangers had died as well. Three others dead and more than eighty wounded.

Estimates placed the Somali dead between three hundred and three thousand. The date was still celebrated in Somalia as "Ranger Day," the day the Somali clan militia beat the United States Army. And they had.

Trisha had never thought before about the parallels of an undertrained, over-armed militia beating the U.S. Army and the USS *Constitution* beating the British. Now wasn't the time to be bringing the idea up with Billy.

"You asked if I ever did anything not in the best interests of the team."

"Shh." Trisha brushed her hand over his chest. "It's okay. Just let it rest." She wondered if he was aware just how tightly he was holding her, as if she were some lifeline he couldn't quite grasp.

His voice was tight when he at last found the words. "I'm the last person you want in Somalia. I volunteered, practically forced my way in when the opportunity came up. But I don't have a cool head about it. I still want to hunt down and kill every single shooter from that day. I don't care that there were tens of thousands of them. I want them taken down so badly. It's not right. I shouldn't be there. I can't be trusted."

She'd have sat up to look at him if she could, but his desperate grasp wouldn't let her move. It barely let her breathe. His voice was ragged with the exhaustion and the strain.

"Look, tough guy. I'm going to ask you a couple questions you asked me once."

"Okay." Billy's hand actually shook where it wrapped around her. What did it take to make a SEAL's hands shake? Had the man ever been more vulnerable than this moment? She'd bet his hands had been steady enough when he buried his mother. He'd been hurt, sad, but somehow this was worse for him. She didn't need to know how, but she hoped she could help him fix it.

"Have you missed a single mission because of this?"

"No." His voice was soft.

"Have you held back or hesitated or corrupted your mission even the least little bit since you volunteered for Somalia?"

"Never! I wouldn't do that."

"Didn't think so." She patted him on the chest and waited for him to remember that he had asked precisely those questions of her while she'd been freaking out over being shot.

It took a minute. Maybe two. Then his death grip around her waist eased enough for her to breathe again as he understood that he hadn't betrayed his own commitments to serving what he believed in.

A low chuckle rippled through him. "Okay, hotshot. I think you got me with that one."

"Have you made a single action of revenge for your father's death?"

"Not even that. As I said, you got me."

"No. I haven't had you yet, but I'm about to."

Bill didn't need more of an invitation than that.

Trisha O'Malley had worked under his skin like a drug until he couldn't stop needing her. He'd tried. For three days in Galkayo he'd done the dance with the pirates and done his best to forget about her, and it hadn't worked in the slightest.

She sat up and over his hips and started to strip down, but he stopped her. He wanted to enjoy this, because he had a bad feeling about tonight's mission. And he wanted to show this woman how truly amazing she was while he was still sure he had the chance.

He trapped her hands in his and pulled the lower hem of her shirt back into place. Then he began tracing her form through the fabric, smoothing out her T-shirt so that not a single wrinkle interfered with his investigation.

She glared at him with those crystalline blue eyes, but he ignored that. Her glares didn't scare him anymore. It was simply her instant-on temper response. He had been with a redhead or two in his time, but they had been calm, steady women. Actually one had been a total ditz worthy of the worst blond jokes, but very sweet. Few would dare accuse Trisha of being sweet, and she definitely had the fiery temper so often associated with her coloring. Maybe Bill was losing his mind, but he was thinking there was a very sweet woman deep down inside one Patricia O'Malley.

She might not like the name, but he did. It was more true to who she was on the inside. There was a quiet, thoughtful girl in there named Patricia who had sat silently with him beneath the maple trees of Vermont. Who had planted flower seeds upon his mother's grave and beamed at him when he'd imagined himself piloting the USS *Constitution* over the high seas. Patricia was the woman slowly melting in his arms.

He traced each rib as he worked his way up to follow the line of where ribs met breast, as sweet a curve as any that ever existed. When he let his fingertips map the terrain of her breasts, her eyes fluttered closed on a sigh.

This was a different woman. She'd always made love to him. Active, even aggressive, and occasionally wild. Now she was passive, letting herself become lost in the sensations of his investigation.

He shifted their position so slowly that perhaps she didn't even notice, until she lay back upon the narrow bed and he knelt on the floor beside her. He couldn't tell what he felt. Like a man at worship before the most amazing gift he'd ever been given, or like a lion toying with his prey before he devoured it. He'd started at the former and felt well assured that he'd get to the latter.

Trisha's hair was soft between his fingers. It had

grown in the month he'd known her, gone from a chop cut done with a knife when she was bored with it, to a soft frame for her exquisite face. At rest, she was also different, rubbing her cheek into his palm as he brushed the lightest of touches over her closed eyelids. Lips that were…

He sounded like he was on a mapping expedition. Well, maybe he was. Studying the terrain for possible strike and extraction zones, seeking out the strengths and weaknesses of what lay before him. Discovering responses that appeared to be a revelation to Trisha as well as to himself. He slowly stripped her bare and gloried in what he found, both the familiar and the new.

She gave herself to him, giving of her body and of who she was without holding back, without caution, without question. Absolute trust. It was the most incredible experience of his life. No one knew both the past and the present version of him. No one knew what drove him.

No one except Patricia O'Malley. And from her he received the absolute faith and surrender that didn't give an inch of ground but gave absolutely everything else. Too humbled to speak, he simply buried his face in her bare belly as he knelt before her. She slid her hands into his hair and simply held him there.

It was a long time before he removed his own clothes and set about devouring this woman and satisfying the both of them. A long time when he didn't think, didn't act, but simply existed in a space that wasn't one person and a team, but was two people together.

—∿—

Trisha knew she was done for when Billy rested his head on her bare stomach. She knew that against all odds and beliefs in how the world worked, she actually had found the one and only man for her. And it was scaring the shit out of her.

She felt his uneven breathing as emotions dug through him, emotions he might never be able to give voice to but that ran deeper than any ocean beneath a ship's keel.

Keeping her eyes closed, she let the images travel through her. Images of how he'd looked. Raging at her for rescuing him. In the sunlight of that waterfall in upstate Vermont as they swam and played. Naked, scarred, and so powerful it was impossible to credit except he was there before her, flesh and blood, warm and alive. And the way he looked at her when they made love, as if he could see all the way down into her soul.

When he moved over her, when he shifted from the tender investigation of her body, which had to be one of the most romantic things any lover had ever done for her, she wasn't ready for the flight of emotions.

As his mouth took her in, suckled upon her, she felt a draw all the way into her very core. She could imagine a child with this man. A child she had never wanted nor imagined until this moment. When he at long last drove into her, and he swallowed her helpless cry with his kiss, she felt truly joined to another for the first time in her life.

She'd never let him go. She wrapped her arms and legs about him, rising to his rhythm. Burning to his every touch, she finally exploded beneath him and he showered her with all the passion and desire that he normally kept locked so deep inside.

Chapter 27

Two more Black Hawks had flown in from the aircraft carrier during the daylight hours. They were Sea Hawks adapted for the Navy. The big change was that they had hinged tails for improved shipboard stowage. They also could be rigged for antisubmarine warfare as fast as the *May* could have her armament changed out. For this mission, these two birds were configured for simple transport.

With them aboard, the *Peleliu* was at its deck capacity without having to fold rotors or shift any craft down the elevators. It made the ship feel suddenly crowded and hectic. They'd also steamed within forty miles of the coast to improve flight times. No other assets were close enough to be in position in time, so it was the *Peleliu*'s operation.

At the preflight briefing, it became clear that the Navy guys were just as happy to leave the forward missions to SOAR. Not that they were any less gung-ho, but their equipment simply wasn't up to the rigors required by this mission. Had some mines that needed sweeping? They were your guys. Nap-of-the-earth flying in the dead of night into a hot battle zone and bringing everyone back out? That was the Night Stalkers.

"The plan is based on the same methods General Garrison used in the Battle of Mogadishu," Billy had told the briefing room.

Trisha was proud of him that he managed to say that without flinch or hesitation. It was a good plan that they'd found no way to improve on it even after sleeping on it. What little sleep any of them had gotten. She couldn't speak for the rest of the crew, but hers had been short. Actually, Lola's, Connie's, and Kee's husbands looked terribly pleased with themselves as well despite the late session last night, this morning, whatever it had been.

"Similar," Billy continued, "except for the addition of an amphibious assault on three key locations. We believe this mission will have a high probability of success. Unlike the Mog, all personnel will fly in full armor with night-vision gear, extra ammunition, and canteens. We also will be flying at night where our superior technology should create a significant advantage. We will not be caught unprepared this time."

There were many glances exchanged around the room. A couple of the senior guys on the *Peleliu* had been offshore for the Battle of Mog and powerless to help. The mess was partly caused because they'd flown during the daylight when the Tier One targets had been located, rather than waiting for the safety of night. And because they had assumed easy victory, they'd only gone prepared for an easy half-hour smash-and-grab operation. After eighteen hours of open warfare against thousands, food, water, ammunition, and medical supplies had been in desperately short supply.

Even after the briefing, when everyone was loading up on the flight deck, Billy stood in a whirlwind of constant questions. Everyone was turning to him, though he was far from the senior-ranked person involved.

Trisha watched as Michael arrived to clarify a point. Lieutenant Commander Boyd Ramis wandered over to report the ship's position. AMC Archie double-checked which chopper Bill would be on and how he wanted the assets spread. Rangers, Navy, Delta, SOAR, it didn't matter. They all came to him.

It was a miracle to watch. Bill had been aboard barely a month, but no one questioned whose operation it was. He personally had made a cohesive team of a wide range of some of the nation's top military assets. A born leader. She'd never seen him look better than all dressed in battle gear standing on the deck of the *Peleliu* with the sun setting behind him.

Heavy leather boots, khakis covered by an armored vest covered by desert camouflage and a utility belt that bulged with munitions. He again wore both a machine gun and a sniper rifle.

Trisha and Roland loaded up. The *May* was once again in her battle configuration, miniguns and rocket pods hanging to either side, and they checked her over extra carefully to make sure everything was ready.

They'd have twelve hours from sunset to sunrise. And for the half hour at either end, it would be best if they weren't over Somalia. They had debated about wanting to run the operation in the dead of night versus getting caught with their feet still on the ground at daybreak if something went wrong. It was decided that the latter was a greater risk, so they'd fly as soon as it was full dark and forego the advantage of a 3:00 a.m. attack.

Dusty James was the first one off, just past sunset. He was headed to an untracked stretch of desert most of the way from the coast at Hobyo to inland Galkayo. True desert, it received less than two inches of rain a year. That meant that even the Somalis who still belonged to nomadic clans—and there were many—would be unlikely to cross there.

Dusty and his transport Black Hawk, the *Vicious*, were delivering a crew of four to set up a FARP, a Forward Arming and Refueling Point. In this case, the FARP consisted of a large bladder of Jet A fuel, along with a couple of high-speed pumps for the Little Birds, and fresh ammo cans and rockets in case something went wrong and the battle got hot.

A C-130 would be off the coast in two hours in case a Black Hawk needed refueling. The Navy's Sea Hawks didn't carry midair refueling probes like their SOAR counterparts, so they each had long-range auxiliary tanks that they would draw down first and drop once empty.

Trisha already had the rotors spinning when Billy swung by to check on her.

"Hey, hotshot!"

"Hey, sailor!"

"Remember, you're my personal hammer. I want you off my left shoulder as much as possible."

"Loud and clear, Billy."

"That's Lieutenant Billy." He grinned at her.

Trisha saluted. "Yes sir, Mr. Lieutenant Billy the Scottish SEAL, sir."

"I love you."

She opened her mouth, but nothing came out. He'd said it just as casually as could be. No way she'd misheard it. She tried to respond, but couldn't figure out how. It was as if her nerves no longer remembered how to fire.

"I know, pretty strange," he continued blithely. "Bound to cause all kinds of problems. But it's true. I love you, Patricia O'Malley."

"Oh shit!" It was the only reply she could come up with.

"Yep!" He acknowledged her complete discomfiture with a knowing smile. "Gotta go." He kissed her, to which she could barely respond, and was gone.

Roland was eyeing her a bit strangely. But she couldn't even send him a Billy-sized scowl.

She was in so much trouble.

Chapter 28

Boyd had wanted Bill to stay on the *Peleliu* in the command center, but he'd refused. The only way he'd kept the ship's commander from ordering him to remain aboard was by insisting that he'd be more effective communicating and reacting if he was on site.

That had been one of the hard-won lessons from the Battle of Mogadishu—the communication lines had been too long. General to command control to air mission commander, then on wholly separate radios, often with different encryptions and a spread of frequencies, in order to talk to SOAR and the convoy. Beyond that, Delta and Rangers had been split off yet further, with individual team members dangling out in the wind. When a group leader was hit, that whole section had been cut off and coordination had collapsed even further.

That issue was mostly solved in the modern forces, but it was still a hot button for every student of modern military history. Keeping the communication chain as simple yet redundant as possible was a powerful motivator.

Bill did stick AMC Archie Stevenson aboard for the *Peleliu*'s commander. He felt a little guilty for doing that. But, with the two drones aloft, he would have an exceptional view. Also, like Mission Control to the Apollo capsules, it would allow the Navy to have just one voice to communicate with the people out on the front lines. He couldn't afford an extra bird for the AMC to circle high, either. Their assets on the ground and in the air were going to be thin as it was.

The real truth was, Bill was a SEAL. And all of a SEAL's training was about being in the field. He never understood the UAV pilots who could fly their drones from the Utah bunkers. The mental disconnect was too far, and Bill often wondered if that was one of the stresses that led to such a high burnout rate for them.

He climbed aboard the front left end of the outside bench seat on Dennis's *Merchant of Death*. Rather than tying himself in, he just faced forward so that he could wrap a leg around either side of the bench.

Michael climbed aboard *Mad Max*, then shot him a casual salute that he returned. In moments, a D-boy sat at the point of the other side bench seats. The remaining four positions on both birds were then taken by Rangers. They'd lost some of their swagger during Michael's "Lessons from the Mog" lecture. He'd been a first-year private for that outing, hell of an indoctrination.

While waiting for the last of the loading and pilot checks, Bill had a moment to himself. The first one since he'd woken to see Trisha smiling down at him. She'd gotten him half-aroused while he still slept. Once awake, the other half got with the program quickly. It may have been less than five minutes from waking to shower, all they could afford, but she had made it a spectacular five minutes. He cursed the Navy for making shipboard showers too small for even the most creative of couples to share.

He'd never told a woman other than his mother that he loved her. He'd actually never expected to say it aloud to anyone else. Somehow the picture in his head

had included a woman who would simply understand
how he felt about her and it would be enough. As stupid
as he knew it sounded, he'd imagined that late in the
shrouding darkness of the night, she would whisper it
into his ear, expressing the feeling for both of them.

Bill had certainly never pictured leaning into a roaring chopper and practically shouting out, so that he
could be heard by her copilot as well, that he loved a
pint-sized lieutenant of the U.S. Army's SOAR. Or that
her response would be, "Oh shit!" Of course with Trisha
O'Malley, that was so absolutely true to form that it
made him feel like everything was right with the world.

He was just as glad there was no one coming up to him
with any more questions or they'd ask why he was grinning like a goon as they lifted into the night sky on one
of the most dangerous missions he'd ever been a part of.

———~~~———

Trisha flew up between the oil tanker *Bateau* and the
cargo ship *Evangeline* at exactly twenty hundred hours
and zero seconds. Her altitude was less than ten feet
above the waves, just five hundred yards off the coastal
town of Hobyo. No radar on these pirated ships would
be able to pick her out of the surface clutter, even if they
were running.

Roland flipped on the jammer that had been added
to their usual load and ran through the line of several
different band antennas running along the *May*'s tail
boom. Now there was no way that any communications
would be sent from either ship—not radio, cell phone,
or anything else. The only unblocked frequencies were
those used by the team's encrypted radios.

Less than five seconds behind her, *Max* and *Merchant* slid to a hover over the command deck of either ship. Fast ropes, two inches of braided wool fifty-feet long, were dropped to dangle from the hangers on either side of the chopper. Four Rangers, wearing heavy gloves so that they didn't burn their hands, grabbed on and descended them like fire poles. They landed on the ships' decks three seconds later, their weapons drawn within a second of landing.

Max, *Merchant*, and *May* all lifted to a hundred feet and set up an overlapping circling pattern that would cover both ships as well as make the choppers exceptionally poor targets. The three Delta operators and Billy, who had remained perched at the front end of their benches on *Max* and *Merchant*, wielded their sniper rifles like scythes. Trisha and Roland sat ready to unleash their miniguns if needed, but the pirates never knew what hit them. Half went down fighting, and the other half came out with their empty hands in the air.

By the time the Navy LCAC hovercraft surged up alongside to board another dozen Rangers onto each ship, both of them were taken back from the pirates. The additional Rangers rounded up the survivors and set perimeter security on each ship. Once they both announced all clear, Trisha switched off the jamming gear and the three choppers dove back to wave height. They circled wide around Hobyo and headed inland to their main target of Galkayo.

Less than a minute later, Lola Maloney reported that the *Vengeance,* with two Delta snipers aboard, and a SEAL team in a high-speed Special Operations Craft-Riverine gun boat from the aircraft carrier *Harry S.*

Truman had taken back the small merchant moored off Eyl a hundred and fifty miles to the north with no loss of life. They'd caught four pirate guards fast asleep.

That ship had been held for over a year, so the chances of a shore watch were considered low and the ship got under way toward international waters immediately. Even if its departure was noted, the pirates on shore wouldn't be likely to connect it to any larger plan or attack. The pirates would be more likely to wait for morning to see if the merchant ship had sunk like the container ship *MV Albedo* had in July 2013.

The two ships captured by Hobyo would have to wait within sight of the shore until the strike team sent the all clear from the inland strike at Galkayo to free the hostages. The chance that someone would miss the Hobyo ships at eight at night was too high. They needed the element of surprise at the Galkayo site if they wanted to take the hostages without a major gun battle.

Trisha and the other two Little Birds headed for the FARP to refuel in the desert. Lola would cut south to meet up with the C-130 tanker plane for a midair refuel before turning inland to meet them. The Little Birds didn't have that kind of capacity.

They stayed low, following the terrain tightly. They were actually in more danger of being spotted by a nomad with a satellite phone than by radar in this country, at least until they got nearer to Galkayo airport, but there was no reason to expose themselves more than they had to.

The first stage of Billy's plan had gone off without a hitch.

"High five!" Trisha called over the intercom. She

removed her right hand from the cyclic for a moment and Roland took his left off the collective. They smacked palms, then both put their hands back on the controls and returned to flying fast and low.

Bill climbed down off the narrow bench seat of the Little Bird as soon as they reached the FARP and landed. He tried shaking one leg out, then the other, but the feeling wasn't returning quickly. Everyone wore night-vision gear, so the only light in the area was an infrared beacon. A native could walk by within a few hundred feet and not see anything on the sand.

The ground team scooted him out of the way to begin refueling the bird. The thick rubber bladder was four feet by eight and about eighteen inches high and filled with Jet A fuel. Even as they began fueling up *Merchant of Death*, they were unrolling another hose toward the *Mad Max*.

Someone came up and offered him a box of M118LR cartridges for his sniper rifle. Someone was being efficient; they were even the long-range spec rounds that would be best for his rifle. So he began refilling the magazine he'd partially burned up during the taking of the Hobyo ships.

Michael came up beside him and took a half-dozen rounds out of the box and began refilling his own. He wasn't moving any better than Bill was, which made him feel a bit better about it. Michael was dressed much like Bill, except that he wore the uncovered MICH helmet favored by the Deltas. He had the four-tube night-vision gear seated in the front clip of the helmet and had it tipped down over his eyes. Like an alien with four eyestalks, the tubes cast a soft green light back around Michael's eyes.

"Long damn ride," Bill greeted him and checked that the twenty-round magazine was full. Then he slapped it on his chest armor, to make sure the cartridges were well seated, and placed it in the rifle.

Michael nodded. "Long damn ride. Those seats are meant for short-haul missions. You know that most SOAR companies wouldn't even try this kind of reach. And these guys do it like it's the most normal thing on the planet."

"I know." Bill watched Trisha as she settled the *May* on the far side of the fuel bladder. He didn't want Michael to think they were having just a conversation about her. "The whole crew is incredible. Can't say I was ever a big fan of the Night Stalkers, but they're changing my mind for me."

"Henderson, then Beale, created a very unique team here. That's why I fly full-time with them."

Bill was feeling a little stupid so he looked away from Trisha as she climbed down and did some limbering exercises as well. He focused back on Michael.

"You fly only with them?" Michael was the top Delta operator on the planet. He should be... Well, Bill didn't quite know where else he should be, but it still sounded strange.

Michael nodded. "I'm a permanent liaison with SOAR Fifth Battalion D Company. We've found it creates a particularly strong alliance to keep at least one member of Special Forces Operational Detachment-Delta embedded with each battalion."

Bill pictured it in his head. SEALs could do something like that. They flew with the Night Stalkers a lot. Maybe that would be a way for him to stick around if Trisha wanted him to. Maybe even if she didn't want—

"I was looking for a second," Michael continued, "because this company is so active. They're the newest battalion and this team is both the youngest and the most decorated. Even without Beale. D Company truly is the tip of the spear."

"Wow!" Bill had known these guys were hot, but never knew they were that far out on the edge. But if Michael said they were, then they were. Without question. Bill scanned the other D-boys clustered together and checking over their weapons. All excellent soldiers. He liked the guys he'd spoken to, but none of them stood out from the other operators.

"So who are you thinking of bringing on?"

"You." Michael nodded as soon as he saw that Bill was no longer breathing. For all Bill could tell, his heart had stopped beating as well.

Michael walked away to check in with the rest of his team.

"Hey, sailor!" Trisha's slap on his back almost sent him tumbling into the sand.

"Ow! You're hard." Trisha shook her hand. She'd slapped him on the rifle across his back. That was the one drawback to the ADAS display on her visor; it only worked when she was wired to her chopper. The FARP was so dark, she'd almost killed herself half a dozen different ways trying to get to Billy. Practically impaled herself on one of the ever-present thorny acacia bushes. The only scent on the air was the sharp kerosene bite of Jet A totally overshadowing the rusty smell of the desert wind, neither of which had offered her any nighttime guidance anyway.

Billy would probably have to escort her back if she wanted to survive the hundred-foot return journey. Next time she wandered away from her helicopter, she'd remember to clip on a battery-powered NVG like Billy's so she could see what was going on.

"Uh, hi." He sounded dazed. Just a guy in mid-mission mode.

"So, pretty smooth on Stage One, huh? You done good."

"Yeah."

Trisha wished she could see his face. He was being even less chatty than usual, which was saying something. "What's up, Billy?"

"I, uh, just got a job offer. I think." She could tell by the angle of the soft green glow the night vision splashed across his eyes that he wasn't looking in her direction, but rather over toward the cluster of dim green glows that must be the D-boys.

"Anything good?"

"Damned if I know, Patricia. Damned if I know."

"That's Trisha." Though she actually was liking the way her name sounded when he said it. Something she hadn't allowed anyone to call her since Catholic school, like that had taken so well.

"Not Patty?" His voice was coming back to normal.

She reached out to find his arm. Finding a spot not covered with armor or a pouch of ammo, she punched him on it.

"I guess not. You good to go?"

"Sure." She was. The *May* was running clean and Roland would be overseeing the refuel. They'd have two hours of fuel and should need less than half of that. Nothing to rearm at this point as they hadn't fired a single shot during Stage One.

"And?"

Damn him for knowing there was something more. "That thing you said earlier…" She didn't know where to go with it.

"You mean, that I love you?"

"Yeah, that. I, uh, don't know what to say."

He reached out and grabbed the D-ring on the front of her SARVSO vest. It was there as a lifting hook if she ever crashed and needed to be airlifted out, or to attach a safety line in order to move freely around a larger helicopter while in flight. He pulled her in by it and wrapped an arm around her. Even separated by their vests and the rifle they each wore across their chests, he felt good.

"Don't worry about it, hotshot. It'll come to you."

"And if it doesn't?"

He shrugged. "Then we'll deal with that when we have to."

Gods, she felt stupid. Of all things. A wonderful man had said he loved her and she, the woman, who was supposed to be so much more in touch with her feelings, didn't have a clue what to say.

Billy was clearly waiting for something. He was in the middle of a mission and exuding confidence in every direction, because that was his job and his training. And she really wanted to say something, but "love" was way too scary.

"Did you say 'we' would deal with it?"

"Yeah." There was a roughness in his voice. He was being casual, but it was costing him.

"I like the way 'we' sounds. That counts for something, doesn't it?"

His arm squeezed her more tightly for a moment. A clear yes. And it did. It counted for a lot.

It felt as he if might have just kissed her on top of her helmet. "You better get back. Looks like we're almost all refueled."

"Sure thing, Lieutenant. Except I can't see shit in the dark."

He laughed and led her back to the *May*.

Chapter 29

GALKAYO WAS GOING TO BE FAR TRICKIER. THE PIRATES would be nervous. They had more than thirty hostages, all in a single location. They'd be keeping tight guards around them. So Bill and Michael had cooked up a different tactic, a variation on Mog.

Unlike that strike, which had been in the most populous and most dangerous center of the country's largest city, they'd now convinced Hassan Abdullah Abdi to gather the hostages at a single secure location, his compound. Even if only for one night. He had thankfully built it on the southeast edge of the city, up on a bluff. It wasn't for the view, as he'd built a large wall around it, too high to allow a view of the surrounding desert. It reflected old-style, colonial thinking, from when ground forces were your only threat.

What made it defensible against ground attack had also made it ideal for Bill's air attack plans. *Merchant* and *Max* had refilled their bench seats at the FARP with the other four Delta operators and four of the Rangers' best.

At precisely twenty-two hundred hours, ten at night, they came in fast and hard. Most cooking fires in the surrounding homes were dying out by this time, and little electricity reached this far.

Trisha flew into the power lines feeding the compound, catching the twin lines in a line-cutter that hung between her skids and the bottom of her fuselage. She and Lola had assured Bill it was possible to cut the lines without endangering the chopper, if you knew what you were doing. Apparently Trisha did. He saw the *May* fly clear right after the blackout hit the compound.

Two small courtyards had been identified that allowed the Little Birds to touch down, just long enough for the teams to jump off the seats. Their skids barely touching the soil before the birds were gone again to act as eyes in the sky for inbound reinforcements.

The ground troops broke into four three-man teams.

The instant the Little Birds were clear, the *Vengeance, Vicious*, and *May* climbed into the sky to circle different sections of the compound with weapons at the ready. Between the six miniguns and the two ships with rockets, they should provide excellent coverage.

In another sixty seconds, the two louder Navy Sea Hawks would each deliver four more Rangers outside the front and back gates to secure against reinforcements. The Sea Hawks would climb aloft to assist those teams from above with their lesser machine guns.

Bill's team, which included a Delta and a Ranger, headed for the main house. As expected, the large steel door was locked. The Ranger slapped on a breaching charge, and they ducked behind large stone planters to either side of the door, each holding a dead palm tree.

"Fire in the hole!" The Ranger lit off the charge and the bolt mechanism disappeared. They were almost back to the door when a stream of gunfire roared out the new hole in the door and into the empty courtyard.

Bill pulled the pin on a grenade, counted to three, and tossed it through the hole. Two seconds later, the force of the explosion slapped the door open, and no gunfire followed it.

Leaning into the opening, the D-boy let off six shots in three quick double-taps, then announced, "Clear."

The three of them moved in, dropping an extra shot in the heart of each of the gunmen and kicking their weapons clear of dead hands just to be sure.

A second team moved in close behind them. That meant the guardhouse was secure.

―✺―

That was Trisha's cue. As soon as she saw Michael's team enter the main house behind Billy's, she fired her first infrared illumination rocket. It burst over the center of the compound, giving them three minutes of light for their night-vision gear that would make the compound even brighter than daylight for them without offering any assistance to the Somali pirates and guards.

Then, per plan, she targeted the pair of Land Rovers parked close to the main house. Three rockets away and the SUVs were history, lighting up the night with visible fire that glared so brightly with heat that it was hard to look in that direction through the night-vision gear.

Vengeance took out four parked technicals with rockets. They purposely left the large truck. In case everything else went wrong, they could try driving the hostages out.

Gunfire streamed up toward the choppers from a third-story window. A burst from the *Vicious* cut that off.

With *May*'s jammer running, none of the baddies would be able to call for help. But this was Somalia. Billy had warned them. It was a country with eight million people and fourteen million guns. Children were taught how to shoot by the time they were seven, and not BB guns, but AK-47s and RPGs.

That was another thing that had happened in the Battle of Mogadishu. When Task Force Ranger arrived, they were facing twenty or so armed men. By the time they exited the building less than ten minutes later, they were facing a hundred. Before the night was over, more than ten thousand men, women, and children had fired at them. All that had happened without much planning. A firefight had started and everyone simply came running.

For the moment they had the advantage of surprise, but that wouldn't last for long.

Sure enough, she saw a tracer-line stream down from one of the Sea Hawks hovering over the back gate. Every fifth bullet was an infrared tracer round. It wouldn't look like much to the naked eye, a dull red line, but through night-vision gear it reported a long, heavy burst and allowed the Navy crew chief to see exactly where his bullets were arriving. The size of the resulting explosion on the ground, though she couldn't see it outside the wall, indicated it was a technical that had been roaring up the road. They weren't supposed to be responding that fast.

"First technical down, Billy," she called to him. It was one of the markers of the battle's progress she'd been told to announce.

The compound below them had more than a dozen buildings. The guardhouse had been cleared by one of the ground teams. That so few guards had been there didn't bode well. What intelligence Bill and Michael had gathered said about thirty shooters would be there. Maybe more after picking up the fifteen hostages from Garowe. If they weren't in the guardhouse, then where were—

"Check the heat signatures of the pool house." AMC Stevenson looking down from his drones.

Even as Trisha turned to look, the ADAS screamed in her ear. She slapped the bird hard left. An RPG flashed by just feet away. Gunfire erupted from the pool house, and she answered it with a pair of rockets and a burst from the miniguns.

They scattered. That's clearly where the guardhouse shooters had been restationed. Either it held more people or the pirate lord was just that smart to know any attack would have identified the guardhouse as a point of first attack.

Two of the pool-house shooters dove into the pool with their guns and then resurfaced, bracing their rifles on the edge of the pool to shoot at her. They were hard to hit that way, only their heads and guns showing above the concrete lip.

"In the water." Roland called out the suggestion.

"Do it!"

He fired a rocket, their seventh and half of the total they carried. It impacted in the pool and exploded. Whether the shock wave killed or merely knocked out the shooters didn't matter. The gunfire from the pool had ceased.

Bill and Michael's teams were moving fast inside, clearing room by room. They could hear the battle raging on the two floors above them. Gunfire directed at the choppers and the other two ground teams. That was the outside teams' job. Secure the compound and keep the upper-floor occupants busy.

The most likely place for the hostages to be was in the basement. Hassan Abdi wouldn't have put them in a remote building; he'd like having tight control on them. He was a very smart pirate. Hopefully this one night they'd be smarter than he was.

Bill sprinted ahead while others were clearing rooms, and Michael fell in close behind him. Just around the corner from the main stairs, Bill stopped. He felt the quick double-squeeze on his shoulder from Michael indicating he was ready.

Bill dove across the stairway, managing two wild shots before he tumbled past the far wall.

A stream of gunfire tried to follow him. Michael, shooting left-handed, leaned around his corner and fired rapidly. Two bodies tumbled down the stairs. Bill heard another land, but it apparently remained on the landing above.

"Hassan," he called up the stairs.

"Bill! Thought you were dead, man." The pirate's accent reflected his London education before he'd returned to Somalia. His parents had taken him out of the country to save him from the civil war of the 1990s, and he'd returned to extort millions of dollars from shipping insurance companies.

"Sorry to disappoint."

He and Michael were ready for it when the grenade rolled down the stairs. They'd each moved well down the walls on either side of the stair so they were well-shielded when it went off.

The loud boom in the enclosed space hurt his ears even through his helmet. Concrete dust filled the air.

They counted five long seconds, then Bill stepped back into the stairwell and shot Hassan, poised on the top step to listen, twice in the head and once in the heart. Michael took out the shooter behind him, then lofted a grenade of his own up the stairs.

The explosion above didn't elicit any more screams, but it would certainly make anyone else think twice about coming down.

The three choppers were in a constant dance over the compound. Sometimes one shooter, sometimes a half dozen would pop up, fire a dozen rounds, and then disappear. It was like an awful game of Whac-A-Mole.

Trisha figured that the estimates had been low. There were more like fifty or sixty shooters in the compound, though that number was dropping rapidly. She couldn't imagine the ten thousand or more that had fought in the Battle of Mogadishu. The core problem here was that they were spread far and wide over the compound so it was impossible to stop more than one or two at a time.

The two heavier Black Hawks circled fast, three hundred feet above the edges of the compound. Not above ground fire, but far enough into the dark to be plenty invisible. That left the center as her flight pattern, and she bobbed and swirled as they found and hit back at targets.

"We've got the hostages," Billy announced.

"Still too hot for extract," Trisha called back. "Keep them inside the main house." The transport choppers might survive a landing, but the chances of hostages getting hit in the crossfire while running out the door, down the steps, and over to the choppers were way too high.

A vehicle roared out of what had been identified as an animal barn on the far side of the compound. It was an animal alright. A beast.

"ZU-23!" She shouted over the radio and flung her chopper skyward. A technical with a ZU-23-2, a twin-barreled antiaircraft gun, was a lethal opponent. The beast could shoot eight one-inch shells a second up to a mile away in any direction. Almost any direction. Straight up was hard when mounted to a small truck.

Fire raked toward the *May*, bright streamers of shells lancing upward that made the ADAS feed squeal over her headphones as well as making bright arcs across her visor. She managed to get clear, straight above them. The problem was that she didn't have any way to attack straight down.

"*Vengeance*?" she called out. No need to complete the question.

A pair of rockets streaked in from above and blew earth skyward right in front of the vehicle. The technical caught air as it flew through the shower of dirt, jumping the twinned craters. The driver hit the ground and had the vehicle skidding sideways in a sharp turn even as it landed. He kept it moving. He was good and he was still active.

Trisha knew the *Vengeance* would be out of position for a dozen seconds following the necessary maneuver to fire those rockets.

"Going vertical." Trisha twisted the cyclic and cranked the collective all of the way up. She forced the chopper nose down toward the ground and went into free fall. She kicked the left pedal and Roland fired off two rockets, no chance to target the miniguns.

She pulled back hard on the cyclic and kicked the pedals back to the right.

The rockets' explosions went off behind her just as she pulled level, barely five feet off the dirt and racing straight at the towering compound wall. Half prayer and half luck combined to climb enough to clear the parapet by about three cat whiskers.

Trisha circled hard. The technical was missing its front end. She'd blown the engine and the cab right off the truck.

Despite the crazy tilt of the truck bed, someone was still trying to fire the ZU-23. A barrage from one of the Black Hawks ended that.

"You see anything else, Roland?" They both were scanning, but the compound had gone suddenly quiet.

"Fire in the hole at the barn," came in on the D-boy frequency. The barn blew apart. Instead of just a clean bang, the explosion rippled and roared for several moments afterward indicating a lot of other weaponry had been parked there rather than animals.

That's when Roland grunted and slammed against Trisha. Then he collapsed forward against the cyclic joystick.

———

Bill knelt well inside the front door of the main building watching the battle; Michael knelt beside him. They had thirty nervous hostages lying on the floor. The Rangers and D-boys were serving as rear guard. To keep this floor secure, Delta snipers sat at the base of the two sets of stairs to the upper stories, picking off the occasional person braving the descent.

There was a brief pause after the antiaircraft gun was destroyed, and then the barn blew.

That's when Bill saw Trisha's Little Bird nose down hard.

He'd barely been able to breathe when she did the dive straight down on the technical with the ZU-23. Not in all his training had he ever witnessed a move like that. Diving straight at the ground from less than two hundred feet up, she'd killed the machine. Not totally dead, but she was absolutely the one who'd killed it.

Then, as soon as he'd for one little instant hoped they'd be all clear for loading, the *May* had jerked in the sky. It gave a sickening twist that no pilot would do intentionally.

The chopper twisted from nose down to almost onto her side.

No fire, no burst of flame.

He sprinted forward. It was stupid; he knew that even as he ran. But it didn't matter that he couldn't help her up in the air. It didn't matter that he was exposing himself. He had to get to her.

Dragging back on the cyclic didn't work. Roland was too heavy and Trisha could see the ground coming up far too fast.

She shoved the control sideways, and he flopped into her lap. That got his weight off the controls.

A hard correction and she managed to get the chopper right side up and the throttle wide open so that the turbine screamed for lift.

The *May* hammered into the ground hitting one skid

first, then after a crucial moment of indecision, flopping down onto the other skid and coming to a rest upright. Her crash-tolerant pilot's seat slammed against the stops and jarred her body. She dropped the collective to kill any lift. If she took off with Roland lying across her lap, she'd have no control at all. The *May* had a distinct list to one side, so the skid must have partly crumpled. But the chopper was still running. Hadn't buried her rotor in the dirt.

A small element of her thousands of hours of training kicked in and she reached up to flip the control on Roland's seat belt harness without even looking. Under normal setting, the harness was designed to let the seat's occupant move as much as needed to reach the control console or lean over to look out the door. It would only lock up in a crash, just like a car seat belt.

On its new setting, it would retract, but not release. Once she got Roland upright, it would hold him tightly in place. It was built that way for moments exactly like this, when an injured pilot had to be pinned back, clear of the controls.

She reached down to drag him upright and froze.

An unexploded RPG was buried through the side of his helmet. A dud. The Kevlar could stop small-caliber bullets, but not this. It must have come up over the wall from outside the compound so that the ADAS mounted on the chopper's belly had been below the edge of the wall and unable to give warning.

Billy raced up beside her, and she'd never been so happy to see anyone in her life. He had his sniper rifle braced to his shoulder as he ran. Michael was three steps behind. They knelt to either side of the *May*'s nose facing in opposite directions.

Trisha's racing heart slowly came back under control.

They were firing. There were people still in the compound firing, though the fire lessened moment by moment as the four separate teams worked their magic.

Time to worry later. Time to deal now.

She dug for a pulse under the edge of Roland's helmet but didn't find one, nor did she expect to.

Well, she wasn't going to fly with an unexploded RPG in her cockpit. Gritting her teeth, she grabbed the tail of it, imagined she could feel it pulsing with evil.

She shouted, "Fire in the hole!" Then, with a single clean jerk, she pulled it out and threw it as far as she could out the door opening.

Bill almost swallowed his tongue when he saw the RPG come tumbling through the air out of Trisha's chopper. He dove away from it, knocking Michael sprawling as he did so.

The explosion behind them was a sharp report, and he could feel the ground he was lying on pulse once with the fury of it. He remained still a moment longer to let the shock wave of dust sweep over them, then rolled to his feet to check Trisha.

Leaning into the chopper, he shouted into her face. "You okay?"

She was shoving her copilot back into his seat. Bill reached across to help, but she batted his hand aside. Another push or two and the harness held Roland in place, back against his seat. By the way his head hung, Bill knew he was gone.

"You okay?"

"Good enough for now. Let's get out of here."

He wished he could see her eyes, but she didn't raise her visor.

She reached down and began pulling up on her collective.

He stepped back and covered his face against the cloud of dust thrown up by her rotor blades. Then she was aloft and gone.

A quick scan of the yard indicated that the four three-man fire teams who had landed inside the walls were ready to move. No other resistance fire was going on. Any pirate shooters were dead, injured, or smart enough to lie low until the invading force was gone.

"Let's load."

Within seconds, the two Sea Hawks landed close beside him, as near as they dared to the main building's front door. They loaded the Hawks with a dozen hostages and two Rangers each.

They labored back into the sky. The *Vicious* came down from her guard station and gathered the rest of the hostages and all except the point men for each of the Little Birds.

Finally *Max* and *Merchant* came in and Bill, Michael, and the last two D-boys climbed aboard.

With heavy covering fire from *Vengeance* and, Bill could hardly believe it, Trisha flying alone in the *May*, the two Little Birds ducked down to pick up the front- and back-gate Ranger teams.

As they departed, he heard a harsh sizzle nearby. He leaned out into the wind and spotted *Vengeance*.

She was living up to her name. Chief Warrant Lola

Maloney had just fired a pair of Hellfire missiles into the main building.

All three stories went up with a roar that shook the night.

Chapter 30

BACK AT THE FARP, BILL RUSHED OVER TO Trisha's chopper.

"You okay?" He came up beside her.

"I guess." She slid up her visor.

Screw security. He pulled a small red flashlight out of a hip pocket and flipped his own NVGs out of the way. He had to see for himself.

Trisha's face was drawn, and he'd wager pretty pale. He wanted to tell her how incredible she was, but it didn't seem right with her sitting next to her dead copilot.

"I guess Roland is fine there." Trisha didn't turn to look at her strapped-in copilot. "I'll fly him home."

"The hell you will." Bill turned and shouted over to the *Vengeance* that had landed nearby. "You guys have a body bag?"

The reaction was galvanic. It was the first anyone else knew about any mortality. Lola Maloney rushed over and did a quick inspection that Bill recognized as totally professional.

"Medic?" he asked her.

"Former CSAR."

Combat Search and Rescue. Good person to have around. Maloney took over in that efficient way of someone who'd seen worse, much worse and too many times, and she had Roland extracted quickly from the *May*. Then she was back at Trisha's side.

"Are you okay?"

"Would people stop asking me that?"

To Bill's ear, she sounded more Trisha-style pissed than just-lost-her-partner numb. But with a high degree of stress overlay.

"Lieutenant O'Malley…" Maloney suddenly sounded like a kick-ass officer rather than an easygoing SOAR pilot. "Do you judge yourself capable of flying, or would you like to trade with my copilot?"

It was an elegant solution. No loss of face, she'd still be at the controls, not relegated to being a back-end passenger. And trusting that Trisha was a good enough pilot to assess her own mental state.

Trisha blew out a breath and squared her shoulders. "I'm okay to fly, sir. Let's get it done."

Maloney nodded a sharp acknowledgment. "I'll go find you a copilot."

"No need," Bill wasn't letting Trisha out of his sight at the moment. "I'm certified in type."

Maloney gave him a meaningful nod, one that told him he'd better not screw this up or he'd have yet another woman trying to beat the crap out of him. Then Maloney squeezed Trisha's shoulder and returned to the *Vengeance* where they'd already taken Roland's body bag.

Bill fished around in back, found the spare helmet he'd worn when flying with the motorcycles aboard, and pulled it on. In moments, he was wired in.

Trisha didn't get out of the chopper. She just sat there unmoving.

So Bill kept an eye on the refueling.

―᪲―

They were aloft and almost back to the coast before Trisha was able to find any words at all. Billy had offered her silence and she appreciated that.

"Thanks, Billy. I wouldn't have liked having Roland here growing cold. Thanks for taking care of it."

"It's done."

"It's done," she agreed, though they both knew it wasn't. They both had been through the "team member loss" counseling sessions that were sure to follow this event as well. Though no one in her own crew had been killed before, she had seen a chopper disintegrate in a ball of fire not a hundred yards ahead of her. Another time it was a crew chief who took a round and would never walk again. For the duration of this flight, though, it was done.

"Bill?" AMC Stevenson's voice crackled over the radio.

"Go ahead." She liked how close and assured he sounded.

"The Navy team that entered Hobyo on the hovercraft has just reported the successful recovery of fourteen hostages. They're 'feet wet' and headed back to the ship. No losses."

"Roger. Job well done."

"Well done," Stevenson echoed.

The plan for the Hobyo hostages had been elegant in its simplicity, Sly's masterpiece. The massive LCAC hovercraft had cruised right up the beach and into town at the same moment the choppers had descended on Galkayo. When the hovercraft reached the building that was believed to hold the hostages, they simply drove the eighty-ton craft through the surrounding wall and parked in the front yard. When the hovercraft gate dropped, twenty Rangers had stormed the building. Chances were that most of the hostages' feet never hit the ground, they were hustled aboard so fast. Total contact time was under three minutes, compared to the seventeen in Galkayo.

"I also have a special communication on a private frequency." Stevenson again.

Billy selected the pre-agreed channel. Trisha wondered, What next? He didn't have anyone else to lose, did he? If she could free up a hand, she'd reach over to rest it as a comfort on his arm just in case the news was bad. That's when she realized he did have someone else to lose, someone he loved. But at least she was sitting right beside him.

Trisha had seen him storm out of the main house, despite the active crossfire, to protect her in her chopper. Would he have done the same for Dennis or Max? Maybe. But not a pell-mell kind of race that had left Michael eating his dust. Unable to free her hands, she leaned her shoulder against his for a moment.

"I don't know if your team wants to know this or not," Stevenson was hesitating which wasn't good.

Okay, it was bad news for the team, not for Billy. At least she could share in that, though she'd kind of had enough bad news for one night.

"Proceed." By his tone, Billy felt the same way. Wasn't it enough that they had just freed every hostage north of Mogadishu as well as liberated three of the four held ships?

Another ship. Must be.

"Remember the yacht guy, Wilkin Benson Jr., and the *Gracie* up in Bosaso? Well, he went and hired a mercenary team. They just went in to try and recover his own yacht from the pirates. Apparently he's no better at hiring mercs than he is at cruising."

Billy cursed an impressive streak, even for a sailor. Which, she realized, might well be the first time she'd heard him swear. When he finally calmed down enough, he asked the crucial question, "Did the idiot go in with the team?"

"We have a report of four new hostages now in captivity there, and he's one of them."

Chapter 31

BILLY CLICKED OFF AND CONTINUED TO SWEAR QUIetly, his expletives getting more colorful and imaginative as he went. She'd have to remember a few of them. They were really creative and perhaps even anatomically possible if enough force was applied.

Trisha kept her attention on her flying and the other choppers around her. The Black Hawk and two Sea Hawks with the hostages reported "feet wet." The hostages would be aboard the *Harry S. Truman* within twenty minutes and calling home. The news would be global by morning.

Their own flight, which had stopped at the FARP only long enough to refuel and then destroy the equipment, still had forty minutes of flight to reach the *Peleliu*.

"You know..." Billy sounded angry enough to damage her bird with his fists. "The instant they hear about us grabbing all of the hostages and ships, they're going to move those hostages into the deep desert where we'll never find them. And the ransom will be astronomical. Did you know that young twerp Benson Junior is a senator's son and tried to bribe me with a presidential pardon if I rescued him, back when he thought I was a pirate?"

Trisha had to laugh. The degree of disgust in Billy's voice was so complete. Even on this horrid day, she'd managed to laugh. It struck her that was exactly what Billy had been trying to do. Help her find her center to continue her flight. To remain steady while in the air. He was such a good man.

Trisha had been doing her own calculations while Billy had been cursing.

"You know, if we change our heading in the next few minutes, everyone in this flight has enough fuel to make it to the aircraft carrier in an hour and a quarter."

Billy turned quickly to look to the north as if he could see it two hundred miles away across the arid land and the salty sea.

"It's almost two hundred more past that to Bosaso."

"Isn't the French *Mistral* up there somewhere? We could refuel on her."

They both turned to the clock on the central control panel, though the time was repeated inside their helmets on the visor.

It was twenty-three-thirty, half an hour to midnight. A three-hundred-and-fifty-mile flight with refuelings would get them to Bosaso about oh-three-hundred.

She counted thirty seconds while Billy thought about it. A dozen battle plans must be going through his mind as he juggled assets in his head. That would also mean they'd been flying almost continuously for eight hours before they even entered the third battle of the night.

Billy clicked on the radio's general frequency. "Flight, this is Lieutenant Bruce, turn heading five-zero, make maximum speed for aircraft carrier *Truman*. Captain Stevenson, we'll need someone to hook us up with the French *Mistral*. Everyone, we've just received report of four more hostages in Bosaso. We have to go get them tonight before they're dispersed into the desert. Let's do it."

The only answer was that they all turned in unison to
the new heading and lifted to fifty feet above the water
as they broke clear of the coast.

At the aircraft carrier, they lined up formally in an aisle
from the *Vengeance* to the elevator that would take
Roland's body down to the carrier's morgue. There
would be time to write letters and inform parents after
the mission. For now, all they could offer were their
salutes and honor to the fallen.

The hostages who had arrived a half hour earlier
wanted to come and thank them and talk to them and
do whatever hostages wanted to do when released from
months—or in a few cases, almost two years—of captivity. Again, there'd be time for that later.

While their birds were serviced and reloaded with
fuel and ammo, they all gathered in the flight-deck-level
briefing room of the tower. A service crew had even
tackled straightening the skid on the *May*, though they
didn't have the parts to replace it. The little chopper was
better, though it still leaned distinctly to the right, as if
tipping its hat.

Bill had Connie and Big John check the rest of the
systems on *May*. Trisha and Connie had traded hugs
before he dragged her into the briefing.

Food was brought in and Bill began the briefing on
the ship's layout. He took twenty minutes reviewing the
ship itself. When last seen, it had been anchored a mile
down the coast, west of Bosaso. The main port of the
northern half of the country, Bosaso was really little
more than a pier and a breakwater.

"At last report, the yacht was still directly offshore from the compound where we did the first hostage rescue last month. It is also placed far enough away that the local officials can pretend that they don't notice a hundred-and-fifty-foot luxury yacht that just happens to be anchored there week after week. As they probably have a stake in the final payout, this isn't hard to understand."

He had almost no information on the failed recovery team of mercenaries.

"The only reason we know anything is that Wilkin Junior was on the phone with his personal assistant right before he was taken. Apparently, they'd thought that rescuing his own ship would make a good news piece to launch his own political career, separate from his father's legacy. That's how we know there were at least four survivors at that time. He had the good sense to set down the phone but leave it active as he was captured. We don't know the size of the initial team."

"So we don't know where they actually are?" Dennis asked around a mouthful of meatloaf.

"Wilkin Junior's team would have targeted the ship directly, probably a seaside approach in a Zodiac rubber boat launched from another boat farther out at sea, perhaps even a passing freighter. Did the pirates leave them aboard, or take them to the same compound as the first hostages or to a third location? This is a crucial unknown. Therefore, we will have to take the pirates holding the *Gracie* as hostages. If we determine that we are unable to recover the yacht, the senator, who is apparently fairly sick of his son, has given us permission to sink her. Probably take it out of the boy's allowance."

That got the laugh he'd been looking for.

He scanned the crews. They weren't tired yet, but they would be after flying another four hours. They'd be exhausted and their bodies shaken by such a long night of flying before they could even begin the battle.

After reviewing the half-dozen different scenarios he'd worked up with Stevenson as they flew to the carrier, which could only be solidified when more intelligence had been gathered, Lola Maloney stepped to the front of the room.

"Okay, crew, you have five minutes to flake out, then we're aloft. This isn't any worse than a lot of flights the Night Stalkers have made. Even though it may be stupider than most." Again the laugh. She was a good leader. "The key fact is that civilian lives are on the line. And there's one thing we know for sure…" She didn't even have to complete the sentence.

The crews chanted out the 160th's motto in strong unison: "Night Stalkers Don't Quit."

He checked Trisha, and she gave him a sharp nod of ready even as she spoke the words aloud.

Amazing damn woman.

She'd better come to her senses soon or he'd have to tell her again how much he loved her.

The *Mistral* represented the latest in amphibious-assault-ship technology. With a sixth of the size and crew, she claimed she could deliver over eighty percent of the force support of the *Peleliu* when she was at full capacity. The wonders of a design that was thirty years newer.

The French welcomed them with sparkling water,

croque monsieur ham and cheese sandwiches, and immense efficiency. They'd cleared the flight deck of their own choppers and were already steaming north by the time the three Little Birds, the *Vicious*, and the *Vengeance* arrived. It was the first visit of the secretive stealth helicopters to a French vessel and the commanders kept the deck clear of gawkers, though they were clearly struggling not to gawk themselves. Despite the interest, there just wasn't time for tours either of the ship or the choppers.

The French captain had come himself to greet them. "By steaming north at full speed," he said, "we will be placing ourselves approximately eighty miles closer by the time at which you complete the operation. Therefore, we calculate that no in-flight or waypoint refueling will be required."

That was a relief. Coordinating a FARP this far afield would be a difficult operation. The United States would have a C-130 aloft to cruise the shore just in case an emergency refueling was required. Though Bill would bet that the C-130 pilot was no more excited than he was about setting up a FARP on a Somali beach somewhere.

They barely had time to chew and stretch before the birds were refueled and they were aloft once more.

Once they were airborne, AMC Stevenson began feeding Bill information from the drones he'd sent scurrying north. At least one of them would have insufficient time to return before it ran out of fuel. It would be ditched at sea when its mission was complete. Another couple hundred thousand dollars that the U.S. Armed Forces should be charging Wilkin Benson Junior.

Heat signatures on the boat showed little activity. The

Gracie was still right where they'd left it a month before. And, the good news, the compound ashore was still occupied. The problem was that it was heavily occupied.

It was a tenth the size of the Galkayo compound and had no such luxuries as a pool. But neither did it have an outer wall stout enough to fend off any outside forces that wanted to come and join the fight. Four technicals were parked around the outside perimeter. The main building still appeared to be unusable from the damage caused by Trisha's rockets.

They briefly discussed involving the Puntland military. The autonomous state had driven most of the pirates out of its territory and even begun creating a slim form of stability in the northeastern part of Somalia. While the ground forces would be welcome, all it would take was a single sergeant with a clan brother on the pirate crew and the element of surprise would be gone.

The French had offered to send a pair of their Tiger attack choppers, but between the *Vengeance* and the *May*, the SOAR team had that covered. And they'd already had to leave behind some of the Ranger force who had flown in the Navy Sea Hawks. The plan was a lean force and a fast strike, operating way out at the limits of supportability by other forces.

This would be a U.S. Army operation with no one the wiser. Army plus one Navy SEAL, Bill had to remind himself. Had Michael been serious about recruiting Bill to join SFOD-Delta? Had Colonel Michael Gibson ever not been serious about anything to do with the military? Even though Bill knew Delta occasionally recruited SEALs, he'd never thought about leaving his team before. Of course, he'd been on the outside of his team for the last six months preparing for, then infiltrating the Somali pirate community. He wished he had someone to ask.

Maybe he did.

"Hey, Trisha?" he asked her over the *May*'s intercom.

"Yeah?"

"Remember what I said about getting a job offer?" He let his hands ride along on the helicopter's controls. It was always a good practice for both pilots to stay engaged, and he liked feeling her constant small adjustments transmitted through the linked cyclic, collective, and pedals. They were as smooth and unconscious as if the chopper had become but an extension of her body. And the heavily weaponized *May* actually was a good extension of this particular woman.

"Yeah, right. Sort of forgot that what with you telling me you loved me and all. What's the offer?"

He smiled that she managed to say the word "love." It wasn't something she'd managed in prior conversations. He decided against pointing it out as progress.

"Michael." Bill realized that he only needed the one word to have a whole conversation with Trisha.

"Wow! That's major." Her voice was soft and drawn out. "To be asked to join Delta…" She let it trail, clearly considering the implications.

"Not just Delta. He wants a second embedded liaison with SOAR's Fifth Battalion D Company."

"That's us. That's…" She flew in silence for several minutes as she processed what he'd spent a fair chunk of the last few hours chipping away at.

"Okay. Twenty questions time, I guess."

He didn't even have to tell her why he'd mentioned

it. She'd understood that he needed help and was willing
to offer it.

"So, let's first set you and me aside. As well as what
that might mean for that 'we' you mentioned earlier."

It was a huge point to ignore, but he could see why
she was doing it that way. "Okay."

"First."

He could feel her correct left, then right for some
small turbulence in the air he would have just ridden
through, perhaps not even noticed if she hadn't made the
adjustments. As a result, their path was just that much
straighter. On the ADAS projection across his visor,
he could see that only Lola in the *Vengeance* made the
same corrections. He suddenly felt he'd been pretty arrogant to insist on sitting as her copilot. He was a better-
than-average pilot, even by SEAL standards. He'd be
bottom rung in SOAR, if that.

"How have you liked all of the testing Michael has
been handing out to you as his right hand this last month?"

"He's been doing what?" Even as Trisha laughed
at him, his view of these last weeks shifted. Michael
had slowly included him in more and more actions.
Leading the oil tanker attack together, the hand-to-hand
wrestling match, letting Bill take the lead on tonight's
mission planning and execution. Even fighting side by
side tonight and every conversation they'd had since the
moment he'd come aboard now shifted into that new
focus. It had been an escalating series of tests, and he'd
never even seen it.

"I warned you about Michael." Trisha was laughing
at him, but it was hard to complain. He'd been well and
thoroughly duped.

"You did warn me, but I didn't see it coming, not a single bit. In answer: I've liked it a lot. He's an amazing man to work with. And the skills the other operators have are truly exceptional, even by SEAL standards."

"Okay, question two."

Clearly she was enjoying herself. He hoped the questions got easier from here.

"Team, and being a part of one, is an essential part of who you are. How would you feel about leaving SEAL Team Nine for Special Forces Operational Detachment-Delta?"

So much for easier.

The twenty questions, which had numbered more like thirty-five, had helped Trisha with the monotony of the long, overwater flight from the *Mistral* toward Bosaso. Now the reports were coming in fast enough that they had to stop the game.

Trisha had carefully not returned to that initial question that she'd set aside as a premise. About that one question, she was stuck with every "What if?" scenario on the planet. "What if he went away after this assignment?" had been at the top of her list for longer than she'd care to admit. "What if he did stay, but she then did her predictable blow-up-the-relationship thing?" No way that would be pretty if they were then trapped in the same unit.

And the third question for her ranked as a real kicker she'd rather not think about but couldn't help herself. "What if he did stay and she didn't destroy the relationship? What then?"

That question had plagued her while some calm, rational part of her mind was working up the questions to ask Billy. It had followed her ashore as they dropped back to nap-of-earth flight levels and left the Arabian Sea to cut inland just south of Ashira, then climbed through the narrow valleys of the Karkaar mountains.

She'd expected a riot of inner protest. A lie-on-the-deck-and-scream-and-wail kind of feeling. Instead she found a silence she didn't recognize or understand.

It was only as they shot over the Gulf of Aden so that they could circle back to approach Bosaso from the sea that she noticed it wasn't silence. It was quiet. It was like all of her emotions simply went quiet and calm.

All except one. And that one spoke plenty loud. She started to smile... She really should tell Billy.

"Three minutes to contact," Billy the SEAL-soon-to-be-Delta announced on the common frequency.

Okay, maybe this wasn't the best moment.

So she said the words very quietly to herself and was surprised at how easy it was to say.

"Love you, Billy Bruce."

Chapter 32

BILL HAD DEBATED THE ALLOCATION OF TEAMS. HE hated to put Trisha back in harm's way, but it made the most sense. He and Trisha knew the pirate's compound in westernmost Bosaso far better than anyone else.

"*Merchant* and *Max*, your teams go on either end of the *Gracie*. *Vengeance*, you're their hammer on high. *Vicious*, you're into the compound with the *May*. Remember, folks, maximum three minutes contact, then I want us gone with or without the ship. We can always scuttle her from the air."

How many missions had gone like this? All the planning, preparation, transport, and infiltration, and it all came down to just a few minutes, or occasionally a few seconds, of contact. It had always struck him as odd, like they were the tiny lethal tip of an immensely long lance.

"Okay, Billy." Trisha interrupted his thoughts. Her voice sounded command tough. "You don't do a damn thing with the controls unless I'm hit. I've got it covered. You worry about two things, spotting for me and running the operation. *May*'s HUMS, Health and Usage Management System, will tell me if anything goes wrong. I'll take care of the weapons as well. We clear?"

"Clear." He wanted to salute, but there wasn't room in the tiny cabin. If any pilot could handle that huge a volume of information and still fly, it was Patricia O'Malley.

AMC Stevenson made a final report at two minutes out. "Two technicals still remain outside the compound, both on the east end closer to Bosaso city. Perhaps ten shooters inside. Several bodies in the guard shack and four more sitting in what Lieutenant Bruce identified as the remains of the main building. We are designating these as possible prisoners. They haven't moved in two hours. I have only three warm bodies showing on the ship. They also haven't moved since initial overflight two hours ago. Best of luck, teams."

"Sixty seconds," Billy said mostly to himself over the intercom. They'd be in radio silence now, only mission-critical calls until they were clear of the coast.

Trisha decided that even if this wasn't the best time, she really didn't give a damn. She cranked up the throttle but eased down slightly on the collective so that she'd have the extra power when she needed it. It wouldn't be a question of "if."

"It's oh-three-hundred," she said over the *May*'s intercom.

"Uh-huh," Billy acknowledged as he leaned forward, straining to see the ship that would be coming into sight in just moments.

"Thirty days ago, at precisely this time, I was on my way to rescue your ass."

"Hell of a first meeting. Thirty seconds."

"I love you, Lieutenant William Bruce."

"Uh, sure." Five-second lag. "Wait!" Three more. "What?" He spun to face her so fast that she was glad he'd taken his hands off the controls.

"Fifteen seconds, Lieutenant Bruce."

"What? You do? Shit!"

———

They blew by the *Gracie* at close to two hundred miles per hour and crossed the shoreline with the *Vicious* in close formation.

Crap! Damn the woman. No time to think!

He needed to mark this moment somehow.

"Great!" was all he managed, then he spotted the technicals. "Hit 'em!"

Coming in at ground level, low enough to look straight into the startled eyes of the men lounging against their big fifty-caliber machine guns, Trisha unleashed a pair of rockets. Men were diving aside as the two trucks blew sky high in unison.

Trisha peeled off, up, and left before quite flying into the fireball.

Vicious, who only had her miniguns for offense, was already over the main building. Two streams of fire raked upward from the guardhouse, and only two heat signatures were placed in that building. The *Vicious* pounded it down.

Trisha fired up the *May*'s miniguns and did a fast spin, raking the parapet of the surrounding wall, and launched another rocket into a garage. The same spinning-top move she'd used in the courtyard a lifetime ago.

And this woman loved him? That was… For lack of anything better, he settled for one of her phrases, "so cool."

Per the plan, *Vicious* dove down into the main building. A half-dozen Rangers spilled out of the bird and sprinted to the four bodies lined up against the wall.

"Billy, two o'clock low."

ore she'd even finished, he pulled up the rifle
ging across his chest and dropped the armed Somali
sprinting across the yard toward the grounded chopper.
The two of them continued to concentrate on the shooters that the ADAS was reporting both inside and outside
the walls. Her minis did the heavy lifting, and he sniped
out the left-side doorway.

When he could, Bill kept an eye on the ground team,
but it was like disconnected blinks. Rangers wielding
bolt cutters. Prisoners halfway back to the chopper.
First aboard. Only one last Ranger on the ground,
kneeling, facing outward, his rifle at his shoulder. The
Vicious aloft, her miniguns blazing. The *May* falling
back and away.

Then they had no more targets. They were aloft.
The compound dropped behind them, then beach, and
abruptly water. Time came back under his control.

The *Gracie* had her bow turned toward the sea.
She'd been bow to the west when they flew by before,
hadn't she?

On his visor Bill could see four men kneeling on the
stern deck facing aft, hands on their heads. Two Rangers
stood guard, identifiable by their exposed IR reflector
shoulder tabs and their rifles aimed at the pirates. A third
moved down the line pulling out zip ties and binding the
pirate's wrists.

An abrupt movement at the bow drew his attention.
A Delta operator swinging a long knife at the anchor
line. It parted and the ship headed out to sea under the
Vengeance's watchful eye.

They disappeared back into the dark, five helicopters
and one ship. Almost no one had seen them. As if they

hadn't been there. They were Night Stalkers, and he found it was very easy to imagine flying with them.

"So." He settled his hands lightly on the controls and felt Trisha's constant, tiny adjustments transmitted through them. "So, you love me, huh?"

She turned to him, but he had to imagine the grin in the darkness.

"I do."

Chapter 33

"LAST DAY YOU GET TO WEAR THESE. YOU SURE YOU'RE okay with that?" Patricia tugged on the lapel of Bill's Navy dress white uniform as she arrived beside him.

He looked down at her and merely nodded. He couldn't muster more because he'd never seen such an amazing sight as Patricia O'Malley standing at the altar in a wedding dress.

The setting didn't hurt. It was spring at the Old Round Church in Richmond, Vermont. Outside, the air was kissed with the first blooms, though the scent of snow still lingered in the higher reaches of the Green Mountains.

Military uniforms glittered in the pews on both the bride's and the groom's side of the church. Many of those who remembered his mother fondly filled the seating in the wooden balcony that swept three quarters of the way around the church's second story.

Colonel Gibson stood as his best man in his dress blues, the same color Bill would be wearing after today. He had finished Delta school, as much as it ever ended, just this week and his official commission awaited his return from their honeymoon.

He'd been introduced to Mark Henderson and Emily Beale. He'd never felt threatened by a woman before. Well, other than Trisha.

They'd held the rehearsal dinner yesterday as an afternoon picnic out at the lower pool of the Huntington

Gorge waterfalls. Beale had come up to him and taken his hand in hers as if to shake it. Then she'd clamped down in a way that proved she was still strong from flying Firehawk helicopters over forest fires, as well as not forgetting any of her Army training. The stunning blond was tall, and he didn't have to glance down far to look into her eyes, which were almost as bright blue as Trisha's.

"If you don't treat her right, I will ram a fire-retardant hose up your backside and then deliver a few thousand gallons under pressure. I may be out of the service and merely the maid of honor, but she's the fourth I've stood beside, and I watch out for my girls. Are we clear?" Her smile was absolutely charming, and he didn't doubt for a second she meant it.

"Yes, sir. Yes, ma'am. Uh, yes."

Then her grip eased but didn't let go. Now they maintained a friendly handclasp as she turned to look at the rocks around them and the crews picnicking around the pool at the base of Huntington Gorge.

"Aren't they amazing?"

They were. The quiet mechanic Connie with her enormous husband, Big John Wallace. The exotic sniper Kee, sitting with AMC Stevenson and Dilya, who was their flower girl. The teen was reading earnestly to Beale's own one-year-old daughter, one of the most beautiful children Bill had ever seen.

Lola Maloney, the long, lean, and strong commander, lounging back against Tim, her weight lifter, gunner husband. Even Dusty James was there with his lovely wife, Amy, who was still in SOAR training. They were an amazing team. Dennis and Max would be at the

wedding along with members of his SEAL team and his
new Delta friends.

"I'm proud to be flying with them." Then he turned
back to face Beale. "I wish you still were. Trisha tells
such stories about you."

"She's sweet."

"She is. But they all share serving under your command. I'm leaving my team to join this one. And I've
learned that the main thing that made this a team was
you. You and your husband."

She'd squeezed his hand once but didn't speak. She
was blinking hard when she moved away to sit by Dilya
as the teen read out loud to the infant about the wonders
of dragons.

They were amazing women, all of them. Especially
Patricia O'Malley.

As she'd walked up the Round Church's aisle beside her father, her figure sleek in a form-fitting dress
and bare shoulders, her long hair all up in one of those
things women did for weddings, he'd never seen a
more beautiful sight.

Unless it had been that morning as they knelt together in the dawn light before his mother's grave.
Flowers had bloomed there. Daisy and buttercup.
Indian blanket and even the black-eyed Susans that
matched Trisha's wedding bouquet.

They had knelt on the dew-filled grass together and
remembered those who had fallen and those who would
continue to fly.

There she hadn't been some perfect woman in an
incredible dress. She hadn't been his soon-to-be-wife or
his fellow soldier.

For that brief time, they had simply been Billy and Trisha, two people who knew they would always be in love.

Pure Heat

The Firehawks Series
by M.L. Buchman

~~~

These daredevil smokejumpers fight more than fires

The elite fire experts of Mount Hood Aviation fly into places even the CIA can't penetrate.

She lives to fight fires

Carly Thomas could read burn patterns before she knew the alphabet. A third-generation forest fire specialist who lost both her father and her fiancé to the flames, she's learned to live life like she fights fires: with emotions shut down.

But he's lit an inferno she can't quench

Former smokejumper Steve "Merks" Mercer can no longer fight fires up close and personal, but he can still use his intimate knowledge of wildland burns as a spotter and drone specialist. Assigned to copilot a Firehawk with Carly, they take to the skies to battle the worst wildfire in decades and discover a terrorist threat hidden deep in the Oregon wilderness—but it's the heat between them that really sizzles.

~~~

"A wonderful love story...seamlessly woven in among technical details. Poignant and touching."
—*RT Book Reviews* Top Pick, 4.5 Stars

For more M.L. Buchman, visit:

www.sourcebooks.com

Betrayed

Rockfort Security Book 2
by Rebecca York

New York Times and *USA Today* Bestselling Author

—◆◆◆—

To trust

Rockfort Security operative Shane Gallagher has been brought into S&D Systems to find a security leak. Confidential information has been stolen, and Shane suspects Elena Reyes, a systems analyst with the access and know-how to pull it off. As he finds excuses to get close to her, their attraction is too strong to ignore, but how can Shane trust the very woman he's investigating?

Or not to trust

Elena has spent her life proving herself, but now she's risking it all: everything she's worked for, and her growing feelings for Shane. Much as she wants to trust the devastatingly sexy, hard-as-nails investigator, she can't let herself fall for him…the stakes are too high.

—◆◆◆—

"Rebecca York delivers page-turning suspense." —Nora Roberts

"Rebecca York's writing is fast paced, suspenseful, and loaded with tension." —Jayne Ann Krentz

For more Rebecca York, visit:

www.sourcebooks.com

Bad Nights

Rockfort Security Book 1
by Rebecca York

New York Times and USA Today Bestselling Author

—⁓—

You only get a second chance...

Private operative and former Navy SEAL Jack Brandt barely escapes a disastrous undercover assignment, thanks to the most intriguing woman he's ever met. When his enemies track him to her doorstep, he'll do anything to protect Morgan from the danger closing in on them both...

If you stay alive...

Since her husband's death, Morgan Rains has only been going through the motions. She didn't think anything could shock her—until she finds a gorgeous man stumbling naked and injured through the woods behind her house. He's mysterious, intimidating—and undeniably compelling.

Thrown together into a pressure cooker of danger and intrigue, Jack and Morgan are finding in each other a reason to live—if they can survive.

—⁓—

"A brilliant stroke of genius. It's a page-turner for sure." —*Night Owl Reviews* Reviewer Top Pick

"Terror, torture, and temptation...a heart-in-throat thriller and a soul-satisfying romance." —*Long and Short* Reviews

For more Rebecca York, visit:

www.sourcebooks.com

Hell for Leather

Black Knights Inc.
by Julie Ann Walker

New York Times and *USA Today* Bestselling Author

Unlimited Drive

Only a crisis could persuade Delilah Fairchild to abandon her beloved biker bar, let alone ask Black Knights Inc. operator Bryan "Mac" McMillan for help. But her uncle has vanished into thin air, and sexy, surly Mac has the connections to help her find him. What the big, blue-eyed Texan has against her is a mystery…but when the bullets start to fly, Mac becomes her only hope of survival, and her only chance of finding her uncle alive.

Unstoppable Passion

Mac knows a thing or two about beautiful women—mainly that they can't be trusted. Throw in a ticking clock, a deadly terrorist, and some missing nuclear weapons, and a man just might find himself on the wrong end of the gun. But facing down danger with Delilah is one passion-filled thrill ride…

"The heat between the hero and heroine is hotter than a firecracker lit on both ends… Readers are in for one hell of ride!" —*RT Book Reviews*, 4.5 Stars

For more Julie Ann Walker, visit:

www.sourcebooks.com

Born Wild

Black Knights Inc.
by Julie Ann Walker

New York Times and *USA Today* Bestselling Author

— ⌇⌇ —

Tick…Tick…

"Wild" Bill Reichert knows a thing or two about explosives. The ex-Navy SEAL can practically rig a bomb blindfolded. But there's no way to diffuse the inevitable fireworks the day Eve Edens walks back into his life, asking for help.

Boom!

Eve doesn't know what to do when the Chicago police won't believe someone is out to hurt her. The only place to turn is Black Knights Inc.—after all, no one is better at protection that the covert special-ops team. Yet there's also no one better at getting her all turned on than Bill Reichert. She has a feeling this is one blast from the past that could backfire big-time.

— ⌇⌇ —

"Drama, danger, and sexual tension… Romantic suspense at its best." —*Night Owl Reviews* Reviewer Top Pick, 5 Stars

For more Julie Ann Walker, visit:

www.sourcebooks.com

Thrill Ride

Black Knights Inc.

by Julie Ann Walker

New York Times and *USA Today* bestselling author

———

He's gone rogue

Ex-Navy SEAL Rock Babineaux's job is to get information, and he's one of the best in the business. Until something goes horribly wrong and he's being hunted by his own government. Even his best friends at the covert special-ops organization Black Knights Inc. aren't sure they can trust him. He thinks he can outrun them all, but his former partner—a curvy bombshell who knows just how to drive him wild—refuses to cut him loose.

She won't back down

Vanessa Cordera hasn't been the team's communication specialist very long, but she knows how to read people—no way is Rock guilty of murder. And she'll go to hell and back to help him prove it. Sure, the sexy Cajun has his secrets, but there's no one in the world she'd rather have by her side in a tight spot. Which is good, because they're about to get very tight...

———

"Julie Ann Walker is one of those authors to be put on a keeper shelf along with Nora Roberts, Suzanne Brockmann, and Allison Brennan." —KirkusReviews.com

For more Julie Ann Walker, visit:

www.sourcebooks.com

About the Author

M.L. Buchman's romances have been named in *Booklist*'s Top 10 of the year and NPR's Top 5 of the year. He has also written and published thrillers, fantasy, and science fiction. He is happiest, no matter how clichéd it may seem, when walking on the beach holding hands with the mother of his awesome kid…or when he's writing. In addition to his career as a corporate project manager, he has rebuilt and single-handed a fifty-foot sailboat, both flown and jumped out of airplanes, designed and built two houses, and bicycled solo around the world. He is now making his living full-time as a writer, living on the Oregon Coast. You can keep up with his writing at www.mlbuchman.com.